INTERRUPT

INTERRUPT

Toni Dwiggins

TOR

A TOM DOHERTY ASSOCIATES BOOK
NEW YORK

This is a work of fiction. All the characters and events portrayed in this book are fictitious, and any resemblance to real people or events is purely coincidental.

The telecommunications technology described in the book is as accurate as the author could make it. However, the "D language" is a fictional update of AT&T's actual "C language," and the speech recognition material is an extrapolation of the state of the technology at the time this book was written.

5ESS®, 4ESS®, and 1AESS® are actual switches produced by AT&T. The facilities described in the book as using the 5ESS do not necessarily use this switch in reality.

AT&T has not in any way sponsored or endorsed this book.

INTERRUPT

This book is printed on acid-free paper.

A Tor Book
Published by Tom Doherty Associates, Inc.
175 Fifth Avenue
New York, N.Y. 10010

Edited by David G. Hartwell

Tor® is a registered trademark of Tom Doherty Associates, Inc.

Library of Congress Cataloging-in-Publication Data

Dwiggins, Toni.
    Interrupt / Toni Dwiggins.
        p.   cm.
    ISBN 0-312-85345-9
    I. Title.
    PS3554.W54I55   1993
    813'.54—dc20   92-21569
                                                                     CIP

First edition: February 1993

Printed in the United States of America

10 9 8 7 6 5 4 3 2 1

For Chuck, the best kind of engineer

ACKNOWLEDGMENTS

I learned what is on the other end of my telephone hand-set from several engineers and technicians who graciously introduced me to their network. If there are factual or technical errors in the book, they are mine alone. My thanks and appreciation go to Dave Naumann, Bob Denig, and Mark Robbins, from Pacific Bell; and to John Katzfey, Jacqueline Levy, My-Hanh Do, and Bob Graber, from AT&T. They are at least part of the reason that my phone always works.

For their support and advice, I am deeply grateful to Sue and Wally Worsley. To Dan Kolsrud, thanks for the name and the words of wisdom.

Finally, my most enthusiastic thanks to the people who shepherded my book to life: Lisa Bankoff and Harriet McDougal.

INTERRUPT

1

●

There was something alluring about an engineer like Andy Faulkner.

Interrupt's face scorched, and the cold wind stung.

Like me, Interrupt thought. Committed. An engineer with passion.

Couldn't be better.

Interrupt gazed at Faulkner's house. The house, unlike the man, was a disappointment.

Hard to make out details because the storm had killed the streetlights. But moonlight tore through the clouds to show enough. Boxy house, too large for the small lot. Garage sticking out at one end toward the street, like a thumb. Middle-class house, streets full of houses just like this all over Silicon Valley. Probably all that Faulkner could afford, the house of an engineer with more commitment than business sense.

The wind picked up, with a vengeance. Interrupt shivered

violently and moved. No one else on the street, no one at the windows. Everyone huddled inside their houses around candles and emergency lanterns. If anyone looked outside and caught a figure in the shifting moonlight, they would see a telephone lineman. They'd feel safe, because nights like this belonged to someone in uniform.

Interrupt stepped onto Faulkner's sodden lawn. A tall walnut tree canopied the front lawn, but provided no cover. Close to the house, hugging it, huge oleanders clumped around the front and side windows. Someone could hide in those oleanders.

Interrupt shouldered into the wet flower jungle and moved around to the side window.

Now the movie scene came to mind, the scene in which the intruder stalks up on the old house. The house in the scene was better than Faulkner's: it stood alone, it had three stories with sharp angles and, Interrupt dredged up the word, dormers. The power hadn't gone out, so it was lighted up inside like a stage. Outside, the intruder moved confidently through the night, closing in on the bushes below the lighted windows.

The scene stopped, cut cold. Interrupt pressed close to Faulkner's window and felt a quick spurting of the heart, like the oleanders quaking uncontrollably in the wind. Not fear, not an attack of nerves. Just gut-level thrill.

Through the window, the living room flickered by the light of a camping lantern, like an ancient fire-lit cave. Interrupt gazed inside and whispered, "Bingo."

There was the phone; beside it, hooked to it, was the TDD.

And there they were, Faulkner and the boy, seated facing each other at a table, Andy snaking his fingers at the boy and the boy snaking back. Sign language. Almost primitive, like the cave-lit room.

Interrupt had expected the boy to be frail. He had a frail-sounding name, Wayne. But, even seated, the boy looked tall like Faulkner, although kid-skinny, and his hands and arms already showed musculature.

Faulkner had his back to the window, and his face showed only occasionally in profile. An admirable face. Clear, strong features, especially in the slanting light from the lantern. A draftsman could have drawn it, getting in a few clean lines the almost-straight brow and the wide mouth and between them the hard angles of the nose and cheekbones. Suddenly, Faulkner turned toward the window and the lantern light took him full in the face, caught the wide-set dark eyes, boyishly somber. Interrupt froze, but Faulkner apparently did not see through the window. Faulkner grinned and two sculpted lines appeared under the eyes, marks of experience quickly sketched in by the draftsman. Then the grin disappeared and Faulkner turned soberly back to the boy again, the private amusement masked.

Andy Faulkner had a fine engineer's face, Interrupt thought, a fine Stanford engineer's face.

Interrupt imagined being the draftsman, grasping a mechanical pencil, hexagonal casing, its ultra-thin point a polymer lead strong enough to withstand the slashings of a driven hand, scoring straight horizontal lines down the paper, then slashing across them with hard straight vertical lines until a black lead grid canceled out the face in the drawing. The lead broke and Interrupt flicked out a new point like the tongue of a switchblade.

Then Interrupt let the drawing hand uncurl and pressed closer to the window, for inside, Faulkner and the boy were grasping hands across the table.

Wayne locked onto Andy's hand with a fierce grip. The kid was getting stronger, Andy thought. When had he grown this strong? Andy had to focus immediately on his own grip or he

13

would have lost it right then, and any remaining urge to smile passed.

Next time, he thought, I won't be giving him this much of an advantage. He won't need it.

He could feel the ungiving Formica under his elbow and the pressure from Wayne's push all the way up his arm through his shoulder and back. He tensed his muscles and tried to pull their forearms up to vertical.

"Give?" he said, and when Wayne didn't respond he turned his head so that the light from the lantern fell more fully on his face. "Give, Rambo?"

Wayne shook his head. With his free hand he fingerspelled "Look who's on top."

"Not for long." Andy grinned this time, psyching.

Wayne grinned back.

There was a noise at the window and Andy snapped his head around to look. Dark shapes, movement, it was the oleanders slapping against the glass. The wind was picking up. He turned back to Wayne, but the boy had followed his father's movements and still looked toward the window.

With his free hand, Andy touched Wayne's free hand and the boy turned to him.

"Wind in the trees," Andy said.

They tightened grips.

Andy channeled his strength into his hand and tried to curl Wayne's wrist inward to weaken it, but Wayne knew the trick as well as Andy, he'd learned it from his father, and he blocked it. Their locked arms held at a 120 angle, with Andy on the downside.

"Give?" Wayne fingerspelled.

Andy shook his head.

"Give?" Wayne mouthed it. No sound came; Wayne could have produced an approximation of the word but he wouldn't.

He had stopped trying to produce words when the expressions of the hearing registered confusion, or worse, amusement.

Andy's arm was beginning to ache. Next time, they'd start at a 110-degree angle. "I don't give," he said, his breathing a little tight. In a couple of years, Wayne was going to be able to slam him down at the start and then it would be time to begin the matches as equals.

Andy could remember the first time his father had arm-wrestled him from a vertical start. Joe Faulkner had simply sat down, placed his elbow on the table, and held up his open hand to Andy at ninety degrees. Andy had been surprised, and then he'd been proud as hell. He lost, and he kept on losing, but Joe never asked if he wanted to start with an advantage again and Andy would have been humiliated if he had. Finally, Andy won a match. He knew he had really won it, he knew his father hadn't let him win, for Joe Faulkner believed that everything, *everything* in life must be earned.

Andy watched Wayne's face. He supposed that was the way he himself looked when he was concentrating hard: squinting, teeth clamped together so tight that the jaw muscles ticked. Wanting to win so badly that it hurt.

For a moment, he was going to let the boy win.

But that's not the way they played it. Wayne was given an advantage at the start, less and less as he got older and stronger, and from then on it was each contestant for himself.

Andy became conscious of the wind again. It was spiraling up to a howl, rattling windows in their casings. He stopped himself from turning to look.

It was humid in the half-lit room. Sweat made their bare arms gleam and slicked the palms of their locked hands.

Andy loosened his fingers to get a better grip. Instantly, with a small grunt of victory, Wayne forced his father's hand back. Andy felt his wrist give, felt the weakness ripple up his forearm. He sucked in a deep breath and pushed back.

Wayne's face was rigid with concentration.

Andy poured every bit of strength into his hand. "Give?" he mouthed. He didn't have a breath to spare.

As their arms shuddered toward vertical, thunder crashed in, splitting their hands apart and roaring through Andy's head. Thunder almost on top of them, taking the roof off.

Andy jumped, knocking his chair over, and stared in amazement at Wayne.

Wayne had clapped his hands to his ears. His mouth opened as if he were going to speak; his eyes widened, ringing the green irises with white.

"My God," Andy said.

They both stood frozen in the vacuum silence that followed the thunder. Then Wayne dropped his hands from his ears and began signing rapidly.

"I know," Andy signed. He crossed to his son and took hold of his shoulders. "I *know*," he said.

Wayne had heard the thunder.

It meant nothing. Once in a great while, very rarely, a sound was loud enough, at just the right frequency, to touch Wayne's residual hearing. It meant nothing, but for seconds Andy and Wayne had been in the world of sound together.

Thunder roared again, farther away. Wayne did not flinch.

Andy almost reached out to touch Wayne's ears, as if he could find the blocked neural circuits with his fingertips and rewire them, as if he could pour in sound.

The boy could hear? He jumped at the thunder, so he could hear. No. He just felt the vibrations, or he jumped because Faulkner jumped. The boy couldn't hear, because there was the telecommunications device for the deaf hooked up to the phone. He couldn't hear, and he used a TDD.

Relax.

Interrupt checked the time. Eight forty-one. Sooner or later,

16

the boy would use the TDD. Used it a lot, according to the phone records. Interrupt's hand rested on the lineman's mobile phone dangling from the tool belt. Worst possible case, Interrupt would have to call the boy's TDD line. Not as elegant, but an alternative.

Patience.

It began to rain again. Interrupt barely felt it beneath the oleanders, but the raindrops snapped loudly on the gutters overhead.

Interrupt allowed the movie scene to continue.

The three-storied house was wood, painted white. A symbol, of course: white for innocence, defenselessness. The intruder watched at will the pretty young woman inside. She came into her living room carrying a paper bag, pulled dead flowers from a vase, dropped them in the bag, then passed into the dining room. More dead flowers into the bag.

The flowers were obviously a symbol too. Heavy-handed, but it worked.

As the young woman moved from room to room, the intruder shadowed her outside, circling the house. The scene played on, now revealing the intruder's face: full of rage. Finally, the intruder located what he was looking for, a thick black cable snaking down the side of the house. Here, the scene cut to a close-up of a black rotary telephone on a hallway table inside.

Interrupt could not help smiling. The close-up was to make sure the viewer understood that the cable was a telephone line, the cable and pair connecting her phone with the central office.

Now the intruder knelt beside the cable and caught it in the jaws of a heavy-duty bolt cutter. Close-up of the hands, the flexed tendons showing the force that was needed to snap the cutters shut. The cutting sound, savage. And then the severed ends of the cable with the twisted wire pairs suddenly exposed. The intruder had cut the line, and her phone was dead.

Something soft, wet, and cold dropped onto Interrupt's hand from the oleanders, and Interrupt hit out, unthinking, like a wild thing.

"What the . . ." Andy spun around to the side window. He could see nothing but darkness out there.

Wayne came beside him and peered out too.

Andy snapped down the blind. "Wind again in the bushes," he signed.

It hadn't been wind in the bushes. Andy grabbed one of the flashlights from the table and pulled open the front door. Wind caught him in the face as he swept the porch and front yard with the tunnel of light.

Wayne was right behind him.

Andy turned. "Maybe something fell. Cat knocked over the trash can. I'm going to check."

Wayne stabbed a finger at himself.

"Wait here." Andy thought quickly. "In case of the phone." Andy followed Wayne's glance at the TDD. The light wasn't flashing now, but if it did, Wayne would not want to miss it. His son was already nodding yes.

Andy stepped outside and pulled the door firmly shut, curling his hand tighter around the flashlight handle.

Stupid. Should've got out to the street as soon as Faulkner pulled down the blind.

A door slammed, from the front of the house.

Interrupt began to sweat. Only one way to go. Around to the backyard and pray there's a way out.

Interrupt crouched and ran, soft-footed and bent over like some kind of quarry.

A familiar pressure built just behind the eyes, and it started to hurt. Losing control. Interrupt winced and rounded into the back. The whole backyard was fenced. Bad luck.

18

Where was Faulkner? Coming through the side yard?

Get hold, Interrupt thought. *Plan it.*

There was a patio back here, a big slab of concrete, and a basketball setup, and grass, and along the back fence more oleanders. Have to be the oleanders again.

The headache was building, sickening.

Interrupt bolted across the grass, nearly tripping on a garden hose that snaked into the oleanders. Once more, into the slick jungle.

Light stabbed into the backyard, and behind it, a tall figure moved cautiously.

Interrupt's head throbbed.

In planning this night, in laying it all out step by step, Interrupt had briefly considered bringing the automatic but decided it was unnecessary. You took a gun if you planned to shoot something. Interrupt had shot targets—bull's-eyes—and pierced rats on the run. But the plan for this night had certainly not involved shooting.

Now, sweating, hurting, trapped quarry, Interrupt clutched at the tool belt for a weapon.

Faulkner was prowling through the backyard, searching with the light. Hunting.

The *pain*. Interrupt tried to hold the pain back with fingers pressed hard against skull.

Faulkner's flashlight swept the oleanders and caught Interrupt full in the face, blinding. Then it moved on, then it zigged back and slashed across Interrupt's chest. And moved on.

What did the man *see*? Was he playing?

He was coming toward the oleanders, slow. Still cautious.

Interrupt crouched lower and, as Faulkner's light arced by again, saw something briefly gleam by the base of an oleander. Interrupt glanced out at Faulkner, calculated his path, waited, waited, then reached for the gleaming object on the ground.

19

The nozzle of the garden hose. With the other hand, Interrupt slipped the bolt cutters off the tool belt.

Faulkner stepped forward, paused, took another step.

Interrupt pulled the hose up taut, then yanked it to the left. It caught Faulkner across one ankle, with the other foot raised to take one more cautious step.

Faulkner pitched forward and fell facedown in the grass.

Interrupt came fast out of the oleanders, but there was no movement from Faulkner. Stepping cautiously, like Faulkner, Interrupt approached the form on the grass. The flashlight was still in Faulkner's hand, its beam stabbing down into the earth.

Interrupt got a double-handed grip on the bolt cutters, gummed with granules of something from the oleanders; raising the cutters to strike, Interrupt inhaled the thick wet odor of pollen. Head throbbing, almost giddy with the pollen, Interrupt came down on both knees.

Faulkner lay still.

Something was wrong. The ground, Interrupt thought. It was soft, saturated with rainwater, spongy. Why was Faulkner not moving? Interrupt fingered the pollen granules on the cutters, bothersome, like dried scabs of glue, and bent close enough to hear the soft hiss of Faulkner's breathing. Bent this close, Interrupt could see the depression in the lawn, the network of gray metal pipe and faucets and the vicious spiked disk that kissed Faulkner's temple.

He was breathing. Knocked cold but breathing. "Thank you," Interrupt whispered, to no one, to God maybe.

Suddenly, sounds came from the side yard. Heavy *thump thump* along the concrete walkway, big-kid heavy-sneakered footsteps.

Interrupt shoved back into the oleanders.

The boy appeared, spotted his father, and stopped cold. He made a sound, a harsh expulsion of breath, and then he started moving. His big sneakers sank into the earth, he walked with difficulty like someone walking through wet sand. He reached his father and came down stiffly on one knee, then grabbed Faulkner by the shoulders and rolled him over.

Stupid kid, too rough with a possible head injury.

Another sound, a groan. Interrupt couldn't tell if it came from the boy or Faulkner. Then the kid panicked, sprang up, and charged across the patio and through a back door into the house, propelling the door into the wall so hard that Interrupt could hear the doorknob sink into the drywall.

The kid's noise receded into the depths of the house, and it fell quiet in Faulkner's backyard. The wind was gone, Interrupt noticed that now, and the roof gutters no longer clattered with rainwater. Interrupt came out into the open, padding on the spongy grass. Like insulating foam. The yard was sound-proofed.

Faulkner lay quiet. The kid had probably gone for help.

Interrupt circled to the front yard. No one there, no one on the street, no alarms raised.

Not gone for help, *called* for help. Interrupt spun toward the front window. The blinds were open there, and Interrupt found an angle to see inside without having to wade through the damned oleanders.

Inside, the boy was at the TDD, shoulders hunched, stabbing the keyboard. Then he went after the telephone.

Serendipity. Interrupt had not planned it this way, the mess out back, but things worked out. Engineers had a saying for the unexpected: if you can't fix it, feature it.

The boy was banging on the switchhook.

The phone is dead, Interrupt itched to say. Sorry, boy, but you can't call whoever it is you're trying to call. Let's see, the doctor? An ambulance? 911? You typed in the number on your TDD, didn't you, and you got an answer, somebody to help, and then you were cut off. Couldn't believe it, could you?

You keep on trying to call for help, boy, but the phone's dead. Bingo.

The boy wouldn't give up. He picked up the phone, turned it over and over, even shook it. Silly kid.

Interrupt let out a long, slow breath. The headache was gone. And then, no point in pressing serendipity too far, Interrupt wheeled and strolled out to the sidewalk. Just someone in uniform going about the night's business.

Joe Faulkner stood like Paul Bunyan, bigger than life, straddle-legged, one foot resting at either end of the bridge span. Andy looked up at his giant of a father and shouted; he had to shout to be heard. Joe's voice rumbled down at him. Look at my bridge, boy, here's a piece of engineering for you. Why don't you build something like this? And Andy shouted up, I can build a bridge that moves your voice around the world in an instant. And Joe laughed, thunder splitting the sky.

Splitting his head.

His head hurt.

Hands on his head, clumsy strokes. Andy opened his eyes. Wayne's face was inches from his.

"Andy?"

Andy turned his head. Helen, too, knelt beside him. He saw her hair piled up in its topknot and smelled the peppermint on her breath.

They were outside, in the backyard, on the wet lawn. His shirt and jeans were wet, soaking his skin. He groaned and shoved up onto an elbow.

"You okay? You all right?" Wayne's hands stopped in mid-air.

"Are you dizzy?" Helen's professional voice. "Nauseated?"

Dizzy, and his right temple was sore. "Let me get up."

"Andy."

He struggled up, Helen grabbing him under one arm and Wayne taking the other. Dizzy, he looked down at the ground where he had lain and saw the garden hose. "I tripped," he said.

They led him inside and released him on the couch.

"I tried to call," Wayne was signing, "911, but the . . ."

Helen brought the lantern over and held it close. Andy blinked. "You called 911?"

"No," Helen said, "he couldn't." She stared into his eyes. "Your pupils are equal."

Wayne came closer, hands flying. "You wouldn't wake up, so I ran in and called, but the line went dead, and I ran back out and you were still . . ."

"So he came and got me." Helen prodded his neck. "Hurt?"

"No," Andy said. "I thought you were retired."

She tightened the belt of her bathrobe. "You take what you can get."

"Thanks."

"Thank your son."

Wayne stiffened. Wayne, Andy saw, was a mess. Dirt on his hands, dirt and grass stains on his sleeves. Wet patches on the knees of his jeans. Dirt streaked across his face. Red eyes. "Nice work, Spock," Andy said gently. He stood, for Wayne, and braced for dizziness. His head stayed clear.

"Andy," Helen said, "take it easy."

"Am I all right?"

"How do you feel?"

"Wet." He needed to change clothes. What about the phone? "What about 911?" he said. They stared at him; he was out of synch.

"Phone is dead," Wayne signed.

"Phone dead?" Andy turned to look at the instrument. "Not in this house. It's not allowed." He walked over to the phone gingerly, the wet jeans worse than his sore temple. The

TDD was switched on, but the screen was blank. He typed in a few letters, but got nothing on-screen. He took the telephone handset from its TDD cradle and put it to his ear. Silence. The one thing a telecom engineer did not want to hear when he picked up a phone. He hung up the phone, waited a few moments, then took it off-hook again. Still silence. He depressed the switchhook but could not get dial tone.

"Mine's out too," Helen said.

Andy turned to face them. "The storm must have knocked out a line somewhere." He switched to signing. He wanted to be sure Wayne understood. "Maybe a tree blew over and snapped a cable. Or rainwater soaked through a . . ." How to sign *splice?* He fingerspelled.

"When fixed?"

"Soon."

"Tonight?"

It depended. A big storm like this, surprising in late April, could cause havoc. "I don't know."

Wayne half turned, lowering his hands, making a sign. "Shit."

The nice thing about sign, Andy thought, was that you could pretend you hadn't been looking. He excused himself and went to change clothes.

He dressed in the dark; he had left the lantern in the living room for Wayne and Helen. There was a beeping and he thought, the phones are dead, and anyway he didn't have a phone in the bedroom and then his head cleared once more and he turned to his bedside table and picked up the pager. Here, in the dark, reading the flashing green numerals on his pager, he shivered. He didn't know whether he was shivering because he felt cold and sore, or because he was being paged to come into the office when he wasn't on call.

2

The streets were dark as far as Andy could see. He drove past the shadowy houses, every one of them cut off. His stomach tightened. He couldn't do a thing about the power, but he thought of every dead phone in each dark house and he softly cursed.

Impatient, he sped into Sunnyvale. The border between Mountain View and Sunnyvale was unnoticeable, even in daylight. One town simply bumped up against another in this crowded valley, and to the hundreds of newcomers arriving every day, to the dozens of scrappy high-tech start-up companies hustling for venture capital, to the dozens of little high-tech companies going under, one town was much like another in Silicon Valley. But Andy knew the boundaries. In the office, mounted high on a wide wall, was a map of California, Nevada, and Hawaii. Studding the map were white lights, each one representing a local telephone switch office. When there was trouble, a light would corrupt to yellow to orange and then to red. If the alarm was local, Andy would check the boundaries to find whose phone service was at risk.

There were around a couple of dozen cities in the entire country that had more phones than people, and three of them—San Francisco, Palo Alto, and Sunnyvale—were in Andy's territory.

The huge AT&T building loomed up ahead, the only thing lighted in a dark neighborhood, thanks to its standby power system.

There was just enough light in the parking lot so that he could make it to the door without tripping, Andy thought sourly.

He slapped his ID badge against the security pad and buzzed inside the building. The joke went that the color scheme—orange and brown stripes along the wall, dull red carpet, yellow signs—intentionally mimicked the colors of the alarm lights.

Light blazed out through the double glass doors of the Regional Technical Assistance Center. Andy buzzed inside.

The R-TAC reception desk was empty. Colson's office, door open, was empty.

Andy glanced up at the wall map. One light had corrupted to red. Local. Andy scanned the boundaries: Sunnyvale, Mountain View, part of Santa Clara. A central office.

He found Lloyd Narver in his cubicle, rigid, staring at his monitor, hands flat on his thighs.

"Good evening, Mr. Narver. What did you do to my phone?"

Lloyd swiveled his chair to face Andy. "You didn't pay your fucking phone bill so we cut off your fucking service." He continued, tone mild, "It's a central office. I couldn't think of anyone else to call in, so I called you." Lloyd was the only one to wear a tie to work, even on night calls, and the joke was that it was the tie that kept Lloyd cool. Tonight, the tie was mustard yellow and avocado green, in thin vertical stripes. Awful, Andy thought, but not awful enough to be intentional.

"All right, I'm on it." Andy started for his cubicle.

"Andy-man."

Lloyd's tone stopped Andy. He turned, looked down the hall at the unwavering red light.

"We lost the whole office." Lloyd sounded calm.

"The whole office." Andy's pulse raced. You just didn't lose a whole office. Lloyd was joking. He couldn't think of anything to say, couldn't think of a comeback, because it was such a damn stupid joke.

"Five-E, Andy."

"Thank you, Lloyd. I know they run one of our five-E switches. What I don't understand . . ."

"Listen to me closely. The only switch in that office is our baby. AT&T electronic switching system número five-E. And our baby croaked. That office ain't switching even one telephone call."

"How many lines out of that office?"

"Forty thou, I think."

Andy thought he saw a tic at the corner of Lloyd's eye. "The power is . . ."

"The power is on. The cables are live. But the switch is *not processing calls.*" Lloyd held up a fist, thumb stabbing downward.

"Both switch processors? Primary and backup?"

"The juice is on, but they're not processing calls. They loaded the backup tape. Nothing."

"Jesus."

"Yeah."

"What have you come up with?"

"Nothing. Remote diagnostics comes up with zilch. I get called in, I do the whole routine, but I'm coming up dry. So

I call you. You and I don't get it fixed, Andy-man, we're gonna have to call Colson."

"All right, give me a crack at it."

"Pac Bell is screaming," Lloyd said softly. "Fucking screaming."

Andy didn't blame them.

The central office was operated by Pacific Bell, one of the seven local telephone companies cut loose in the 1982 breakup of AT&T. The Balkanization of the phone system, telco people called it. Pac Bell handled the local calls in California, but they bought their switches and the software that ran the switch processors from AT&T, Northern Telecom, and a few other companies.

The switch processors were powerful computers, and inevitably there were glitches. But half of the computer system's memory was devoted to self-maintenance, and it usually fixed its own problems.

If a problem was thorny enough, it was turned over to the company that had provided the offending piece of equipment. R-TAC took about twenty calls a month on problems with AT&T's 5ESS switch. Still, the customer wouldn't be aware of the problem, because the switch processors worked in tandem. The telco believed above all else in redundancy. It ran the biggest computer system in the world, and every critical component of the vast system had a twin, so that if a piece on the front lines faltered, its place would instantaneously be taken by the backup. And the customer's phone would continue to work.

Except when an entire office went down, an entire switching system that took over forty thousand individual telephones down with it.

Andy could think of only a few instances of total switch failure, and those were due to major fires.

Switches just did not die. There was the story of a maintenance tech who had been canned and gotten angry and had come back with a gun and shot a switch. The guy had fired right into the central control unit, like shooting someone in the brain. But the switch, unlike the human, had a duplicate brain. The backup central control unit had taken over and the switch had not gone down.

Now, somehow, they had lost one of AT&T's most sophisticated electronic switching systems, the 5ESS.

"When?" Andy said.

"Eight fifty-nine."

Just about when Wayne's TDD had gone down. Andy checked his watch. The switch had been down well over an hour.

"I know, Andy." Lloyd shrugged. "It doesn't happen."

"Do you have the trouble reports?"

"They're on your workstation."

"Then let's *go*," Andy said, more sharply than he intended.

"Don't get a feather up your ass. Just get the switch up." Lloyd straightened his tie. "You're the genius, Andy-man. Lead on."

Never panic. That was the rule.

Andy strode into his cubicle and put his portable TDD beside the phone. For the first time, he couldn't call Wayne and he didn't like it. And if there was a problem, Helen couldn't call him.

The screen on his workstation was crammed with numbers and symbols. The alarm box on the screen held one word: CRITICAL. He couldn't help feeling a thrill. The highest alarm level he'd ever worked on was a MAJOR.

He studied the trouble reports. From the central office on up the line, they had run every conceivable diagnostic on the five-E. And they had all punted.

Andy slapped down the trouble reports and tapped in a command on the keyboard. The screen slowly scrolled a picture of the five-E system. He always found it elegant, and he always found himself sucked whole into it the way Wayne was sucked into Nintendo.

His pulse beat harder, but steady, as he followed the scroll. He would find the glitch, wherever it had intruded—into the circuits, into the software, wherever. He suddenly stopped the scroll, tapped a key, and the screen responded to his query with an enlarged diagram. He shook his head, let it scroll again. His fingertips just brushed the keys.

"All right, I'm with you now, I'm *there.*"

Everything looked right, there was no sign of a glitch, there was no problem, certainly nothing that could take down the whole switch.

The back of his throat constricted, and he swallowed.

Keep looking.

As he touched the keyboard, pulling away one layer of the switch to reveal another, he relaxed. If something was there, he would find it. Right now, he owned the five-E.

He flicked a key and probed into the central control permanent memory. He was into the software, millions of lines of code. He would find the glitch and trap it in one of the error legs.

"I'm talking to you," he whispered to the five-E. "Come on, show me."

It was as if the current were flowing from the five-E over the lines and into him, and from him back into the five-E. A circuit.

His shoulder muscles burned as he worked the keyboard, and his temple throbbed, but his eyes kept skimming code, smooth, not missing a loop. He was speaking the language, he was fluent. Whomever had written the high-level language for the processors had written poetry.

"Andy!"

He whirled around.

Lloyd stood at the door, staring.

Andy caught his breath. "What the . . ."

"What the fuck did you do, Andy-man?"

"What?"

Lloyd thrust a fist in the air. "Score one for R-TAC."

"What happened?"

Lloyd let his arm fall. "Don't you know?"

"What happened?"

"The switch is up." Lloyd leaned over, looked at Andy's screen. He reached around Andy, typed in a command. A window appeared on the screen, a status report. Inside the alarm box, the words now read: CRITICAL RETIRED.

Andy was still high on the five-E, and he tried to clear his thoughts. "Who retired the alarm?"

"Then you didn't do the fix?" Lloyd's tone was flat.

"No. I was working on it."

They stared at each other. Lloyd finally said, "Fairy godmother." He tugged at his regrettable tie and eased out the door.

Andy shoved back in his chair. He clenched and unclenched his hands, releasing the keyboard tension from his fingers.

The switch was up. The phones were working.

On-screen, the alarm box was now blank.

A 5ESS had failed and then come back to life. Why?

One thing was certain: it wasn't a fairy godmother. The obvious answer was a bug in the software. It took a long, intricate program to tell ESS what to do—millions of lines of computer code. Bugs were inevitable. The more code, the more bugs. The best a programmer could do was to track and crush the more formidable bugs and then apply defensive programming techniques to try to neutralize the rest. But bugs were hardy; some always survived. Checking out this one would take a long, ugly D&D session. Well, he had lost plenty of nights to debugging and donuts.

It must be a bug.

But . . . a bug that fixed itself?

He had to get back in control here. This was something new. He felt like a stranger to the five-E and he didn't like it. Maybe the fall had dulled his senses. Whatever. He keyed his workstation back into the guts of the switch.

What the hell was in that machine?

3

A hand was on his shoulder.

"Mr. Faulkner?" Someone lightly shook him, then withdrew the hand.

Andy jerked upright. His head ached.

He stared.

A woman stood over him. She wore jeans, heavy boots, a blue workshirt. A slash of grease marred the Pacific Bell logo on her shirt. Slung low on her hips was a wide leather belt, dangling wire strippers, duckbill pliers, screwdriver, voltmeter.

"Who are you?" His voice was thick. Lord, he must have been asleep for hours.

She held up her hands and flashed him a smile. "He told me to wake you. The guy out there. Lloyd."

"You're a friend of Lloyd's?"

"Nope."

"Uh . . . this is a security area. You're not supposed . . ."

"It's okay." She pulled a key from her pocket, showed him. "Look, Mr. Faulkner. Andy, right? Lloyd was really busy when I came in, and he asked me to do him a favor and wake you."

This was a joke. Lloyd, you jerk. He suddenly hoped she wasn't one of those strippers that people hired and sent to some guy's office to rattle him. Dressed as a *lineman?* Her hair was red-blond, in a braid. Wavy strands had come loose around her ears.

"Sorry. It wasn't such a good idea." She didn't smile again. Her mouth, unsmiling, was pretty.

"It wasn't a bad idea." He felt grubby, unshaven.

The switch. He came alert. He had found nothing that could have caused the number five to crash. And then he had fallen asleep? "I . . . What time is it?" He looked to his watch. Six-thirty. "Oh, sh—" He cut himself off, grabbed for the phone.

"Oh, shit," she offered.

She moved back, as if to give him privacy in his own cubicle, but she watched him make the call. He got Helen and apologized. No time for him to get home and get Wayne ready for the school bus.

He glanced at her. Her eyes, light brown, almost gold like wild grasses, seemed sympathetic. She was going to stand there and listen if he didn't ask her to leave.

Helen was putting Wayne on. Andy switched to the TDD. This caught her interest and she craned forward.

Andy typed in, "Good morning. Sorry didn't make it."

"What time you home?"

"Don't know." Distracted, he stopped.

"Work-a-holick. Bye." The connection broke.

Andy carefully replaced the handset. He stood, facing her.

No dizziness, he noted; just confusion. "Who are you?" He cleared his throat. "I like to know who's waking me up."

"Nell Colson." She stuck out her hand.

He took it, and she waited for him to let go.

"Colson? You're Ray Colson's . . ."

"Daughter."

Andy hadn't known that Colson had a daughter. But then, nobody knew whether he'd ever had a wife.

"That was your son on the phone?"

"My son?"

She smiled again. "I'm not a detective. Ray told me you had a deaf son."

"*Ray* told you about my son?"

"And then the TDD." She gestured at the phone. "We learn about all the equipment in training. So, clearly you were talking to a deaf person, and I made the obvious guess."

"Good guess."

"Is he totally deaf?"

Andy choked back a word. "Ray didn't tell you that?"

"He just said deaf." She gazed at him levelly. "I'm sorry. Did Ray tell me something he shouldn't have?"

Andy shook his head.

She was tall, like her father, and a lot more curious.

So what was the big deal? "I'm just surprised, Miss Colson, that Ray told you anything about my son. Around here, he doesn't talk about personal things."

"No, no one would call my father a gossip." She hooked her thumbs in the tool belt. "The way it works is, I ask Ray questions, and as long as I'm not asking about company security or something, he answers. I was interested in the people he worked with and he answered my questions. I'm sure he found the conversation . . . *pointless* . . . but he humored me." She had Ray's "pointless" down cold.

"I see. But Ray doesn't work with my son."

Her eyes narrowed, hooding the gold. "When he told me about you, there was something in his voice . . . respect maybe. Interest anyway. That's something, with Ray. He said you had some fire in your eyes. So I got interested, and I asked him a bunch of questions."

Andy took a step backward and braced against his desk. "He doubtless meant bloodshot eyes. We work crazy hours."

"No," she said, "fire."

He could think of nothing to say.

She glanced at the phone. "The woman you were talking to . . . Helen. She's . . . ?"

"No one Ray would know."

She was finally embarrassed. He watched the blush spread down her throat, into the neck of her soiled workshirt. "I'm sorry, that's none of my business."

It wasn't, but he realized his pulse was racing. "It's okay. I love being interrogated at dawn."

She looked startled.

"That was a joke," he said. Idiot, try again. "You can ask me anything you want."

She shook her head.

"Go ahead."

"I just wondered if that was your wife on the phone."

Thanks, Lloyd, real cute. Do me a favor, miss, go on in there and wake Mr. Faulkner. Nobody calls him Mr. Faulkner, but linemen who look like you don't usually wake him up. Just go on in there, like Venus rising from the half shell, and reduce him to gibberish. It'll be easy.

"She helps out with my son," he said. "I'm not married."

"Ray didn't tell me you were good-looking."

Jesus, Colson's daughter. He wished she wouldn't look at his reddened, unshaven, grinning face. "Yeah, well, Ray didn't tell me he had a good-looking lineman for a daughter. You are a lineman? Line person."

36

"Lineman," she said. "That's what we're called."

"Okay."

"Well," she said, "my father . . ."

They moved to the door.

He saw Lloyd and Speedy Lewison lounging outside Candace Fuentes's cubicle. Lloyd looked refreshed and shaved, Andy noticed, despite their long night. Speedy looked beat. Speedy always came in early, and he always looked as if it half killed him to do so. Andy could hear Candace's hoot from inside. Candace only came in early if there had been a night call that she missed. In her opinion, all male engineers were inferior and their work had to be checked.

Reflexively, Andy checked the map on the wall. All lights white.

"Colson's . . . your father's usually not in till about seven-thirty." Andy gestured down the hall toward Colson's office.

"I know. I couldn't wait."

Clearly, she wanted him to ask why. "Why?"

"I found a tap."

Lloyd and Speedy turned to look; Candace came out.

Nell grinned, letting them in on it, but addressed Andy. "I found a wiretap. I was checking out the lines, over in Cupertino. A piece of somebody's roof came off in the wind and took out a cable. Anyway, I'm checking the damage, and I find a *tap*."

Candace moved closer. She glanced at Nell's tool belt, then turned her face up to Nell. Her dark pageboy flared.

Lloyd had remarked once that Candace looked like a doll, like some prim little girl had patiently turned Candace's hair under in the pageboy and dressed her in an unending wardrobe of pleats.

Candace did look like a doll next to Nell, but Nell could hardly have been the prim little girl.

"So what did you do about this tap?" Candace asked.

37

"Reported it. We're not in the business of tapping phones."

"We?" Candace said.

"You know." Andy patted Candace's shoulder. "We who labor in the public interest."

"He really buys that," Candace told Nell. "That's why he's such a nerd."

Lloyd shrugged. "He's fucking brain-damaged."

"He's a romantic," Speedy said. "We're all romantics. Our phone system's an engineered miracle. We'll cross swords with anybody who messes with it." Lloyd, in his cataloging of the group, had once called Speedy a romantic, because of the dark hollows beneath his eyes, blacker than his skin, because of his gaunt frame, and because he wore satiny shirts that billowed. Any shirt on Speedy would billow, Candace had added.

Speedy saluted Nell. "Find some more taps."

"Are you joking with me?"

"We've got a phreak," Andy told Nell. "You know about phreaks?"

She nodded. "They're into free phone calls."

"This one's into our E-mail," Candace said. "Electronic mail, on the computer system. He leaves cute little messages."

"He does more than that," Andy said, "he snoops. He knows a lot of stuff he shouldn't know . . ."

"He'll leave a message about a failure somewhere," Candace cut in, "and then challenge us to get it fixed. I left a message for him once. I told him he's a strange, pitiable creature who hasn't got the balls to interact with people face-to-face. I signed it 'Lady.' He tried to initiate a dialog with me."

"He?" Nell asked.

"Acts like a he. Can you see a woman playing games like that?"

Nell shrugged. "How does he get in?"

Andy said quickly, "We don't know. Bulletin board, maybe. That's a telco computer network. If you know the code you can log on and gossip." He realized he was competing with Candace for Nell's attention.

"Your wiretap," Lloyd told Nell, "is some guy who thinks his wife's cheating."

Ray Colson came into the room.

"Morning."

"Hey, boss man."

"Morning, Ray."

"Nice day. Storm's over."

"Good morning," Colson said.

Nell smiled.

Andy wanted to talk to Colson about the five-E, but he didn't want to do it in front of Nell.

Colson surveyed them one by one, precise, like an oscilloscope registering electrical variations. Lloyd had said about Colson that he didn't see the human form when he looked at you, he saw electrical waveforms instead. Waveforms could be calibrated on a scope, and could be triggered at different points by proper adjustment of the control knobs.

Andy looked at Colson more closely than he ever had before. Nell's father. She didn't get her sunny hair from him; Colson's thinning hair was dark. He had a strong, angular face, with shadowed eyes and a sharp nose. Only around the mouth did he resemble Nell, and his finely rounded lips, almost always compressed, were at odds with the rest of his face.

Nell hooked her thumbs in her tool belt. "Hi, Ray."

"Nell." Colson nodded.

Andy waited for Colson to hustle her off to his office. Surprisingly, Colson didn't seem to mind standing in front of the group with his daughter, whose existence he had never bothered to mention. Neither did he act as if he knew what to do with her.

"I found a wiretap."

Colson's face displayed interest.

Nell described the line damage, the tap, how she reported it, what Pacific Bell was going to do about it.

"Whose tap was it?" Colson had his full oscilloscope focus on her.

She said, cool, "Probably some guy listening in on his wife."

"That's a bullshit theory." Colson's lips compressed, and he looked away.

Nell strode across the room, the tools on her belt clattering. She stopped at the double glass doors and looked back at them. Her lips compressed, but her mouth twitched up at the corners. Andy couldn't tell whether she was angry or amused. She was Colson's daughter, all right.

She waved to Andy. "Sorry I woke you."

Someone snickered. Speedy. Andy felt the heat rise in his face, the second time in one morning.

Colson was focusing on him. Nothing was more vital to Colson now than Andy. Jesus, Andy thought, Colson wasn't suddenly going to become the vigilant father. Andy looked levelly at Colson. It could have lasted minutes, or nanoseconds. Then Nell pulled open the door and Colson reoriented himself toward his daughter.

"Nell."

She paused, holding open the door.

"That Pacific Bell van in the back parking lot, the one with the 'E.T. Phone Home' bumper sticker. Is that yours?"

"Yeah."

"Next time, park it in the visitors' lot."

Her lips formed a tight, straight line. This time, Andy thought, there was no question. She was angry. She released the door, and it closed with the sound of a sharply indrawn breath.

Colson turned back to the group, unbuttoned his shirt cuffs, and folded his sleeves in neat segments up his forearms. "In my office, people, I want to hear about that five-E."

* * *

Colson's office, in the telco hierarchy, was midlevel. It had a wooden desk and table and two visitor chairs, whereas the engineers' and programmers' cubicles each had a metal desk and no visitor chairs. Colson never conferenced in the cubicles.

The 5ESS group crowded Colson's office. Candace and Lloyd took the chairs; Andy and Speedy settled on the table.

Colson folded the trouble report and creased it with a thumbnail. He pointed at Andy. "Good work."

"I didn't *find* anything, Ray."

"You followed procedure."

Colson was being honest in his praise, Andy knew, but it was low-level praise. The only thing Colson truly admired was brilliance, and when somebody on the team showed it, Colson rewarded it with a look of startled appreciation.

Outside Colson's office, there were sounds of more R-TAC people coming through the glass doors. Power supply people, specialists on other switches. But the 5ESS group considered themselves the R-TAC elite: trained to the apex in both hardware and software, high priests of the five-E.

"So, does anybody know what happened last night?"

The five-E team was silent.

"Candace?"

"I checked out the reports this morning, Ray. I haven't found anything yet."

"Well, if *Candace* can't find it—" Speedy began.

"Speedy?" Colson said.

"—then why ask me? I'm mortal."

"Distressingly," Candace said.

"Lloyd?"

"I've been on it the whole night, Ray. It went down, it went up."

"Andy?"

"I don't like it. A total switch failure, out of left field. Then it fixes itself."

"So we don't know anything," Colson said.

"What about a virus?" Speedy put in.

"Not likely," said Andy. "The program boots normally, no flaky error messages . . ."

"If it's a virus, I'll eat it," said Lloyd. "We're not talking about a P.C. here, we've got a mainframe processor with the best data integrity in the business."

"There's no such animal as one hundred percent data integrity," Speedy said.

"It's not a virus, it's a garden-variety bug," Lloyd said. "Somebody forgot to reenable the memory protect and we ended up with a stack overflow. Whatever. It'll either pop up again and we'll trap it or it'll bury itself and we can forget it."

"I tend to agree," Colson said.

"So do I," said Andy, "but it's a bug that took down the whole five-E. Let's pursue it now."

Speedy groaned. "Do we really want to waste our precious bodily fluids sweating over this?"

"The fucker's fixed. It's processing calls," Lloyd said. "Andy's so fucking dumb he couldn't figure out why it went down, and he hasn't noticed that it's back on-line."

"You're jealous," Candace told Lloyd. "Andy's so compulsive he can't give up and admit defeat. I'll cover for him. I'll find the problem."

"No, no, *I'll* find it," said Speedy. "I got up early for this."

Andy suddenly yawned, bone-weary. He rubbed his hands across his face and flinched when he touched his sore temple.

The team stared. "You feel all right, Andy?" Colson finally asked.

"Fine."

Lloyd stroked his tie. "Hard work always gives him a headache."

"Okay," Colson said. "Anybody want to punt this up to PECC?"

Nobody on the five-E team wanted to punt it up to PECC, AT&T's Product Engineering Control Center. If PECC punted, the problem went all the way back to Bell Labs, where the engineers who had designed the problematic piece of equipment could scratch their heads over it. Andy had put in a spell at Bell Labs, wrestling with speaker verification algorithms. The work had been sexy, fun, but he found himself putting in seventy-hour weeks and feeling guilty as hell if he took a weekend off. Then one day in the halls he had run into a research engineer walking backward. The guy always walked backward, someone said, because he had a problem with balance. Andy had decided that it was time to take a break from research.

Nobody, including Colson, wanted to admit defeat and punt the five-E failure up to PECC or back to Bell Labs.

Colson laced his fingers. "Speedy, you're on it. Candace, take the new alarms. Andy and Lloyd, nice work last night, now go home and sleep."

The phone rang. Andy was always amazed watching Colson on the phone because Colson's features would soften, his mouth would relax. With the handset at his ear and the switchhook under his fingers, he was interfacing with a piece of equipment and he was happy.

Colson hung up. "That was Pac Bell. They're cutting over to a number five in Palo Alto tomorrow night. They want someone from R-TAC to hold their hand." Colson's gaze registered the team, one by one. "You, Andy."

Candace flicked up a hand. "I'll go too. I love cutovers."

4

•

Across the street, people hurried through the dark to the nondescript door in the huge brick building, knocked, and were admitted. Like some secret society.

The switch office did not have windows. One reason was that people who worked there cared more about computer monitors than a view of the sidewalk. A more important reason—vastly more important, Interrupt thought—was security. If a switch office had windows, a terrorist could throw a bomb through the glass and cripple a community's ability to communicate.

Interrupt did not need windows.

"Andy Faulkner, AT&T," Andy told the woman with the clipboard. "From the Regional Technical Assistance Center."

She found his name, crossed it off, and rummaged through a box full of badges to find his ID.

A cutover always drew a crowd. A cutover was like a road test on a new car, like a presidential election—an event that dozens of people had worked toward for months and in some cases years, a climax of effort and guesswork and hope and risk, a moment of truth when there could be only success or failure.

Andy walked into the cavernous switch room. For a moment, he stayed back in the shadows and watched. If Joe Faulkner had been alive, Andy would have brought him here, would have dragged him along the way that Joe had dragged Andy to his bridge openings.

When they knock out the last scaffold on your bridge, Dad. You know what it's like. You're up for two days and nights, you're a bastard half the time and a prince half the time. You poured your guts into it and now it's out of your hands. Some guy in a hard hat is going to pull out the last piece of timber and all you can do is wait and watch and see if it stands on its own. So look at this, *engineers* built this. They don't know shit about lift spans because they're electrical engineers, but you look at this switch and tell me it's not a damn fine piece of engineering.

Tall blue and white steel cabinets filled about a third of the room. Shoulder-to-shoulder in row after row, a silent army in blue and white.

Okay, Andy thought, a bridge is prettier. But look at the boards, Dad.

The cabinets held racks of circuit boards, thousands of them. Each board, studded with components, was a miniature city with power and life and purpose.

At the front of the steel rows was a giant cabinet, eight feet tall and ten feet wide. Fan vents slitted its top and bottom. On its face was a control panel with rows of lights like duplicate eyes. The administrative module, the general of the army. At its side stood another cabinet, the communications module, the colonel, passing messages to and from the rows of switching modules, the troops.

Thick packets of cables wound up from each of the cabinets to a catwalk that arched over the entire switch, a line of communication from general to army.

Each module was driven by a processor, and each processor had a duplicate, a standby waiting to leap into service should its active counterpart falter. A ghost army.

It was the 5ESS switch, state-of-the-art, AT&T's finest, standing tall and proud in its brand-spanking-new coat of blue and white.

Already, people milled around the switch. Drinking coffee, holding plates from the celebratory buffet, joking, checking their watches. Looking at the switch, grinning, telling each other it was going to crash and they'd all be out of jobs.

It was nearly midnight, an hour and a half to go, and already they were wired. Middle of the night and nobody yawned. It was the coffee, it was the cutover adrenaline.

Andy made his way to the control center, a glassed-in corner of the room. Techs in swivel chairs monitored workstations, minor alarms flashed red, printouts littered the floor unread. Andy flagged the supervisor as he put down one phone and started to pick up another.

"Andy Faulkner from R-TAC."

The man paused, stared at Andy's badge. "Oh, hey, great. Get some food."

"Everything normal?"

"Yeah, normal. You know, last-minute stuff. Glad to see you here, but I sure in the hell hope we don't give you anything to do."

"Right," said Andy, "I'm just insurance. Mind if I stash this in a corner?" He held up his portable TDD.

"Sure thing. I'll page if I need you. Go get some coffee."

The phone rang and the supervisor snatched up the handset.

Andy went back out to stare at the silent switch. It was not yet on-line, it had yet to process a single customer call. But there was energy in the room, and the source was the number five.

He stopped a passing tech. "Where's the crossbar?"

He followed the tech's instructions, out a door, down a hallway, up a flight of stairs, into another hangar-like room.

The crossbar switch was like some old, old friend—reliable, plain, chattering amiably. Nothing fancy, simply rack upon rack of electromechanical relays opening and closing with a tinny clacking as the switch processed calls. The crossbar sprawled over twice as much floor space as the new ESS and took thousandths of a second to perform the same switching operation that the ESS could polish off in millionths of a second. The crossbar wasn't sexy, it couldn't deliver call forwarding, call waiting, speed calling, three-way calls, voice-bridges, 800 numbers, or any of the other services supplied by ESS.

Telephone people called the crossbar POTS. Plain old telephone service. And it was doomed, because technology was advancing and the customer expected the utmost of technology.

"Andy, Andy," a voice behind him said, "what a pleasure."

Andy turned, grinning. "Amin!"

Amin al-Masri took Andy's hand and shook it vigorously. Amin had the lean small build and whipcord strength of a boy, and hair that had begun graying prematurely but had never completely turned.

"You are here officially," asked Amin, "or just because you love telephones?"

"Both."

"Very nice. I take a certain credit for that."

"Credit freely given."

"I am an invited guest."

"Of course. They wouldn't dare cut a switch next door to Stanford without inviting you."

"Yes, but I am also here watching one of my chicks. One year out of the nest and he's updating his professor's phone service." Amin smiled sweetly up at Andy. "Now two of my chicks."

Andy nodded, pleased.

"You haven't called me in, let's see, is it eight months? Since you came back to California."

"You're busy."

"I think you're busier than I am. You're happy at R-TAC?"

"I like it. It's good work."

"You don't miss working in speech recognition?"

"I'll get back to it someday. You still consulting with it?"

"Dabbling," Amin said. "But there are other tidbits to acquire. I am easily seduced."

More like enthralled, Andy thought. Amin had grown up in an underdeveloped country, Jordan. He had conceived a passion at an early age: that good communication, *telecommunication,* was vital for his people's development. He had come to the United States because the technical education he needed to fulfill his passion was not available in Jordan. He was the best kind of engineer, in Andy's opinion, a romantic. He understood that an engineer can create what never has been. Someday, Andy was certain, Amin would take his technical skills, all his tidbits, back to Jordan.

Amin waved his hands. "Listen. The crossbar is coming to a close."

Indeed, the clacking of the old electromechanical switch was quieter. As the hour turned later, the telephone traffic slowed to insomniacs, teenagers calling in pizzas, lonely elderly calling each other, night businesses, graveyard shifts, emergencies. By 1:30 A.M., traffic would be at its lowest level and the crossbar could be killed with the fewest disruptions. The only thing that would stop the cutover then would be a caller to a suicide hot line.

People were funneling through the crossbar, squeezing up and down the aisles that separated the racks, having a last look.

Andy saw Candace coming down the aisle toward them, waving, and behind her, Nell. "One last look at the dinosaur," Candace said, patting the metal rack.

Nell smiled.

"And who are these ladies?" Amin held out both hands, palms up.

"Candace Fuentes. From R-TAC. Nell Colson . . ." Andy stared at the red-gold braid, the blue workshirt. He focused on the logo. ". . . from Pac Bell. This is Amin al-Masri."

"I am Andy's former professor," Amin explained.

"Stanford," Candace said. "Not a bad school."

"Candace went to Berkeley," Andy explained.

"Aha. Our rival. But top-rate." Amin turned graciously to Nell. "And you, Miss Colson?"

"University of California. At Irvine. It's not Stanford, Professor. It's not even U.C. Berkeley."

"It is the student who makes the difference," Amin said smoothly, "not the school."

Andy had never before caught Amin in an open lie. Amin didn't believe that. Obviously, neither did Nell. Her mouth pulled taut as Ray's.

Candace broke the silence. "So what kind of student was our boy here?"

"He was one of my stars." Amin smiled sweetly. "This embarrasses him, but it reflects well on me, as his professor."

"Yes," Candace said, straight, "we all call Andy a genius."

Andy groaned.

"I'm afraid I'm not," Nell said. She hooked her thumbs into her belt. Only one tool hung from the belt tonight: a pair of heavy-duty wire cutters. "I'm smarter than average, not particularly intellectual, but very quick to learn."

"I will tell you a story of genius." Amin waited for their attention. "Have you heard of Mr. Strowger?"

"Was he a genius?" Nell looked to Andy.

Andy knew the story about Strowger; it was one of Amin's favorite classroom anecdotes with a moral. Amin knew that Andy knew. Andy said nothing.

"Back around the turn of the century, there was an undertaker named Mr. Strowger. Business was bad, because a rival undertaker was getting all the calls from the bereaved. You see, the rival undertaker was married to the town switchboard operator. Whenever someone called the operator, distressed, looking for a professional to take charge of a body, the operator would connect the caller to her husband's telephone."

Nell's mouth twitched. Candace listened intently.

"Mr. Strowger, understandably, thought that this was quite unfair. It was at this point that Mr. Strowger developed his revolutionary theory of telephone service." Amin paused.

Amin always paused at this point. Neither Nell nor Candace spoke.

"So what was the theory?" Andy finally supplied

"Mr. Strowger concluded that the telephone system should be totally unbiased."

Candace hooted. "Unbiased. Professor, you're mixing up philosophy and technology. I thought we only did that at Berkeley."

Amin's eyebrows raised slightly: disapproval. Then he glanced at Nell. Like a small boy, Andy thought.

Amin continued. "And so, Mr. Strowger invented an automatic dialing system. The caller dials a series of digits, which activates a motor, which moves an electrical contact point to positions correlating with the digits, which finally connects with the proper wire to signal the called party. The call goes through automatically." He eyed Candace. "There are no biased operators to appease. The system welcomes everyone on an equal footing. It is called . . ."

"The Strowger step-by-step switching system," Nell said.

Amin stopped cold. "You do know about Mr. Strowger."

"They tell the story in training."

Candace hooted again.

Smarter than average, Andy thought, very quick to learn.

"After the step-by-step came the panel switch," Nell was saying, "and that was improved on by the crossbar. And then of course, the electronic switch."

She was Colson's daughter, Andy reminded himself. She probably learned it all on his knee.

Amin had recovered. "Yes, ESS. This is how technology advances. First there is the human need. We build something to satisfy that need. And then we build it better, faster, cheaper, more elaborately to satisfy the creative need."

"Philosophy," Candace said.

They fell silent. The chattering of the crossbar had slowed, even as the noise around them was building, the hubbub of a crowd eager for the event.

"You know what I like?" Nell suddenly said.

"What?" Andy and Amin responded as one.

Nell held up her wire cutters. "The human touch."

Amin started, as if she had wielded a chain saw.

"ESS is advanced electronics, right? Leading edge stuff. Everything is done by computer, everybody sits at a keyboard and tells it what to do. Well, I like the fact that a *cut*over still means people like me *cutting*."

"The human touch designed ESS," Candace said.

Nell holstered her cutters. "I meant the *common* human touch. Telecommunications isn't just . . . advances in technology . . ." she intoned it, dead on for Amin, "it's wires and cables and duct tape. Real people can look at a cable and say, oh, that's a telephone line. They look at ESS and they don't know what the hell it is."

Andy jammed his hands in his pockets. "Sure. Who could love a switch? Never mind that it does the job, that you can call the deli whenever you're hungry. Real people know whether or not their phones are working. In fact, the guys who engineered ESS are damn close to being real people themselves."

"The guys," Nell said. "What about women? Candace is an engineer."

"He's noticed," Candace said.

Amin watched attentively, as if they were arguing a point in his class.

"Look," said Andy, "it's just a figure of speech. Hey, guys, check out this board."

"In school," Nell said, "in engineering classes, I always felt that guys who used the term 'guys' were talking about *guys*. Men."

"Engineering?" Andy let the surprise show. "But you're not . . ."

"I took some engineering. Ray's genes."

"Pity you didn't finish," Candace said. "The profession could use more women."

Nell fingered her belt. "Why?"

"Women engineers see the big picture. Men get bogged down in details."

Over the din in the room, a voice yelled, "Cutters to their stations, ten minutes to cutover." A cheer erupted, and people pressed toward the back of the room.

"That's me," Nell said. She smiled formally at them and edged into the tool-carrying crowd.

Amin regarded Candace. "I think you overstate . . ."

"Excuse me, Professor, Andy. I have to find a bathroom." Candace threw Andy a quick grin, then strolled away.

Amin turned to Andy, helpless as a freshman in one of his own classes. Andy shrugged. "We have a real way with women."

Amin recovered himself and patted Andy's arm. "Well. I must abandon you also. I must find how my other chick is doing." He slipped into the crowd.

Colson's daughter, Andy thought. Bad idea.

He moved through the lines of cabinets. He should be at the ESS for the cutover. It was his specialty, it was why he was here. But he had no real line job in the cut, nothing to do.

People were moving toward the far wall, toward the terminus of the crossbar cables, staking out a place to watch.

He decided to watch the crossbar cut.

The cutting site was a long aisle that ran the length of the room. The floor was marked off by strips of duct tape into segments; in each segment a bundle of cables spilled out of the switch. The cables were bunched, tied, flagged, stretched out like chicken necks awaiting the axe. Cutters were in position, one to a segment, one to a cable bunch. They shifted, joked, checked their watches, worked the jaws of their wire cutters open and shut. Some were maintenance, old friends of the crossbar; some were installers and linemen, invited by Pac Bell to take part in the ceremony.

Andy found a place at the end of the aisle, sighting down the long line of cutters. He saw Nell, coming in and out of view as the line shifted. She was talking to the cutter on her left, a hefty white-haired man who nodded and grinned and wiped his hand across his forehead. It was bright under the high-wattage lighting, getting warm in the crowded line of cutters. Nell looked like some beach lifeguard, blond and tanned and gleaming, standing lanky and at ease. She put one hand to the nape of her neck and twisted up her braid, and with the other hand pushed down the collar of her workshirt. A bit of strap flashed stark white against her skin.

"Sixty seconds to cutover," someone bawled out.

The cutters straightened, planted their feet wide apart, and nuzzled their blades against the thick necks of bundled cables. A cutter near Andy let loose a rebel yell.

Andy craned, saw Nell with the jaws of her wire cutters in place.

The crossbar clacked in tired intervals, processing the dead-of-night calls.

"Ten, nine . . ." shouted the voice, and the cutters and watchers picked up the count.

"Eight, seven, six . . ." Andy yelled it with the crowd.

The roar rode over the sound of the crossbar.

"Ready . . . and . . . *cut!*" the voice screamed.

Metal snapped against metal as cutters chewed through the cables.

Suddenly, the crossbar, like a dying beast, began a frenzied clacking. It sputtered and chattered crazily, drowning out the final sounds of the cables being severed.

The cutters, finishing, let their arms fall to their sides and gaped at the machine. Someone said, "It's shorting out."

The crossbar mistook the electrical shorts laying waste to its components for telephone calls. It thought that thousands of callers had picked up their phones all at once, and its relays were stuttering open and shut in a desperate attempt to process what seemed to be an onslaught of calls.

Someone ran into the room and yelled, "ESS is up!"

The crowd cheered, and Andy was surprised to find himself relieved.

People moved toward the stairs, anxious to get down and see the ESS. Andy looked for Nell, but she was nowhere in sight. He followed the crowd to the stairs, feeling a quiet pride in the new number five. Behind him, the clacking was dying out as the final shorts shut down the crossbar and the fuses on the frames were pulled.

Downstairs, an admiring crowd surged around the ESS. At the moment of cutover, while the crossbar had howled out, the ESS had come to life and taken over the thirty thousand lines cut off from the old crossbar switch. Quietly and efficiently, the new switch began processing telephone calls.

Andy went into the control room and offered his hand to the supervisor. "Congratulations!"

"Hey, thanks. Thanks for coming, but looks like we don't need you. Your ATT box is slick as snail snot."

Andy grinned. "I'm supposed to stick around for the post-cut diagnostics."

"Good enough. You get anything to eat yet? I'll page if we get any interesting glitches."

Even in the smoothest of cutovers, there were glitches.

Just down the block from the switch building was the hotel. Shabby, dating from another era, still clinging to its street corner in upscale Palo Alto.

Interrupt went inside. The brown and red plaid carpet rasped underfoot, caked stiff with scum. The red-flocked wall-paper had peeled. Although it was the middle of the night, a television in the lobby played to ageless men parked in deep chairs. No one at the front desk, no bellboys to help the lame up the stairs.

Interrupt wore a baseball cap with the bill pulled low and a coat with the collar turned up, but here it hardly seemed necessary.

Beyond the lobby was an alcove that housed the door to the men's room and the pay telephone. It was a black touch-tone, greasy with fingerprints. Not having a handkerchief, Interrupt tore a page out of the telephone book and used that to grasp the handset.

The time was one-fifty. Twenty minutes after cutover.

Interrupt lifted the handset off the hook, deposited coins,

and received dial tone. The new ESS, working beautifully. From memory, Interrupt dialed the number. The connection was made, and a recorded voice said, "You have reached 725-6652. Leave your name and message at the tone."

Interrupt hung up and began marking time.

Fifteen seconds later, Interrupt again deposited coins, dialed the number, and broke the connection with the recording. Forty seconds later, Interrupt punched in a new number, 767-2676, waited for the recording, then hung up. Twenty seconds later, the second number again.

Breaking that connection, Interrupt immediately dialed one final number, nine digits this time: 468377878. It was not difficult to remember because the digits on the touch-tone keypad corresponded to the letters that spelled Interrupt.

Now this telephone line, from this grubby phone, was connected to a maintenance port on the new 5ESS. A port that led into the switch's permanent memory.

"Bingo," Interrupt whispered. The transmitter in the mouthpiece transformed the word into electrical waves and sent them over the line. But there was no receiver on the other end to convert the electrical impulses back into sound waves. There was nobody to hear the word "bingo."

There was only the switch and its memory.

Fingers icy, Interrupt spread open a piece of notepaper and double-checked a telephone number. The trigger. Silence, but for the faint drone of the television, as Interrupt dialed in the trigger.

He hung up, then quickly went outside into the clean night air, down the block to the phone booth. One more call to make, a call that required a different place of origination.

Across the street, the switch building showed its sealed brick sides to the street. Interrupt shrugged. Who needed windows?

* * *

Andy was hungry, hole-in-the-belly hungry. But he wasn't the only one; success evidently bred good appetites. A crowd three-deep pressed toward the food table in a corner of the switch room. When Andy finally got his turn, there wasn't much left. Stale bread, stiffened cheese, browning fruit, a scattering of cold cuts amidst the parsley. He helped himself.

Then, over the intercom, his name crackled out like a gunshot.

His stomach tightened. He abandoned his plate and headed back to the control room.

The supervisor looked up from a terminal as Andy came in. "A call just came through for you from a TDD relay operator." He looked at Andy, curious, then handed him a slip of paper.

Andy read the message: call Wayne, and his home number. It was too damn late for Wayne to be up, Andy thought. His son had been interested in the cutover, had wanted to know if it would affect his TDD. Andy took the desk across from the supervisor. He hooked up the TDD to the phone and dialed Wayne's number. The indicator light on the TDD blinked as his home phone rang, then shone a steady red. Someone had answered, but he was getting no message on his TDD screen.

He snatched the handset out of the TDD cradle and put it to his ear.

"Hello?" the sitter was saying.

If Wayne had wanted him to call, why hadn't he answered on his TDD? "This is . . ." Andy began. He heard a click, then dial tone, then nothing.

The phone was dead. He depressed the switchhook, listened again. Nothing.

All right, there was a glitch.

Andy looked up to tell the supervisor, but he was gone. The techs at their monitors were furiously punching in numbers.

Except for the clicking of keys, it was deathly silent in the control room.

Through the glass he saw people gesturing, shoving past one another, swarming around the ESS. Two maintenance techs were running, their tool belts swinging.

Andy pushed out the door. A droning of low voices came from the switch area, as if the ESS itself were softly moaning.

A knot of people hovered around the administrative control panel, their faces blank with surprise. Andy moved closer and his heart chilled: the control lights were off, the panel was as blank as the faces of the stunned techs. The central processors were not working. ESS was brain dead.

Someone tapped Andy's shoulder and he spun around. "We lost ESS," the supervisor said sorrowfully.

From somewhere deep within the rows of switching modules, a voice was rising: "What the hell happened, what the hell happened, what the hell happened, what the hell happened?"

ESS was dead, the crossbar was dead, thirty thousand telephone lines were dead, and not even the caller to the suicide hot line was going to be able to get through.

"Let's get you onto a terminal," the supervisor hissed.

But Andy wasn't thinking of diagnostics. He was thinking that within the space of three days, two ESS number fives had gone down. Both times, the switches died in the middle of a TDD call. His TDDs.

Suddenly, Candace was at his side. She looked up at him, plowing a hand through her dark bangs. "Someone's out to get us," she whispered.

5

•

"How long have you worked for AT&T?"

"Seven years."

"Where did you work before that?"

"Stanford. Graduate school."

"I mean *worked.*"

So do I, Andy thought. "Nowhere. I went to work for AT&T straight out of grad school."

"Why?"

"Because I wanted to work in telecommunications."

"Why?"

"Because I liked it."

"Because you liked it."

"Because I loved it."

"Why?"

"I don't see what this has to do . . ."

"I'm not being mysterious, Mr. Faulkner. I'm just trying to find out why you became a telephone man."

"I'm an electrical engineer, and telecommunications is an exciting field."

Feferman lunged out of his chair and prowled around the conference table, huge and light-footed as a hungry bear. As he passed by, his scent, a piney after-shave, washed over Andy. Colson, three empty chairs away, sucked in his breath as Feferman passed. Buck and Howland, sitting together across the table, did not seem to mind their chief special agent's after-shave.

"Is that all?" Feferman resumed.

"What?"

"Was that your only motivation? Excitement."

"I was good at it."

"You advanced quickly?"

"I don't know. I guess so. I moved around a lot, but so does everybody in the company. I worked in R&D, and in the field . . ."

"So, is that all? Excitement and job opportunities."

"What is it you want?"

"I want to know why you do what you do."

"We've covered it."

"No, we haven't. I went to college too, Mr. Faulkner, not Stanford but I went to college, and I studied psychology for a while. The fact of the mattter is, I almost majored in psychology. I know just enough psychology to make me dangerous, because I never believe the first thing that someone in a difficult situation tells me and I always look for something hidden. You're hiding something, Mr. Faulkner, you're holding back."

"No, I'm not."

"Why did you become a telephone man?"

"I've told you. I chose my work like anybody else does. I found telecom interesting, I was good at it, AT&T was hiring engineers . . ."

"Did it have something to do with your deaf son?"

"Jesus."

"It looks like I've found something hidden."

"My son has nothing to do with this. I thought we were here to talk about the switch failures."

"TDDs, Mr. Faulkner."

"Fine. Let's talk about TDDs."

"Later. I still want to know why you became a telephone man."

"It was interesting."

"I think it's more than that. Remember, I'm an amateur psychologist, and I've read all your files and snooped around talking to your colleagues and ex-bosses, and I've come to a diagnosis. I think you're a zealot, Mr. Faulkner, I think you are driven by some mission, you have some deep emotional need to be a telephone man. I want to know exactly what it is. Why did you become a telephone man, Mr. Faulkner?"

"To pay the rent."

Feferman roared, a huge man's laugh. He stopped pacing, turned to face the high-definition television screen at the end of the room. A camera mounted on top of the television was trained on the room. "Do you have any questions at this point?" Feferman asked the man on-screen.

On-screen was a full head shot of the executive vice-president for technical development. Andy hadn't caught the man's name, just his title. The veep shook his head. "Please continue, Mr. Feferman." He leaned back in his chair and turned his face slightly to watch his own screen. Behind him, through a generous window, spread the haughty New York skyline.

Feferman climbed into the nearest chair; even sitting, he loomed over the others. He pulled a thin roll of papers from his suit coat pocket, opened and smoothed them like a fussy schoolmaster, and passed two pages to each person at the

63

table. "All right, Mr. Faulkner, we'll drop psychology for the moment. Let's have a look at your telephone calls." Feferman stabbed a large white finger in the middle of his pages.

Andy glanced down at his own copy. The top sheet was a printout of the telephone calls made just before the first switch failure. The last listing was Wayne's TDD telephone number, and it had been circled with a heavy-point marker. Then white space, then INTERRUPTION. Switch not processing calls. Andy did not look at the second page; he knew what was there.

Feferman had done exactly as he had done, Andy thought. After the cutover he had asked Pac Bell for the Automatic Message Accounting data covering the time before each switch failure. Normally, the AMA system only generated records for billable calls. But 5ESS had a high-capacity billing feature, which could generate data on all completed calls, including local calls.

Wayne's call to 911 had been a local call. Only someone who knew 5ESS would know that records of local calls could be generated. Andy looked straight at Feferman. "The calls were setups."

"Oh? Well, let's save setups and double-crosses until we've examined the calls," Feferman said.

Andy glanced at Colson. Colson was watching Feferman without expression; his damned oscilloscope look. Hey, boss, Andy thought, I could use some support. He wondered if Colson was intimidated by the chief special agent.

AT&T Security had a fearful reputation; if there was wrongdoing, Security would pursue it doggedly and punish it mercilessly. They were better than the police, they were better than the FBI, because they were telecom-trained and did not give a damn for any kind of criminal activity that did not involve telephones. The chief special agent was their headman and reputedly more single-minded than J. Edgar Hoover.

Technically, his title had been changed from "Chief Special Agent," a longtime title that had recently been judged too independent, to "Head of Security." But everyone in Security, everyone who came in contact with Security, and everyone who tried to avoid Security called Feferman chief special agent. Feferman's reputation had preceded him to California.

"The computer has picked up an interesting correlation," Feferman was saying. "Both switch failures occurred immediately following telephone calls involving Mr. Faulkner's home number. To be precise, Mr. Faulkner's son's number. You have two numbers assigned to your phone line, Mr. Faulkner, each one identifiable by a distinctive ringing pattern?"

"Yes. And they're both listed in the phone book, so anybody could have gotten my son's number."

"Failure number one"—Feferman rustled the papers before him, then held up one finger—"occurred after a call was placed from Mr. Faulkner's son's number to the emergency service 911. Failure number two"—a second finger shot up—"occurred after a call was placed from the Palo Alto central office to Mr. Faulkner's son's number."

A low whistle came from the television screen.

Colson finally spoke up. "Andy volunteered that information himself."

Andy felt absurdly grateful.

"Beating the computer to the punch. Yes, thank you, Mr. Colson, I appreciate Mr. Faulkner's zeal. And, according to Mr. Faulkner's statement, both phone calls were placed with a telecommunications device for the deaf. Since TDD calls are not identifiable as such in the call records, I appreciate Mr. Faulkner volunteering this information. As a matter of fact, the second TDD connection"—Feferman grimaced, as if someone else had made the pun—"so to speak, was brought to the attention of Security by the central office supervisor at the cutover."

"Faulkner's TDD," said Buck. It was the first time either of the local security men had spoken. Buck was young and heavyset, and Howland was a big jowly older man. Sitting side by side, they presented a solid block of dark-suited flesh.

Security hired gorillas, Andy thought, and it worked. Buck, Howland, and Feferman looked as though they would be equally at ease with computer printouts or rubber hoses in their hands.

"Where is the TDD now?" asked the veep.

"There are two of the machines in question, and they are in Security lockup," Feferman said. "The tiger team will have them shortly."

Andy remembered Wayne, hands jammed in his pockets, expression as cool as he could produce, his eyes flecked with panic as Andy took his TDD.

"You have a tiger team set up?" Colson asked with interest.

"That's right," said Feferman.

"I'd like to be on it."

"Thank you, Mr. Colson, but we don't need volunteers."

"You need the best technical people we have."

"Security has access to the best. As a matter of fact, I've selected one of your own people for the team. Candace Fuentes."

Colson's mouth compressed. "You might have asked me first."

"You object? She's expert on the 5ESS, she's familiar with the circumstances, and unlike Mr. Faulkner, her telephones were not involved in the failures. I think she'll be dynamite. You object?"

"Not formally."

"Good." Feferman got up, started circling the table. "There are two issues I want to kick around here. First, how are Mr. Faulkner's phone calls connected to the switch failures . . ."

"You're presupposing that they are connected," Colson said.

Feferman smiled. "I can have our computer calculate the odds of a coincidence. Mr. Faulkner or his son just happened to be on the telephone each time that a total 5ESS failure occurred, the only such times that there have been total 5ESS failures. Would that satisfy you?"

"No. That would be meaningless."

Feferman stopped behind Colson's chair. "The second issue I want to kick around is how Mr. Faulkner himself is connected."

"I'm not," Andy said.

"You're still presupposing," Colson said. He did not turn around to look at Feferman.

Feferman stalked to the other side of the table so that he could see Colson's face. "All right, Mr. Colson, *if.*" He moved on to Andy. "First issue. Let's assume, *assume,* that the phone calls are a cause, and the failures are the effect. That makes the phone calls . . . ?" He was past Andy, looking back.

"I don't know."

"Mr. Faulkner! You're the best. That's what my reports say, you're a brilliant troubleshooter. Please contribute. Cause and effect, so the phone calls are . . ."

He was behind Andy now. Andy's stomach clenched. "A trigger." The after-shave was suffocating.

"Good. And if the calls are a trigger, and the effect is a switch failure, then . . ." Feferman paced.

"We have a virus!" the veep said. He had forgotten to face his camera, he was staring at his own screen, at the images around the conference table.

"We started checking that after the first failure," Andy said to the camera, then to Feferman. "We found no indications of a virus."

"So R-TAC has totally ruled out system contamination?" Feferman growled in surprise.

"We don't rule out anything," Colson said, "we prioritize."

"Did you look at the new generic?" Feferman said. "Our records show that an update of the operating system for the number five was shipped two weeks ago."

"It's clean," Andy said.

"You *think* it's clean. My tiger team will decide if it's clean. My tiger team will sniff every piece of software in the same building with the number five, and if there's contamination they will find it."

"There could have been physical penetration on-site," Buck put in, watching Feferman.

"Especially at the cutover. Too many goddamned people at the cutover," said Howland.

"Faulkner was at the cutover," Buck said.

"That's issue two." Feferman wagged a finger at Buck. "We're on issue one."

"You are checking for any unauthorized visits?" the veep asked.

"I'm checking it down to the janitor's ass." Feferman abruptly settled in a chair directly across from Andy. "Starting with Mr. Faulkner. Okay, issue two."

Andy straightened. "Look, the calls were setups." He paused, expecting Feferman to pounce on the word "setups" again.

"The emergency call was a setup?" Feferman's eyes narrowed, two small dark holes bored into the massive face.

Maybe I didn't trip, Andy thought.

"Mr. Faulkner?"

"I don't know *how* it was set up. But in light of the cutover call, it makes a damn strange coincidence. If you'd like to have your computer calculate those odds."

Feferman did not smile.

"And then the cutover call. I got a message that my son had called me, and so I called him back, using my TDD. But he had *not* called. He was asleep at the time."

"And so?"

"And so somebody else made the call."

"Impersonating your son?"

"Yes, using a TDD, through a TDD relay operator. Look at the call records, you should find a record of the call. Find out where it was made from."

"Thank you for the suggestion, Mr. Faulkner. As a matter of fact, I managed to think of that myself. In the time frame between the cutover and the switch failure, there was only one incoming call placed through a TDD relay operator. It originated at a phone booth across the street from the Palo Alto switch office."

Andy was chilled. He had known from the time he got home on the night of the cutover and questioned Wayne and the baby-sitter that someone else made the call. But this made it real, this was a place. A phone booth. Someone had stood in that phone booth and called the switch office pretending to be his son.

Feferman stood and began pacing, this time relaxed and leisurely. "How long do you think it would take someone to just slip out of the switch office—everyone is busy with the cutover so nobody notices—and dash across the street and make that call? Five minutes? Four minutes? Could be done in less."

Andy was wondering the same thing.

Colson said, "What's your point, Feferman?"

"No one can account for Mr. Faulkner's whereabouts for a good fifteen minutes between the time that he left the control room and the time he returned in response to the page."

"I went to the buffet table to . . ."

"The cutover call was a setup," Feferman said, "but who set it up?"

"Why would he set himself up?" the veep asked.

Andy appealed to the camera. "I *didn't.*"

"Unfortunately, you can't verify that." Feferman strolled behind Andy, trailing his piney scent.

Andy craned to look at Feferman. "It doesn't make sense. Why would I make a fake phone call from my son that could be so easily traced? Why wouldn't I have just told Wayne to call me at the cutover?"

"Because you wanted it to look like someone was setting you up?" Feferman asked in a friendly curious tone.

"Why would I want to do that?"

"Because you were going to make a phone call that would trigger a very costly and distressing failure of a brand-spanking-new 5ESS, and you wanted to have a cover?" Feferman asked, even more deferentially.

Colson was staring at Andy, eyes hooded. Buck and Howland leaned forward, four beefy muscular arms pressing on the table. The veep watched, immobile, as if the camera had caught him in a freeze frame.

"Do you people think I'm an idiot?" Andy said. "If I was purposely triggering switch failures, why would I do it from my own phone? Why would I do it with a TDD when God knows how many people know I use a TDD? Do you think I'm a fucking idiot?"

Feferman was standing across from Andy, still at last. He slowly shook his head. "No, Mr. Faulkner, I think you're the opposite of an idiot. I think you're smart enough to know that phone calls leave records and that records will be analyzed, and that triggers will be found."

"If I'm so smart, then why didn't I invent a more sophisticated trigger?"

"I think you're smart enough to anticipate that my crack tiger team would eventually find this sophisticated trigger."

"No," said Andy.

"You make it look like you were set up, and then you protest that you wouldn't be stupid enough to set yourself up."

"Then it's him," Buck said.

Feferman extended his two forefingers, then crossed them. "We do have a crosspoint here. He has the skill." Feferman wagged one forefinger. "And he had the opportunity." He wagged the other. "But I have to admit I'm still curious about his motive. *Why* did he become a telephone man?"

On-screen, the veep said, "Mr. Feferman, are you making a binding accusation against Mr. Faulkner?"

"No," said Feferman. "He might be telling the truth. Anybody could have gone into that phone booth. Somebody from the cutover, somebody from across town, somebody who flew in on United and got a rental car at the airport and drove into town. That person might be a confederate of Mr. Faulkner; then again, he—or she—might not. Or maybe it's 'they,' we might have a conspiracy brewing."

Andy's head ached. Feferman was draining him, every word drilling into his skull.

"We don't even know yet *how* Mr. Faulkner's calls triggered the failures."

"I advise your tiger team to start with the source code," Colson said.

"Thank you again, Mr. Colson." Feferman sat down beside Buck and Howland, dwarfing them. "So here's what we're going to do. We have a lot of work ahead of us. Day and night, we're going to sleep on cots, we're going to live on sandwiches and coffee, no family time, no days off, we're going to snoop into every corner and hound everyone who so much as blinks at us."

"What about Mr. Faulkner?" the veep said.

Feferman braced his elbow on the table and pointed his forefinger at Andy. He cocked his thumb like a trigger, then snapped it down. "Mr. Faulkner and his son have new telephone numbers. He will also receive a brand-spanking-new set of TDDs, courtesy of AT&T."

Andy looked at Feferman in surprise. That was fine, that was perfectly reasonable.

Feferman turned to Colson. "And I recommend—you understand 'recommend' being a courteous way of saying I demand—that you suspend Mr. Faulkner while we find out who is diddling with the telephones."

"No." Andy whipped around to face Colson.

Colson laced his fingers together and regarded Feferman. Finally, he nodded. "I'm sorry, Andy," Colson said, still looking at Feferman, "but I'm going to have to suspend you."

High and dry, Andy thought wildly, high and dry. It was a telco term for when a phone went dead. You were just hanging out there, high and dry.

"With pay," Colson said to Feferman. "The man has a son."

6

●

"Hello? I don't hear you. Hello?"

"Hello, Lloyd."

"Andy-man!"

"Yeah."

"How you doing?"

"Just great."

"We're all great here. Having a wine and cheese party to celebrate your abrupt departure. Except with you taking a vacation and Candace on a top-secret mission, we have to do your share of the work."

"It'll make you better engineers."

"Hard to get any engineering done with all the security around here."

"Security's tight?"

"Fuck security. I hope they're listening."

A long pause.

* * *

Interrupt flicked the switch, shutting off the tape. Faulkner's voice was strung tight. Joking, just like everything was normal, but he sounded like a man who was sinking.

The tautness in Faulkner's voice made Interrupt relax.

This was a good room to relax in. Cramped, but neat. Spotless as a lab. Electronics parts were stored in see-through plastic boxes, each type of component to its own box. Interrupt had, as a child, played with a tin box filled with electronics parts. Transistors, capacitors, resistors, diodes, fuses, plugs—scoop a handful from the box and rain them down onto a tabletop. They were like tiny multicolored insects with hard exoskeletons. Then one day, Interrupt couldn't remember exactly how or when, the realization came that one could *use* the little insects, make them perform stunning little feats. Mastery of the insects gave one control over things that made the world work. And the silly child, who had spent so much time playing aimlessly with the components of power, began to study them seriously.

Little insects, Interrupt thought, flicking the tape recorder back on.

". . . and fuck Colson."

"It wasn't Colson's fault. He had no choice." But Faulkner sounded ticked off.

"Just following orders. The Nuremberg defense."

"He saved my paycheck."

"Well, he hasn't been crying over your absence here."

"He only cries at beautiful sunsets."

Laughter on both ends.

Then Faulkner, hesitant. "Lloyd, I need a little help."

"That you do."

* * *

Interrupt punched the pause button. Andy Faulkner, telecom star, needs a little help.

A little help from his friends.

So be it.

Interrupt did a short rewind, to be sure not to miss the next part, then hit "play."

". . . a little help."

"That you do."

"I need a look at the code."

"If there's anything in the code, Andy, the tiger team's going to find it."

"Maybe. But I'm the one who's high and dry out here. Maybe whoever trashed the switches left fingerprints in the code. Something. Some record of how he got into the switch."

"You already looked. We all looked."

"We got started. Come on, Lloyd, we had how many million lines of programming code to wade through? I want to look again, I want into that code." A long pause, then Faulkner cleared his throat. "Can you get me the password, get me access?"

No answer, just even breathing.

"I'll say I forced you at gunpoint."

"It's not that, Andy-man. They've gone security mad here. They're redoing the memory protect, they're squeezing data access and program access. We can't debug without a fucking license. You gotta be able to translate Russian into Swahili to figure out the password. We don't even have access to the toilet without a hall pass."

"Can you at least get me a printout of the source code? There must have been five or six copies floating around."

"Security owns them now."

"Then how about the call records?"

"Security."

"Look, I ordered a mag tape of the call records after the cutover. I never got a chance to do anything with it, but it should be in my file cabinet."

"Your file cabinet is in the DMZ. I know. I watched some guy who looked like Robocop slap locks on your cabinet and your desk, and I just managed to stop him before he poured cement into your workstation."

"Shit."

"Don't swear. Colson has a key. Colson glowered and insisted he had to have access to all records in his kingdom."

"Security and Colson are the only ones who have the key?"

"They didn't give *me* a key. You want me to transfer you to Colson and you can ask him for it?"

"I'm off the team, man. Colson's code of ethics is binary, on or off. When you're on the team, it's total loyalty, and when you're off the team you're dead."

"Good point, Andy-man. You're fucking dead."

"Maybe. Where does Colson keep the key? In his desk?"

"We all lock our desks now, Andy. We tear up our phone messages and eat them. We wear chastity belts. You can thank Security."

"How hard is it to open a locked desk? Or a locked file cabinet?"

Interrupt stopped the tape again. What expression was on Faulkner's face when he suggested . . . well, it was burglary, wasn't it? Did his face show pain? Fear? Disgust? *Something,* something gut-wrenching, because Faulkner, too, clearly had a binary code of ethics—right or wrong. It was there in his face.

So do I, thought Interrupt. Right or wrong.

Interrupt let the tape continue.

* * *

". . . a locked file cabinet?"

Another pause. The line hissed faintly.

Finally, "You want me to ask around, Andy?"

"I want . . . I want you to do whatever you're willing to do. Whatever's right. It's my file cabinet, my records."

"What's fucking right isn't always what's fucking smart."

"Lloyd, I need to see those records."

"Why don't you ask your girlfriend?"

"What?"

"Nell Colson. The daughter of the man with the key to the call records."

"What do you mean, my girlfriend?"

"You still brain-damaged? What do you think I mean?"

"She's not my girlfriend." Faulkner sounded embarrassed, like an adolescent.

"She was in here this morning, to see Daddy, but she wanted to talk about you. Were you okay? Were you very unhappy? I told her they were going to shoot you at dawn."

"Great idea, Lloyd. I'll just ask Nell to break into her father's locked desk. Maybe I should get to know her first, what do you think, ask her out to a movie?"

"I think she'd do it."

"But you wouldn't?"

"It's different. A difference in opportunity. She's his daughter, she can get a look in his desk. If she gets caught, she can say she broke a fingernail and she was trying to find a file. A woman can get away with things that a man can't."

"Jesus, Lloyd, you let Candace hear you talking like that, she'll nail you to the wall."

"You disagree?"

"I agree she has a unique opportunity. That's it."

"So ask her."

"Sure."

"Will you forget the fucking Stanford ethics code? *Ask.*"

"Honor code."

"Whatever."

"Thanks, Lloyd, I . . ."

Interrupt cut it. The Stanford honor code. The big-deal Stanford honor code.

The first time Interrupt had seen the word "Stanford" was in *Telephony*. Reading the magazine the way Mother read the Bible, fervently, but always impatient for the next issue while she was content to reread verses she knew by heart.

But this article, this one Interrupt had read again and again.

The article had been titled "Filling the Gaps on Transatlantic Cable." The cables that ran beneath the Atlantic connecting telephone traffic between North America and Europe were vastly inefficient, the article began. Because of the way signals were transmitted, each cable was in use less than half the time. During any given telephone conversation, there were pauses, and these pauses ate up valuable transmission time. But a new technique, called Time Assignment Speech Interpolation, or TASI, promised to double the capacity of the costly submarine cables. The new circuitry could detect the instant that a speech element began, locate an inactive portion of the transmission channel, and assign the unused space to the speech element. What TASI did was wedge portions of one conversation into the pauses that were occurring in another conversation.

Interrupt had sat on a tree stump in the yard, rough and uneven, and admired the beauty of TASI.

But there was more. The article had quoted one of the engineers who contributed to TASI, a research associate at Stanford University's innovative Center for Telecommunications. "At Stanford," the engineer boasted, "we design elegance." The article had described the Stanford engineers as "stars."

In the following days and weeks, reading the article again and again, Interrupt had begun to say it out loud. "At Stanford we design elegance." And, saying it out loud, Interrupt had set a course: to study at Stanford and become a Stanford engineer, one of the stars. That was a promise.

Interrupt stared at the tape recorder. Faulkner was one of the stars.

Suddenly, Interrupt struck out, hitting a row of plastic boxes, and components exploded throughout the room, clattering against the walls and raining to the floor.

Hard little insects scattered and mixed up on the floor. Inelegant.

A scratch bloodied one finger. Interrupt sucked the wound and thought again, there is right and there is wrong.

7

•

Nell was climbing in front of him, picking her way up the
trail with the ease of a browsing deer. This time she wasn't
wearing the jeans and blue workshirt; her short white blouse
skimmed her waist and her pink corduroy pants were rolled up
to her knees, rolled far enough to show how tanned and finely
shaped her legs were. The bulky pack on her back rode
smoothly.

"You want to rest?" Nell called, not looking back.

The pack he carried dug into his shoulders. He turned to
check Wayne, hiking too close behind him in the rutted trail.
The kid wasn't even sweating.

Beyond Wayne, the hill swept downward in a wide slope
and knee-high golden grasses softened its contours. He took a
deep breath. But there was no real sense of height. He let it
out.

They had come well over halfway up. He could see a long

way: there wasn't much on the hillside but stands of oak and scattered poppies. Down below the hills were the red tile roofs of the Stanford campus.

He turned. "We don't need to stop," he said to Nell's back.

This was not the way he wanted it. He had wanted the two of them, without Wayne, in some uncomplicated place—a coffee shop, a park. He would have preferred to just do it over the phone. He had called her, every telephone call now made with a touch of dread. When he stumbled like a teenager, she had spoken up and invited him and Wayne on a picnic. He could think of no way to refuse her invitation.

Up ahead, Nell disappeared into a fringe of oaks. Andy and Wayne followed up the trail, through the trees, and emerged onto the spine of a ridge.

The first thing that caught his eye was a line of telephone poles sticking up along the ridge. They led toward a concrete-block building in the distance. He remembered that Stanford's engineering departments maintained some labs up here.

Nell was under a large oak, tramping down the grass. They dropped the packs and she opened the one he'd carried, pulling out a blanket. He grabbed a corner and helped her lay it out on the flattened grass.

They sat in a triangle on the blanket, and she pulled containers out of the pack and dished up plates of food. Falafels, tabbouleh salad, Greek olives, pears, cans of juice, a box of gingersnaps.

"This looks great," said Andy, accepting a paper plate. There was no way he was going to be able to ask her about the call records.

She handed Wayne a plate, then turned to Andy and whispered, "How did he get to be deaf?"

"He was born deaf." Andy faced Nell. "But he lip-reads. Whispering won't help."

"It can't be fixed?"

Wayne sat cross-legged, hunched forward, eating and watching them with the same taxing attention he gave the television.

"It's a nerve defect. The auditory nerve, it connects the inner ear to the brain. It's like a telephone system," Andy said. Wayne's eyes glazed over; he knew this story by heart. "The outer and middle ears are like the wires coming into the house, and they're working, they're conducting current. But the nerve in the inner ear, the telephone inside the house, doesn't work. And it can't be fixed." Andy took a long drink of apple juice.

"That must have been hard for you. And his mother."

Andy glanced at Wayne. The boy had wearied of the effort of following their conversation. "It was. In fact, she couldn't handle it."

"So she . . . ?"

"Left."

"Does she ever see him?"

"Sometimes." When it was convenient, when Sandra happened to be in town, when he pushed it.

"Did you love her?"

Jesus. He turned away from her, toward Wayne, but his son had stretched out on the blanket, his back to them, and was idly yanking up strands of grass.

"Yes," Andy said.

"You must hate her for leaving."

"Hate?" He stared down at his lunch. His stomach knotted. Did he hate Sandra? He had been angry at her for so long; if he felt anything else, it hadn't yet surfaced above the anger. "She was young," he finally said, "younger than I was." Anger, just anger. "It's better that she left."

Nell snapped the covers back on the food containers. "That's what Ray did."

It took Andy a moment to realize what she was talking about. "Ray left your mother?"

She nodded. "She put him through grad school, and then the bastard left her."

"I'm sorry. Before you showed up, no one even knew he *had* a family."

"He didn't, until I showed up." Her mouth compressed.

"You sound as if you . . . well, hate him."

"I did. I spent a lot of years so focused on him, what I wanted to say to him, what I wanted to do to him, what I wanted to happen to him. I had a picture of him, just staring out at the camera with his look. You know it. He's probably never smiled for a camera. So I would stare at this picture and pretend that he was looking right at me, that he could see the expression on *my* face, that he knew how I felt. God, I really hated him." She suddenly smiled. "I don't hate him now."

He wasn't sure he believed her. Drop it, he thought. Take her hand and say, then Ray doesn't deserve a family, he doesn't deserve your loyalty. And then say, can you help me? Ray has a key to some records that I need.

And then say, I deserve your loyalty? Shit.

"I came up here from San Diego, that's where I was living, that's where my mother is. I was out of school, with no exactly hot prospects for a job, except for another summer selling athletic shoes. I guess I got curious, I thought I'd give him a chance. So I came up here and got a job with Pac Bell to impress my father."

"Why did you have to impress him?"

"I didn't know how else to approach him."

"It's not easy to impress Ray."

"You know what I found out? He's not always a bastard. You know what he did when I finished lineman training? He brought me up here to celebrate."

"Here?"

"Yeah. He brought along strawberries and champagne."

He bought her off with champagne and strawberries. Andy

had never seen Colson take a drink. The team didn't socialize outside work, except for lunches and the occasional beer at Scott's Seafood after work, and Colson didn't even join them for that. Christ, Colson popping a bottle of champagne under the oaks, offering strawberries like some Woodside yuppie.

How about offering her sympathy? I understand. My father was a demanding jerk too. So can you help me? *No.* "I guess you impressed him."

"I'll show you." She grinned and jumped up. The golden beach girl again, sunny and open, not a shadow of hatred in her. She shifted back and forth, on the balls of her feet, a runner ready to fly. "Come *on.*"

Andy rose, and Wayne, coming alert, scrambled up after them.

She grabbed the unopened pack and led them to the nearest telephone pole. Wrapping an arm around it, like an old friend, she said slowly, too loud, "Wayne, this is *my* telephone system, this is the heart of it."

"Just speak in a normal tone, so the words form naturally," Andy told her, eyeing the pack. What was this?

She wet her lips. "Your dad will say the switches are the most important, and you probably think it's your TD1)." Still too loud. "You want to know where the voices are?"

Wayne nodded yes.

Nell pointed up. "Up there. My job is to climb the pole and keep the voices moving."

Wayne craned his neck to follow the pole.

Nice, Andy thought. Wayne liked it. Andy liked her for it.

Then she was opening the pack and setting its contents on the ground, and he froze.

She'd brought pole-climbing gear: boots with sharp gaffs, safety belts with long leather straps, heavy gloves, orange hard hats. Two sets of gear. The smaller pair of boots had stripes of pink reflective tape; the larger pair was clearly for him.

"Nell . . ."

"I guessed on the boot size. I have a good eye for that, but I brought some heavy socks for you in case they're a little big."

He hoped they were a little small.

Wayne was looking over the gear. He understood.

"If you don't want to, that's okay, but I thought you might like to give it a try. It's a thrill up there."

"No, thanks."

"We won't go too high."

"I've never climbed anything."

"I can teach you."

"Great. Can you set bones too?"

She was pulling on her boots. "You won't fall. I'll climb behind you, that's how sure I am that you'll do fine."

Wayne already had a safety belt, was fooling with the strap, grinning at his dad. With his big hands and feet, grinning, he looked like an eager puppy.

Andy took hold of the strap. "Not you, Rambo."

Wayne let go, signed, "You climb."

You're going to have to disappoint him, Andy told himself. Just like you disappointed Joe Faulkner.

Andy had been eight or nine, and the family had been living in upstate New York, in the Adirondacks. The mountainous resort region was known for its gorges and rivers, and the state was still building roads to bring people to the resorts, and bridges to cross the wild waters.

Work had finished on the bridge, and it would officially open the next morning. Joe Faulkner wanted to suspend this consummate moment in time, so he went out to the bridge precisely at sunset. He brought Andy along, because of the Roeblings.

John Roebling had been an iron-willed civil engineer in the mid-1800s who designed dams, aqueducts, and bridges. He also built his son into a civil engineer. He named the boy

Washington after a surveyor he knew and packed him off to engineering school. Joe Faulkner might never have heard of the Roeblings had it not been for their most famous engineering feat. Father and son designed and built the Brooklyn Bridge.

From the time Andy was old enough for bedtime stories, Joe read to him from a biography of the Roeblings.

The sun, Andy remembered the sun, lowering behind the humped Adirondacks, glazing the foamy river with a red glow. Joe walked out on his bridge, carrying a paper bag. Andy walked close behind, arms stiff at his side, staring down at his sneakers.

It was a suspension bridge, a soaring concoction of towers and cables and stiffening trusses. Joe stopped at the middle and leaned on the railing. Andy stopped beside him.

Joe reached into the bag and pulled out a handful of bolts and steel shavings, scraps from the construction. He stuck out his arm and let the scraps fall into the river below. He was nominally Catholic and slightly superstitious, and after every project he fed the water steel so that it would not take down his bridge.

Joe held the bag out to his son. But Andy was frozen; he had looked down and thought he saw his own face in the water below. His stomach churned wildly, like the river, and his face was slick with cold sweat.

This was the worst it had ever been. Every time Joe had brought Andy out to one of his bridges, it had gotten worse. Andy could never tell Joe, and so Joe did not dream that his son was terrified of heights.

"I thought he'd get a kick out of watching you," Nell was saying.

Andy shook off Joe, then he caught Wayne's keen look. He wiped his hands on his pants. His palms were wet and his mouth was dry. He would just tell them no, he didn't like heights, he wasn't a lineman and didn't want to be a lineman, he didn't have to climb this piece of wood, he didn't have to pull some stupid macho stunt to impress his son and Colson's daughter.

How high was the pole, anyway? He didn't look up.

"Okay," he said, tight. If he climbed it, then she owed him one.

The boots were maybe a half size too big.

Suited up, he felt more at risk. All this damned equipment so he wouldn't get hurt. He caught Wayne admiring him, admiring the hard hat and the boots with their gaffs that flashed in the sun.

He couldn't help noticing the way the belt looped around Nell's hips. She had rolled down the legs of her corduroys and tucked them into the boots, but the short blouse still exposed her midriff when she raised her arms to put on her hard hat.

Sex and fear, he thought.

No telephone pole is totally straight, Nell was explaining, so you have to find the side that leans away from you and start climbing there. He found the leaning-away side and shoved against it, hard. If he had detected the slightest movement he would have ripped off his gear.

Strike the gaff cleanly into the pole to get your foothold, she was saying. Heels together, toes and knees out from the pole.

He had one foot off the ground and looked back at Wayne. The boy gave him a thumbs-up and watched with serious attention.

He moved up and checked his position. Heels together, toes and knees out. The belt chafed as he moved the strap up the pole. He would climb it as fast as he could and keep his eyes locked on the worn pine in front of his nose.

He felt a slight shudder in the pole and froze, then realized that Nell had started below him and what he felt was the vibration of her gaff chunking into the wood. He climbed, already feeling his thigh muscles working.

"Keep your butt out," she said.

He wished she were climbing in front of him.

"You're doing fine. Okay? Rest whenever you want."

"Great," he yelled. He was already sweating, his hands steaming inside the rough gloves. He could see blue sky beyond the pole that filled most of his field of view, and a bit of horizon where the sky met the grasses. He would climb slowly, the hell with fast.

"I climbed with Ray, when we came up here."

He jerked his head around and looked down. She was right below him, he saw her orange hard hat, her brown arms, her pink corduroys, and below that the ground, far enough, the grass trampled, Wayne foreshortened, flickering at the edge of his vision. His stomach cramped and he snapped his head back up in desperation and pressed his cheek against the pole. Jesus.

"It was sort of a ceremony," she said, and she was now beginning to pant. "Me becoming a lineman."

If he didn't pull a stupid trick like that again, if he just kept his eyes steady front.

She taught Colson how to climb? So what was this, a reenactment?

"You okay?"

He couldn't answer, but he moved his right leg upward, knee locked into position as instructed, and kicked his gaff hard into the pine. He inched up the strap, brought up his left leg, dug in the gaff. The left gaff wobbled, it wasn't in far enough, sweet Jesus it wasn't holding. He wrapped his arms around the pole and jabbed again with his left foot.

He remembered, with gut-sick clarity, the part in the Roebling biography when tragedy struck. There was a surveying accident on the Brooklyn Bridge project, and it killed John Roebling. Washington Roebling, too, met with an accident on the project, and although it didn't kill him it crippled him for life. The project continued, and the legend was somberly repeated: every bridge demands a life.

Andy's left foot was dangling in the free air.

"Trust your safety belt," Nell yelled, "get back into position."

He got the left gaff in. Was he in position? he thought, paralyzed. She didn't say, she didn't tell him. He could smell the preservative in the wood, he could feel the sun like a heat pump on his back. Then the nausea and dizziness circled him, came at him, hit him like double fists. He didn't dare close his eyes, that was the worst thing in the world. He looked hard at the pole, he gripped it until he thought his fingers would snap, but he had to hold the pole still. Please, God. He was dying.

She was touching him, he felt her hand on his right ankle. She said something but he couldn't hear it.

He swallowed, to hold back the nausea, and said, "I'm coming down." It was a whisper, it wasn't even that. It was a prayer.

He expelled a breath, hard. "I'm coming down."

She heard. She was tapping his right boot, a gentle tug.

Move it. He had to get down.

"Just reverse it, slow and easy."

He got the gaff out and his foot hung in the air. Then the headache came, a third fist, and he knew he wouldn't make it.

She had hold of his foot, tugging it down. He wanted to scream at her to let go, but he flexed and moved down and had the presence of mind to wait for her to let go before he dug in the gaff.

In a prolonged mime they climbed down, Nell tapping his boot when he froze. She didn't coax him and he was deeply grateful.

But for the safety strap lashing him to the pole, he would have collapsed when he touched ground.

She was holding Wayne back, casually, and he was grateful again.

Leaning against the pole, he unstrapped himself and yanked off the hard hat. He couldn't look at them. He held up a hand in a wave to them and walked off stiffly in the opposite direction.

He heard Nell saying to Wayne, "Let's go get some cookies."

There was a stand of oaks, and the knee-high grass, and he fell into it and heaved up his lunch.

On the bridge, on the bridge when Andy wouldn't take the bag from Joe, Joe had looked closely at his son and seen the fear. Andy had not been able to hold back the hysteria, and he sobbed out. Joe grabbed him roughly by the shoulders, shaking him, but Andy couldn't stop. Then Joe had slapped him full across the face.

Andy forced himself to get up, and walked through the oaks until he stopped shaking.

Nell met him halfway back to the blanket, where Wayne waited, and handed him a can of apple juice. He drank it steadily down. She didn't look at him, just walked beside him.

"You think of everything."

"Why didn't you tell me you're acrophobic?"

He concentrated on the oaks ahead and breathed slowly and evenly. The juice stayed down.

"I didn't think you'd notice."

Wayne couldn't wait; he loped over to them and fell into step beside Andy. Andy punched his son's shoulder lightly and let his hand rest there.

Joe Faulkner had said to Andy, days after the incident, that the slap was the only way to bring Andy to his senses. Andy hadn't believed that. He knew that his father had slapped him because he had failed. You're not engineer material, Joe meant. An engineer who was afraid of heights could never build a bridge.

He would get no help from the memory of Joe Faulkner.

He was conscious of Nell on his left side, walking close. He slipped his left hand into his pocket. "Nell, when I called you I called to ask a favor." He figured he had earned it.

"Sure."

"Don't say sure yet." He took a slow deep breath. "I need some records, they're records of telephone calls. They're on mag tape, magnetic tape, you know, a tape reel. The tape is in my file cabinet." Unless the Robocop took it, but why assume the worst? "The problem is, the file cabinet is locked, and I don't have access because I'm suspended." She knew that. "But I need that tape. I can't clear myself without the records on that tape." He swallowed. "Your father has a key to the lock, probably in his desk."

"You want me to ask my father for the key?" She didn't miss a beat.

He had never before been glad Wayne was deaf.

"I don't think that would work. I think the only way is if you could get into the drawer and find the key." *Get into?* Say it straight. Break into, burglarize, steal. Andy turned to look her full in the face. "The desk is locked. You'd have to somehow get the key to the desk, which would likely be on your father's key ring, or you'd have to break into the desk. Then you'd have to go unlock my file cabinet and get the tape. It's in the front of the bottom drawer. And you'd have to return the key to your father's desk, all of this without having anyone see you." Without getting caught.

Her eyes, warming, gold like the grasses, sympathetic and amused like that morning in his cubicle.

"Sure," she said.

Sure. He shivered. Hey, Dad, he thought, it's different with telecom engineers. No lives for bridges.

8

•

No way in. Doors locked, windows locked, she wasn't careless.

Not knowing what to expect, Interrupt brought it all. Pry bar, bolt cutters, glass cutter, duct tape, volt-ohm meter, wire, screwdrivers, whatever implements were handy and could be crammed into the toolbox.

There hadn't been time to plan, hadn't been time to think it through.

The one absolute necessity Interrupt had attached to the lineman's belt: the automatic, with a pair of leather gloves draped over it.

Already, deep inside Interrupt's head, the pressure was beginning to build.

She lived in a duplex. The neighbor's unit was dark; sleeping, or, please, not home. Her unit was dark downstairs, lighted upstairs.

The best place, only place really, was the back patio door. French door, wood frame with flaking paint. Good. Double-keyed dead bolt. Bad.

Try it.

Interrupt pulled on a pair of latex gloves, took the glass cutter from the toolbox, and scored an arc near the door latch. A squeak, like boots on hard snow. Interrupt jerked the cutter away, hand already sweaty in the glove.

Silence. Nothing happened.

Come on, you've cut glass before. Interrupt took a breath. Not like this.

Interrupt forced the blade back to the glass and scored the second arc, then covered the circle with silver duct tape. A hard tap with the heel of the hand and something gave. Interrupt peeled off the tape; a round of glass came away with it. A hole now gaped beside the door latch.

It worked.

But the head pressure was flowering.

Interrupt got out the volt-ohm meter, set it to the most sensitive current scale, and attached the coil of wire to it. Then, hand shaking, Interrupt swept the wire coil around the wood-frame perimeter. According to the meter, no magnetic field. No burglar alarm.

Interrupt slipped the roll of duct tape onto one wrist and, gingerly, reached through the hole in the glass to unlatch the door. It swung open easily. So she hadn't locked the dead bolt; careless, after all.

Swiftly inside now.

Interrupt moved the leather gloves out of the way of the automatic.

From the second floor, light seeped down the stairwell. Interrupt slowly took the steps.

Pain stabbed behind the eyes, enough to bring tears. Damn

her. *Damn* her. Interrupt took the automatic from the belt and flicked off the safety.

Two doors led off the upstairs landing. One to a small room, a study, empty. The other to the bedroom. Interrupt moved in increments, ready to leap ahead or bolt. The bedroom was lighted, empty. The door from there to what had to be the bathroom was slightly ajar, and Interrupt inhaled steam and soap. No sound of a shower running. Then there came a sound—water lapping as a body shifted position.

She was taking a bath.

The headache pulsed like an alarm, and Interrupt nearly groaned out loud.

Gripping the automatic, Interrupt stepped toward the bathroom door.

She splashed, and Interrupt hesitated, and saw the telephone on the bedside table. The telephone. People didn't think twice about it.

Serendipity.

Interrupt snapped the safety back on the automatic and replaced it on the tool belt.

The roll of duct tape still circled Interrupt's wrist. Interrupt tore off a piece, picked up the telephone handset and dialed the lineman's ring-back number, replaced the handset, and taped it securely to the body of the phone.

She had a long cord on her phone; she was one of those people who liked to be able to carry it with her as she moved around. Most likely, she took it into the bathroom now and then.

She should have had a cordless.

The phone rang. *Move.*

Interrupt kicked the bathroom door open and lurched inside, gripping the phone set.

She was already half up, arms flexed, hands planted on the

sides of the tub, going to scramble out and answer the phone. Now she froze, staring gape-mouthed at Interrupt.

"It's necessary," Interrupt said softly.

"I . . ." she said. "What are you . . . ?" Now she twisted to reach for a towel that lay neatly folded on a small table beside the tub. Beside the towel were an open bottle of shampoo and a box of bath salts.

The phone rang and Interrupt flung it into the bath, then backed hard against the wall.

The phone was still ringing when it hit the water. Current flowed through the water, flowed through her, and there was no escape because water, especially water with bath salts, was an excellent conductor of electrical current and she was immersed in water.

Her body convulsed and Interrupt could see, below her breasts, the muscles of her chest seizing up in an uncontrollable contraction.

Bile rose in Interrupt's throat, burning.

Suddenly, her body relaxed, her chest muscles were released, and she struggled in the water like a stunned fish, gasping for air.

The current had stopped, but the duct tape held the handset firmly in place and Interrupt tensed for the next ring pulse. The bell might have shorted out, but the ring pulse should come.

She knew it, she was trying to come up out of the water, trying to regain command of her shocked muscles.

Interrupt slapped a hand onto the automatic.

Their eyes met, for an instant, and Interrupt saw panic, fear, hatred, shock, or maybe it was just bewilderment.

She grabbed the faucet, trying to drag herself up, and she was still gripping it when the next ring pulse came, pumping current through the water, through her, to the metal. The muscles in her forearms were frozen in contraction and she held onto the faucet as if it were a lifeline.

Interrupt's head was pounding.

Suddenly, she let go of the faucet and toppled backward into the tub, banging her head, sending a wave of water out onto the floor, her arm flailing and striking the little bath table. The towel, the shampoo, and the bath salts tumbled into the water. She lay dazed, but then her hands, slick with green shampoo, came out of the water and reached out toward Interrupt, as if for help.

The ring pulse came again, current flowed, and her slack body began jerking again. Now her head sank below the water. Her eyes were wide open, staring, but Interrupt thought panic still flickered there.

When the current stopped it seemed to take seconds for her to surface, trying for air and taking in water.

Interrupt turned away, hearing the desperate sounds of asphyxiation.

Then water lapping gently, then, finally, quiet.

Interrupt turned back to face her. She had not surfaced again. The water was still, tinged an unnatural green by the shampoo.

Interrupt waited, counting out three full minutes, counting in time to the exhalation of each breath. The headache was excruciating, pulsing like a live thing.

Abruptly, Interrupt dropped to the floor and shoved back the toilet seat and hugged the bowl, stomach convulsing, and vomited over and over, helpless as a child.

The room was steamy, stifling, foul.

Interrupt flushed the toilet, found cleansers in the medicine cabinet, and scrubbed the toilet and the floor spotless, scrubbed until the only odors in the bathroom were of cleanser and shampoo.

Then Interrupt fled, through the bedroom to the stairs, craving the clean outside air.

Idiot. Interrupt stopped dead. Idiot. There was no choice but to go back.

It should have been like walking back into a nightmare, but it wasn't. Almost peaceful, because it was over.

Interrupt yanked on the cord to drag the phone out of the water. The duct tape was hard to peel off, and left sticky strands. Interrupt took a bottle of rubbing alcohol from the medicine cabinet, doused a wad of tissue, and gently wiped the adhesive. The telephone, a rose-colored Trimline, smelled of shampoo.

For the first time in hours, Interrupt began to relax. The simple act of scouring the phone was healing.

The telephone. Commonplace thing. No one thinks twice about it; everyone expects it to work. Interrupt had learned that lesson, hard, as a kid. Mastering the components of power that made the world work.

The adhesive loosened.

One day there had been noise on the line, and Interrupt had torn into the phone set to fix it. But something went wrong and it died. Interrupt tore into it again, and then Father came in to use the phone and found his ten-year-old had spread its guts over the table. Father, smooth-shelled but feral at the core, spitting out the warning. *Don't ever touch the phone.*

The alcohol vapors ate at the pressure in Interrupt's skull, easing the headache.

Don't ever touch the phone. At first, Interrupt had burned with humiliation, but then had seen to the heart of things: that mastery of something that everyone needs and few understand *is* power.

The rosy Trimline gleamed, without a trace of adhesive. Satisfied, Interrupt dropped the phone back into the tub. The handset floated free and lodged in the crook of her knee.

Interrupt replaced the rubbing alcohol, closed the medicine cabinet, and left.

Outside, there was only the smell of the night, and the cool air to draw the heat from Interrupt's face.

Back on track now, back in control.

Still, an ugly, ugly night. Damn her.

9

Feferman filled the doorway, giving off the scent of a whole pine forest.

Andy took a step backward. "The police have already been here."

"I know, they talked to me. Now I'm going to talk to you."

Andy moved out of the way and Feferman lumbered in. The big head swung in a slow circle as the chief special agent inspected the room. Andy watched, eyes burning with fatigue. "What does AT&T Security have to do with murder?"

"Murder?" Feferman cocked his head. "Who says it was murder? She's in the bathtub, the phone rings—there's one of those little brass tables by the tub—she reaches for the phone, she's expecting a call, but just then downstairs a burglar is breaking in. She's startled by the noise and she knocks the phone into the tub." Feferman's small eyes locked on Andy.

"I thought you didn't buy coincidences."

"I don't ignore possibilities. You look like hell, Mr. Faulkner."

"I just lost a friend."

"I just lost a member of my tiger team."

"You shit."

"Considering your obvious distress, I'll let that pass. Now. I'm going to listen to the message that Ms. Fuentes left on your answering machine. I instructed the police not to touch, not to even breathe on, anything in this house having to do with telephones. It all belongs to me now, Mr. Faulkner."

"Help yourself." What did it matter?

"You're going to show me where the answering machine is."

Andy spun around and walked into his workroom. He could smell Feferman at his back.

Feferman looked over the racks of electronics parts stacked against the wall, the computer on the desk, the modem that hooked the computer to the phone, the answering machine. "You do a lot of tinkering in here? Freelance stuff?"

"There's the answering machine."

Feferman stuck out a thick stubby finger and punched the play button. Tape noise, then loud, clear, and excited, Candace's voice. "Andy! Dammit, you're not home. Gotta *talk* to you." Tape noise again.

Andy held his breath.

Candace's voice continued. "You know I hate these things. Anyway, look, I've been reading code and call records night and day and I finally got some time off to relax and I just couldn't turn it off. I'm at home, and I've just had a brainstorm. Hold the presses, right? If I'm right, this gets you off the hook and maybe gets someone we both know on the hook. I want to kick it around with you before I call Feferman in the morning. Guess I shouldn't tell you, but screw that, we're on the same team. Just *call* me as soon as you get home."

Tape noise. Feferman slowly rubbed his chin.

Then Candace's final words, light. "Remember at the cutover, the story about Strowger? *Call* me, pal."

The tape stopped, then rewound. Andy watched it spin. She was dead, and there was her voice, alive, on tape. Eternal digitized life, until the tape rotted.

Feferman sat down in Andy's desk chair and revolved to face Andy. "From the top. You were *where* when Ms. Fuentes called?"

"I went over this with the police."

"Go over it with me."

Andy repeated the story. How he and Wayne had gone to Blockbuster but the movie they wanted was out, then they had gone to Fry's Electronics and browsed, then to Happi House for Japanese fast food, then to some yogurt place for a cone. Then home, and some TV. Then Wayne went to bed and Andy checked his messages, and, excited, called Candace back. But her phone was out of order. Andy reported it. But, thinking of the number fives, he got suspicious. Thought of going over to Candace's himself but didn't want to wake up Wayne, and Helen wasn't home. Called the police.

Feferman smiled. "So your son is your alibi?"

"I don't need an alibi, Feferman. I'm not a killer."

Feferman shrugged. "That's not my business. What Ms. Fuentes said to you in her message is my business. She was wrong to call you. She should have called me."

"So *fire* her," Andy hissed.

"That was crude."

"Yeah."

"What's the story about Strowger?"

Andy told him the story about Strowger.

"Does it mean something to you?" Feferman asked.

"No."

"Nothing? Nothing worth dying for?"

"Feferman, she's *dead*. The hell with Strowger."

Feferman spun the chair around to the desk and picked up the phone set. Balancing it on one big paw, he spun back to Andy. "It occurs to me," Feferman said, revolving his hand to showcase the phone, "that the message on your answering machine is a cause and the death of Ms. Fuentes is an effect."

Andy just stared.

"You, of course, listened to the message and perhaps—I'll have to figure this out with a stopwatch and all that—perhaps you had time to pay Ms. Fuentes a visit. The effect."

"She was my friend."

Feferman squinted at the phone. "Or . . . or someone else heard the message, intercepted the call, and subsequently paid Ms. Fuentes a visit."

Andy drew in a sharp breath.

"If that were the case, then it would follow that your lines are wiretapped or your phones are bugged. Did that occur to you?"

It hadn't occurred to Andy. All that had occurred to him since the police had arrived and said "Candace Fuentes" and "electrocuted" had been that he was in a nightmare where unthinkable things were happening. He had sat, after the police left and until Feferman showed up, and tried to understand the fact that his friend and colleague was dead. And, irrationally, he had checked in on Wayne half a dozen times to make certain that his son was just sleeping.

He looked at the telephone resting on Feferman's palm. It was the standard AT&T boxy desk phone, like the telephone that had sat on his father's desk, except that this one was chocolate brown instead of black. Brown had been on sale, a color that went out of style. The color had been irrelevant to Andy. He had cared about what was inside the phone, and AT&T built highly reliable telephone sets.

What was inside the phone?

"I've had some training in detecting wiretaps. Would you like me to examine your phones?" Feferman asked politely.

"I'll do it," Andy said, tight.

Feferman grunted and handed him the phone.

Andy knew zip about wiretapping, but he did know what belonged inside a telephone and what didn't. He disconnected the cord. He got a screwdriver out of the desk drawer, turned the phone set over, and removed the back plate. Everything looked right: the wire pair, the transformer system, the connect/disconnect switch, the dial pulser, the signaling bell. He reassembled the phone. "Nothing."

"Christ," Feferman said, grabbing the handset, "check in the most likely place first."

They bent, heads almost touching, over the handset. Feferman unscrewed the cap on the mouthpiece. The transmitter fell into his hand; he rotated the disk, flipped it over, peered inside the drilled holes. It was a simple carbon microphone, but the black ring inside was not standard.

"That," Andy said, "doesn't belong."

Feferman tossed the transmitter to Andy. "Congratulations, Mr. Faulkner. You've just caught your first bug."

Andy held the thing in his palm. Somebody had gotten into his house and put this thing in his telephone. He kept a spare key under the planter by the back door into Wayne's room so that Wayne could get in when he came home from school, in case he forgot his own key.

Somebody had come into his goddamned *house.*

Somebody, he suddenly thought, had been outside his house the night of the storm. He hadn't tripped; somebody had knocked him down.

The same person who had come into Candace's house? Andy's hand closed tight over the transmitter and his knuckles stood out white. The same person who had gotten into the number fives.

He agreed with Feferman. He didn't buy coincidences.

"Lifting the handset supplies line voltage to the bug, and it picks up whatever is said into the mouthpiece," Feferman said. "The bug transmits a radio signal to a receiver somewhere. Can't be too far away. Maybe we'll find it, maybe we won't."

Andy swung on Feferman. "Then we know someone was listening in. We know someone picked up Candace's message and went to her house and—"

Feferman cut him off. "We know there's a drop-in bug in your telephone. We don't know who put it there." The chief special agent laid a heavy hand on Andy's shoulder. "You could have put it there."

Andy stiffened under the weight of Feferman's hand. "What?"

"As a cover. So we would concoct the scenario we just concocted. You've discovered two things about me, Mr. Faulkner. Remember them. One, I don't buy coincidences. Two, I don't ignore possibilities."

"Feferman, for God's sake, I didn't bug my own phone."

"Who did?"

"The same person who shut down the switches."

"And pinned it on you."

"Yes."

"So this person has it in for you?"

"Yes."

Feferman held up his hands. "But it is Candace Fuentes who is dead."

Andy felt a jolt, something shifting inside. *Candace Fuentes is dead.* How was that possible? How did a person who was as alive as he and Feferman just hours ago cease to exist? If anyone had asked Andy to describe Candace, he would have said, she's quick. She has a sharp mind and a sarcastic tongue, she looks like a girl at a tea party but she's the toughest one on the five-E team. She's somewhere in her early thirties, she went to Berkeley, she's not married. He had never asked her out, never approached her as an available woman, at first because she was a coworker and then simply because she had become a friend. And now the central fact about Candace Fuentes was that she was dead.

"So I'm naturally wondering," said Feferman, "if whatever Ms. Fuentes was talking about on your answering machine was something that worried you." Feferman's heavy face was alive with interest, the black eyes bright, the bear single-mindedly ogling its prey. "A motive."

"Get out," Andy said.

Feferman blinked.

"*Get out.* If you want to talk to me about switches, I'll come to your office. If you want to push your way into my house and hound me, I'll file a complaint with your superior."

"There is no superior. I'm the chief."

"You're a hired gun."

Feferman stood and moved close enough to embrace Andy. His size and scent were nearly overpowering. "Are you trying to antagonize me? I'm going to give you my best advice on that subject. *Don't.*"

"Get out."

Feferman picked up the answering machine, pried it open, and removed the tape. He slipped it into his jacket pocket. "*Now,* Mr. Faulkner, I'm going to leave. If I want you in my office, I'll tell you when to come. If I want to visit you again, you're going to welcome me." He wagged a finger at Andy, then turned and trudged into the living room.

Andy didn't follow. He heard the front door open, then Feferman's voice. "You're going to call me when you figure out the importance of Mr. Strowger." The door slammed shut.

Andy dropped into the chair, still warm from Feferman's body.

If he could have had any wish granted right now, he would wish to be sitting in Colson's office with the team, kicking around some minor alarm that was provocative, not lethal, hearing Candace's high, clear, sarcastic voice assessing the damage.

Suddenly, he lunged for the phone. He got dial tone and jabbed in the number that was jotted on his desk blotter. Then he slammed down the handset; there was no transmitter in the phone. There was the bug, still in his hand, but he was damned if he was going to reinstall that.

He sprinted into the living room and used the phone on the coffee table. The thought came that they hadn't checked this set for bugs, but he didn't care, he just counted the ring-backs and waited for her to pick it up. He was shot through with adrenaline.

Finally, she answered, voice cottony from sleep.

"Did you get the call records?" he said, hoarse.

When she realized who he was and what he wanted, she answered. "Not yet."

"Don't try." For God's sake, Nell, don't end up like Candace.

10

•

Andy opened his hand and spilled the sand down onto Candace's coffin. Then he walked away, fast, his palm gritty where sand grains clung to sweat.

He moved uphill, above the long line of mourners waiting to file past the hole in the ground and release their sand.

A small grove of eucalyptus offered shade, and Andy stopped there. The smell of eucalyptus made him think of Stanford; the trees were all over campus, and on a warm sunny day like this the leaves would release their oils and saturate the air with the astringent odor.

Below, a slight figure in a well-fitted suit paused beside the hole, looked down, and with one elegant movement scattered sand onto the earth. Amin. He turned from the grave and followed Andy's path uphill.

"I am sorry," Amin said, stopping beside Andy.

"Me too." Andy picked out Speedy and Lloyd in the line, and farther back, Colson.

"I didn't really know her. Just that once at the cutover, you understand."

"Nice of you to come."

"Respect for the dead," Amin said softly.

Andy looked downhill.

"Andy, my chick, a quick word. Sometime soon I would like to talk with you about these switch failures."

"Anything to do with switch failures is the business of telco Security."

Amin pressed his fingertips together, steepling his hands. This was a gesture he had used in class for effect, inviting the student to rethink his position. "I am concerned about you, about your difficult situation."

"I'm alive."

Amin broke the steeple and patted Andy's arm. "I hear that you are suspended, and under a cloud of suspicion."

Andy didn't ask where Amin got his information. Amin always had access to information. He remembered Amin as his students saw him, native of Jordan, schooled in Europe and Boston, alighting at Stanford for no one knew how long, consulting and conferencing in Chicago, New York, Los Angeles, Milan, London, wherever the principal people were meeting. A player in the real world. Amin was the processor in his own communications network.

"Andy, I had a thought that may be of use to you. Perhaps, though, this is not the time or the place."

The mourner standing over Candace's grave, bulky and huge even from here, was Feferman. Feferman dropped his sand, wiped his hands, and stepped aside to watch the others in line.

"Now is all right," Andy said.

"Well. If you are certain." Amin waited a moment, discreet, then resumed. "As you may or may not know, I've made a little study, a hobby, of the technical phenomenon of phreaking."

"Phreaking? You think it was a phone phreak who sabotaged the switches?"

"Most probably not. But the phreaking network is buzzing about these switch failures. Possibly, they have learned something useful."

"Then they should report it."

"Phreaks, as a rule, are not drawn to report things to officialdom."

Andy glanced at the mourners. The chief special agent, head tipped back, white face shining in the sunlight, was looking uphill at them. Too far away to overhear, too far away to read lips if he had the skill, but close enough to be curious. The bear sniffing the wind. All he would catch would be the odor of eucalyptus.

"We've had a phreak over at R-TAC," Andy said. "The guy is into everything." Candace, he recalled, had left the phreak a rude message on the bulletin board.

"Andy, I must repeat that I don't think a phreak is actually responsible . . ."

"Why not?"

"Well, it's possible, in that phreaks are technically clever. As are a good number of non-phreaks."

"But this takes more than technical know-how. It takes a certain mind-set."

"Do you mean criminal?"

"Maladjusted, at the least."

Amin stepped out into the sunlight, to a worn granite gravestone. He regarded it a moment, then sank gracefully to the ground, legs crossed, perching on the stone. He looked up at Andy, sweeping his arm in a half-circle. "Please?"

Andy sat on the grass beside him. Amin had held seminars

on the grass outside the engineering building. Never before, though, on a gravestone.

"Let's consider maladjustment. I have had students who were quite bright, in the ninety-ninth percentile. And some of them, in my opinion, were capable of activities that someone might call maladjusted. Perhaps, more accurately, we'll call them skewed. They are concerned with the technical distillation of the problem without regarding the nontechnical parameters, the human dimensions." Amin gazed at Andy. "But then all of us in the ninety-ninth percentile share that weakness to some extent. You, Andy, have certainly been . . . carried away . . . by the thrill of the hunt."

"Carried away? That's not the same as crippling two switches." Andy folded a blade of grass. "Not the same as murder."

"It was murder, then?" Amin did not show surprise.

Remember at the cutover, the story about Strowger. His strongest memory of Candace, Andy thought, was going to be of a voice on an answering machine. *Someone we both know.* Strowger, the cutover, Amin. There was a crosspoint, the kind that Feferman would savor.

Andy stared at Amin. *No.*

Amin was consulting his watch. It was a crafted gold watch, thin, European, not an engineer's watch. Andy remembered it, or one like it, how Amin would always remove it and slip it into his pocket before touching any equipment in the lab.

Amin did not get carried away.

Someone, in the line of mourners down below, was crying.

The eucalyptus oils, like a medicinal inhalant, filled Andy's head and made his eyes water. Now, he thought, he would associate the smell of eucalyptus with a funeral, rather than with student days on campus.

"Andy," Amin said, "would you like to talk to your phreak from R-TAC?"

"You *know* him?"

"No. But my little hobby has given me a certain reputation in the phreaking world. I am considered to be a nonjudgmental interested observer. Phreaks have tremendous egos, they can't resist someone like me. If I put the word out, he may contact me, and I can perhaps induce him to contact you."

"Do it, then."

"For one of my chicks, anything." Amin rose. "I have class in forty-five minutes." He held out his hand.

Andy scrambled up and took it.

"Take care of yourself, Andy."

"Thank you."

Amin headed down the hill, headed back to his students. No one would ever mistake him for a student; not because of his graying hair but because of his bearing, fluid and surefooted, that of a man who had only answers.

A phreak. The thought remained in Andy's mind. He knew no phreaks. Phreaks were like ghosts; they came and went as they pleased, and unless they chose to reveal themselves they remained invisible. It was possible, he suddenly thought, that a phreak knew him.

Later, when he walked back down the hill, there was still one mourner at the grave site. Ray Colson stood erect, hands folded behind his back, gazing down into the earth like a watchful hawk. Then he knelt, probing the grass. He did not look up as Andy approached, and Andy stopped and waited for him to finish his search. As he waited, he noticed the top of Colson's head, how expertly Colson's hair was cut to disguise the thinning.

Colson stood, holding the dandelion that he had torn from the grass. "When I was a child," he said, "we used to call these milk fairies."

Andy had never seen such an expression on Colson's face:

113

open, almost daydreaming. Feeling like an intruder, he fixed his sight on the dandelion.

"I don't believe I ever told that to Nell."

Nell had not come, Andy thought. But then, she barely knew Candace.

As much as Amin knew Candace. From R-TAC and the cutover.

Someone we both know.

Christ, Andy thought. No. Someone we both know. Colson was someone he and Candace both knew, as was Lloyd, and Speedy, and twenty other people at R-TAC, and how many others from field calls and conferences.

Andy turned to Colson. "I thought Nell might have come."

"No," he said, terse again, Colson again. "But I'm meeting her back at the office for lunch, if you have a message."

Andy froze. The five-E team, what was left of it, was here, and Nell was alone at the office.

Colson lifted the dandelion close to his lips and blew hard. The silky filaments exploded into a cloud, then took a long slow fall back to earth.

Like fairies, Andy thought.

Colson watched the bits of dandelion float down into Candace's grave. "More appropriate than sand, don't you think?" he asked, leveling his oscilloscope look on Andy.

11

●

Foothill Boulevard sliced across the back lands of Stanford, the foothills for which the road was named angling upward from its western side. It was two-laned and narrow here, jammed with traffic routed around Stanford. Joggers scissored dangerously close and cars crowded them back.

Andy snapped on the radio, punched the buttons past the all-news station, classical, TalkNet, New Age, heavy metal, reggae, and stopped when he hit old Creedence Clearwater. They used to play this kind of stuff in the lab at Stanford, hard-beat rock, always oldies, loud straight-on music that fed them energy at three in the morning. Andy turned up the volume and rolled down the window and sucked in the tang of California browning—weedy, heavy sage, bone-dry and warm—while Creedence intoned the bayou.

His heart echoed Creedence: heavy downbeat, insistent.

He came to the turnoff, a graveled driveway that cut

through the trees several hundred yards to a dirt clearing. They had left the car here when they hiked up the hills for the picnic. Today, there were a couple of parked cars and, at the far end of the clearing, the van with the "E.T. Phone Home" bumper sticker. White with red stripes girding its flanks, the red starburst logo, and "Pacific Bell" in humble gray block letters.

He parked, shutting off the engine and Creedence, got out, and approached the van.

There was no one in the cab of the van so he walked around to the back and knocked softly on the doors. Her face appeared, screened, at the tinted glass windows. Then the doors flew open and he saw her clearly. She smiled. "Come in."

He climbed into the back of the van and she slammed the doors shut behind him. The window tint filtered the light inside to amber.

There were huge spools of wire, racks of parts, test phones, large green metal boxes, a ladder strapped to one wall and a pegboard of tools to the other. Stacked in the corner were the two sets of pole-climbing gear.

He didn't see a mag tape reel. Disappointment, relief, then disappointment again hit him.

Nell sat on a metal box and invited him to sit on another. She wore the blue workshirt and jeans, but she had on sandals instead of boots. He wondered if the sandals were supposed to offset the Pac Bell truck; if she had something to give him, she wasn't doing it as a telco employee.

"You said on the phone . . ."

"No, I didn't. All I said on the phone was meet me here."

"Okay." He watched her. "I like secret meetings."

"You think this is crazy."

"No, just cramped." The metal boxes were close; their knees jammed together. He tried to keep his breathing even.

116

"Andy, did you ever think that your phone might be wire-tapped? Or your house or your car bugged?"

He was momentarily stunned, as if he had gotten the wrong way across a power supply. He had never thought of such a thing until Feferman suggested it, and now he could not touch a phone without wondering if it was tapped.

"Think about it," she said.

He started to tell her about the drop-in bug, but instead said, light, "Who's going to tap the phone of a telecom engineer?"

"God, you engineers have such egos. You're just like a doctor who won't admit he's sick."

"All right, I'm sick. What do you know about wiretapping?"

"We cover it in training."

After Feferman had left that night, he had examined his other phones and found them clean.

"There are some nasty little bugs out there," she said mildly.

"You want to check out my phones?"

"If you want me to." She grinned at him, pleased, or amused. Then she leaned across him and stuck her hand into the space between the metal box he was sitting on and the wall of the van. She produced a bulging manila envelope, laying it on the box beside him.

He willed himself not to look at the envelope. He watched her eyes, the almost-gold irises widening as she waited for his reaction.

"Did anybody see you?"

"Nobody." She paused. "Almost everybody was at the . . . thing . . . for Candace."

"I wish you hadn't taken the risk."

"There was no risk. I made a lunch date with Ray and asked him for his keys so I could wait in his office."

So easy, he thought.

"It's what you wanted, isn't it?"

"Yes. But after what happened to Candace, what I wanted was for you to stay out of this."

She shrugged. "Too late."

He nodded.

"Do you want me to return the tape?"

"*No.* No more risks." He glanced at the envelope. "I don't want you to take it back."

"Then say thank you and stop worrying."

He took her hand, held it gently resting on his knee. Her fingertips were work-roughened but the palm was soft and warm. "Thank you, Nell."

"Any time." With her free hand she pushed loose curls of hair back from her face, tried to tuck them into her braid, and he saw in surprise that she was nervous.

He was grateful. More than that: he was stirred. He could see the pulse beating in her throat, fast, an alarm gone red.

"Nell." He let her hand go and reached for her, moving his hands to her shoulders, down her back, feeling the heat of her skin through the workshirt. She slid onto the box next to him, pressing close, and laid her head on his chest. He could feel his own heartbeat vibrating through her.

He touched her hair, his hand shaking. He pulled off the band that held her braid and dug his fingers deep into the red-gold plaits. Her hair was slippery clean, like a child's.

Her lips were at his throat, and he breathed in sharply. "Look at me," he whispered.

She tipped her head back. Her face was flushed, her lips still open.

He kissed her. Her hands pressed hard on the back of his neck, she was pulling onto his lap, and he slid his arm under her legs.

As they moved, they knocked the envelope to the floor.

* * *

They lay in a canyon of equipment, a spool of wire rising above their heads, a latticework of racks and shelves flanking them on either side. Andy stared up at the black coils of wire, tightly ribbed, then at Nell. She was tanned all over, a harvest of sand and water and warm beaches, but here amidst the tools her sweep of flesh was stunning. As he continued to stare, she sat up and pulled her workshirt from the tangle of clothes beneath them and put it on. "You're beautiful here," he said.

"Here?"

He waved a hand: the tools, the truck. "Context." He tried again. "Like gold in the gravel." He shoved up beside her, his body stiff from the hard floor. "It's more striking that way." He stopped; shut up, fool.

She held the edges of her shirt but didn't button it. "You're very nice."

He leaned closer to her, touched his forefinger to her cheek, and traced a line down under her chin. He realized he had made the sign for "girl."

She turned to him. "Don't tell Ray about us."

"Ray?" He pulled back. "You're more likely to see Ray than I am."

"When you get back to work."

Andy picked up his pants, held them over his groin. "Why shouldn't Ray know about us?"

"Well," she said, "the records . . ."

He saw. He saw her on the picnic with Colson, the celebration. The strawberries and champagne. She has come all the way up from San Diego, taken a job with Pacific Bell, she won't be an engineer but she joins the telco, just like him, to please him. She wants to impress him, and by God she gets past the calibration, she registers approval on his scope. He toasts her with champagne and feeds her strawberries, he acquired that trick somewhere, maybe that's how he courted her

mother. Then, pleased and probably astounded with her success, she shows off and teaches him how to climb.

Now she looks at the stolen records and she feels guilty.

"You don't want to lose what you started on that picnic
with Ray."

"Whatever it was." Her mouth compressed, then relaxed.
"Well, it *was* something. When I was climbing with him it was
a real father-daughter thing. You know what I mean. The
father passes along his skills and there's this bonding . . .
except"—she laughed—"he didn't actually pass along that
skill."

"You taught him instead."

"No. He already knew how to climb."

"What?" Had Colson been a lineman?

"He was at some ATT facility in Connecticut, about ten
years ago. He took one of his sabbaticals, you know about
those?"

Andy nodded. Colson had his own way of dealing with
whatever stresses deviled him. He simply left. If he had vacation time, he took it; if he didn't, he went without pay. He
never told anyone where he was going, he never checked in
while he was gone, and he didn't always return when he said
he'd return. He'd taken a sabbatical a couple of months after
Andy had joined R-TAC; Lloyd had calmly informed Andy
when he came in to work that Colson had "gone over the
fucking hill." After a six-day absence Colson showed up, unmarked by whatever he had experienced.

"He turned up at the ATT pole farm and taught himself
how to climb."

"Pole farm?"

"Yeah, they test telephone poles to see how they withstand
weather and animal attacks. Anyway, he knew some guy there
who let him climb the poles."

"Ray told you about it?"

"Ray doesn't explain." She shrugged, and her breasts disturbed the drape of her shirt. "He brought the equipment when we went up the hill. It was his idea to climb."

"So you figured out the pole farm?" Andy stopped himself from reaching out to part the edges of her shirt.

"No. Lloyd Narver told me about it."

"Lloyd? How did he know about it?"

"I don't know."

Did Colson confide in Lloyd? "When did Lloyd tell you?"

"A couple of days ago. I was waiting for my father."

"Why?"

"Why what? Why did he tell me?"

"Yes."

"We got to talking about Ray and I asked him a few questions and it just came up."

"Lloyd just happened to tell you that Ray took a sabbatical to a pole farm, how many years ago?"

"It came up. If you must know, he teased me about you, and I bragged about you climbing the pole. We talked about that for a while, and then I asked if he knew how Ray learned to climb."

"Why would you ask him that?"

"Because he seemed to know so much about my father. I mean, no one knows a *lot* about Ray, but Lloyd knew some stories."

"He never told me."

She grinned. "You're jealous."

"No, I'm not."

"You think Lloyd was coming on to me."

"Lloyd's married."

"So?"

So Lloyd didn't come on to women, Lloyd never talked about them, never talked about his wife. "What stories did he tell about Ray?"

She crossed her arms, gave him a hard look. "Maybe I'll tell you sometime."

"What's wrong?"

"Nothing. I love being interrogated after sex."

She was smiling, her eyes glinted gold and warm, but her arms remained crossed tight across her chest.

"Christ, I'm sorry." Andy kissed her softly on the cheek, and when she turned her head, on the mouth. Through the screen of her hair he gazed at the manila envelope. The bulge in the envelope had the shape of a mag tape.

12

●

Andy glared at the computer, turned his back on it, strode across the room to the window, shoved it open. Early-morning fog seeped in.

He paced back to the computer. He had fed it the call records from the mag tape and now it was running his program SORT. But it was taking its own sweet time, plodding through the thousands of calls in a half-assed search for whatever it was that Candace had found in the records.

If indeed she *had* found something there. Maybe whatever she found was in the code, somewhere in the programming that told the switch everything from how to send dial tone to how to wipe its nose. Maybe she hadn't *found* anything, maybe she was just going on a hunch.

Strowger, he thought. It made no sense.

Maybe whatever he was looking for existed only in his fevered brainpan.

His neck was stiff, his eyes ached, and his stomach was acid with coffee.

He went back to the window and let the fog chill him.

He could taste a bitterness along with the fog. It wasn't the coffee. He connected the taste with an urge he had not felt since childhood. It was a single-minded schoolyard desire for revenge.

Andy spun around and paced to the computer.

The computer continued to sort. Scanning the numbers, searching, looking for multiple calls from/to the same number, calls from/to AT&T prefixes, from/to R-TAC, from/to anyone or any place that Andy could dream up or cast suspicion on in his dead-of-night programming. Patterns.

More significantly, the computer was trying to find a match: a pattern that occurred before both switch failures. Whatever Candace had found had to be connected to both failures.

Andy went back to the window. It was gray outside, the gray before dawn, cold weak light that wearied him to the bone. Too damn cold. He slammed the window shut.

Suddenly, the printer clattered. Andy turned and watched, gripped, as if he had never seen a job run before. He tore off the printout.

Behind him was Joe Faulkner's chair, its mahogany arm jutting into the back of his knee, nearly forcing him to sit. The chair had been brown suede once, but had been worn shiny and smooth as the scarred hide of an animal. He let himself down into his father's chair, braced a foot against the wall, and flipped to the last page of the printout.

NUMBER PATTERNS FOUND, 458; NUMBER PATTERNS MATCHED, 0.

Zero.

The rule was, never panic. You crawl through the list and look at the patterns until you find something that means something. Four hundred and fifty-eight patterns. Columns of numbers, the number of the calling party, the number of the called party, the time, the duration of the call.

His eyes were dry, scratchy, burning. He got a red pencil and began to work through the numbers.

When the computer bell rang, it took him moments to surface. On-screen, a window had flipped up with a communication coming in through the modem: "Dialog requested."

Who was calling him at dawn?

As he stared, the communication changed to: "Will reinitiate dialog request at eleven." Whoever it was, was leaving a message. Andy sprang to the computer, hit the hot key, and logged a reply: "Accept dialog. Who's calling?"

The answer rolled across his screen.

"FLAME ON ********** u dont know me but I know u. Congratulations!!!!! Ive agreed to beam into yr system and set u straight. u may address me as Zot."

The phreak, Andy thought. My God. He quickly typed, "Did Amin al-Masri ask you to contact me?"

"Conceivably."

"Are you the phone phreak who's been listening in on R-TAC?"

"Ive told u my address is Zot and if u insist on a label it is COMMUNICATIONS HOBBYIST."

Andy froze. This was going to be like trying to hold a weak signal on a scope: if you moved the wrong way, you lost it. He finally typed, "I apologize. Communications hobbyist. You must know a lot about the telephone system."

"I know everything. More than u."

Amin had told him about phreaks' egos. This one clearly was voracious. Andy thought a moment. Challenge him. He typed, "How could you? I have a Ph.D. in telecommunications and experience in design, research, and troubleshooting. What do you have?"

"Consummate skill."

"You also need information."

"Yr bell telephone journal is available in any tech library. I cn call any switch office and get anyone to tell me ANYTHING cuz I cn use phone company jargon and sound just like one of u ***** they think anybody who talks like that is authentic. I cn get passwords. I cn call an operator and she thinks shes talking to a lineman and she will verify a line for me—patch me into a test loop—tell me anything. Im in yr system WHENEVER I want to be in it!"

He was bragging, exaggerating. Andy didn't know a lot about the phreaking world, but he did share the common knowledge. Phreaking had begun in the sixties, when someone figured out that he could build a device that would produce the same tone signals as those that controlled the telephone switching network. All he had to do was put the device against the mouthpiece and produce the frequencies needed to route his calls and turn off the toll-charge accounting. Soon there was a network of phreaks using these "blue boxes" to make free calls. Then they figured out how to build other spoofing devices, like red boxes that simulated the sounds of coins dropping into pay phones.

The phone phreaks had finally ticked off AT&T. The phone company installed detection equipment on its circuits and began to catch the phreaks. These days, Andy guessed, phreaks weren't making many blue-box calls. Then what the hell were they doing?

Zot might have consummate skill and every issue of the *Bell Journal* ever printed, but he couldn't have the kind of total access he was bragging about. That was the kind of access, Andy thought with a chill, that could get you into the processor of a 5ESS.

Andy typed, "How long have you been a communications hobbyist?"

"TEN YEARS!!!!!! ******* I came online when att was switching over to D so rite off the bat I had to learn the language."

Andy could picture it, the whole phreaking underground scrambling to learn AT&T's new programming language, D.

"I played around for a while," Zot was typing. "At first it was just enuf to be in the system. The telephone switching system is the BIGGEST COMPUTER NETWORK IN THE WORLD and I was HUMBLE but then I learned the ropes. ******** HEY telephone man u shld take better care of those switches!"

Andy searched the screen for the phreak behind the words, the guy who called himself Zot, who with his anonymity and arrogance assumed he had total control. He was a ghost, faceless, no more than an on-screen flicker. Andy typed, "Nobody knows what happened to those switches."

"Nobody."

"You don't know?"

"Even I dont know."

"I thought you knew everything."

"About the system not about sicko *****hackers*****"

"Was it a hacker?"

"I dont know."

"Why did you bring up hackers?"

"Hackers give us a bad name!!!!"

"Hackers or phreaks, what's the difference?"

"Youre a troll. Listen up troll!!! The communications hobbyist is NOT in the business of sabotaging the phone system."

"You're certainly into ripping it off."

"Troll, its there for the taking if u have the skill. Troll if u picked up a pay phone and found an open line u wd use it. Every mister and misses Average American wd use it. BUT THATS NOT THE POINT!!!!! Im really not into free calls that much."

127

"What are you into?"

"Purity. Im into the pure beauty and elegance of the system."

Well, so am I, thought Andy. He typed, "Then you wouldn't want to see it damaged. You'd tell us if you knew anything about a . . ." Andy searched the keyboard, "*****hacker***** who's screwing with the switches."

"Tell who? I wouldnt tell the cops I wouldnt tell the federal bureau of idiots and I wouldnt tell yr security goons."

"Me. Tell me."

"WHY shld I?"

Flatter him. "Because you have access that I don't have. Because I need your help." Andy imagined the phreak, stretching and purring like a cat.

"Yr not a communications hobbyist why shd I trust u?"

"I work with a communications hobbyist," Andy typed. "She goes by the name Lady." He was getting good at this. Lying. The saying was right, he thought; Candace would roll over in her grave. "Do you know her?"

"Lady. A cipher to me."

Andy grimaced. Let it go. "Will you contact me if you learn something?"

"Well well well troll we will see. U cn contact me thru yr friend or I might contact u. WE WILL SEE. ***** FLAME OFF."

The window went blank. Zot was gone.

Nothing. The phreak had given him nothing.

He turned back to the printout. He tried to focus, but his eyes blurred.

God, he was tired.

He went into the kitchen. A black sludge was left in the coffeepot, so he drank tinny orange juice from the open can in the refrigerator. The thought struck him that he had become a phreak himself, angling to get into the system, to get access, a ghost who wouldn't go away.

I know you, Zot had said, but you don't know me.

Did the phreak mean that he knew about Andy because Amin had passed him a message to contact this poor sucker Faulkner, or did he mean that he knew all about Andy and his son and the TDDs, the way someone who was setting him up knew him?

Sunlight suddenly breached the oleanders outside the kitchen window, slivering inside to shine the green counter tiles. Andy leaned into the counter and let the rays warm him.

He closed his eyes.

Sunlight and redwood tables and oaks and worn grass and the smell of frying grease. Rossotti's Alpine Beer Garden, up the road in the hills above Stanford. There were other hangouts: the burgers were better at the Oasis, chili came with the burgers at the Dutch Goose, but on a bright gold California day you wanted to eat charred meat outside with the sun on your back and the air smelling like trees instead of cars, so you went to Rossotti's. Sooner or later, almost every Stanford student made his way to "Zot's."

Even a phone phreak named Zot?

The phreak could have taken the name from a comic strip or a science fiction paperback or a hacker bulletin board. Or it could be that he called himself Zot because he liked the hamburgers at Zot's.

Did Zot mean that he knew Andy because he had been at Stanford with Andy? Maybe he was one of Amin's chicks. If so, did Amin know that his chick was the phone phreak called Zot, or was Zot a ghost to Amin too?

Somebody had set up Andy, and Andy had been a Stanford student.

Stanford.
Prefix 725.

Andy bolted into his workroom. He was already pouring over the printout before he touched down into Joe Faulkner's chair. There were a good number of calls to or from Stanford numbers, especially on the night of the cutover at the Palo Alto office.

He should write a new program, isolating all the numbers with Stanford prefixes, checking for patterns. But it took time to write a program and run it.

He couldn't put down the pages.

Something was there. He knew it the way he knew when he had a bug cornered in 5ESS, and he knew he would find it. His eyes were sharp and his head was clear as he ran through the printout.

Most people could recall, if pressed, every phone number they'd ever had.

725-6652.

It stopped him cold.

Oh *yeah.* He knew that number.

The computer had printed it out as a two-call pattern. Two calls to that number, separated by fifteen seconds. The calls had been made about fifteen minutes before the switch failed at the cutover.

Okay, he told himself, don't jump it. This meant nothing unless he could find the same pattern before the first switch failure. Hands shaking, he turned to the printout for that night, the night of the storm.

Almost immediately, he found the pattern, two calls to 725-6652, less than an hour before Wayne's TDD call and the switch failure.

His chest tightened. The time interval between these calls was over a minute. The time interval between the calls on the cutover night was fifteen seconds. The patterns didn't match. Just like the computer had said. NUMBER PATTERNS MATCHED, 0.

He rubbed his hand across his eyes. But this was it; he felt it in his gut.

He looked again, and his eye caught on another pattern woven in with the Stanford number. Two calls, about a minute apart, to 767-2676.

He flipped back to the printout for the cutover and there it was again. Two calls to 767-2676, twenty seconds apart.

Again, the same number, but the patterns didn't match.

Oh, you *idiot,* he hissed.

He grabbed his pencil and rapidly jotted the times of the two patterns before each failure, subtracting to work out the time intervals. The pencil lead snapped and he cursed.

Finally, he had it. Identical patterns before each switch failure. A match.

The computer hadn't found it because he had told the computer to look for a matched pattern of phone numbers.

This was a matched pattern of time intervals between calls.

The night of the cutover, the guy called 725-6652. Then he waited fifteen seconds. Then he called the number again. Forty seconds passed. Then he called the other number, 767-2676. Twenty seconds passed, and he called that number again.

The night before the storm, the guy called the numbers in a different order, but the times between the calls were the same.

There it was. Sweet Jesus, there it was. But what? *What* the hell was it, other than a pattern of calls, one set to a Stanford number?

He knew the Stanford number cold. 725-6652 was the phone number of Stanford's telecom lab. Anybody who had been an E.E. student in telecom had lived days and nights in that lab, and knew that phone number. He didn't recognize the other number.

Candace had gone to Berkeley. Was the other number a Berkeley number, is that why she had found it?

Andy snapped up the printout. First things first: where had the guy called *from?*

Andy circled the originating numbers in red and carried the printout over to the phone. He dialed the number from the night of the storm. He listened through ten ring-backs, then hung up. Come on, he told himself, you didn't really expect the guy to answer the phone and offer to turn himself in. Maybe throw in an apology as well?

He had better luck with the second number. Three ring-backs, and a peevish male voice answered, "Carolina Hotel."

Andy's heart raced. "Uh . . . is this, uh, which Carolina Hotel is this . . ." *Come on.* "Where are you located, please?"

"Palo Alto." The voice wasn't offering any more.

Keep him on the line. "Do you have any rooms available?"

"How should I know, fella? You gotta call the front desk."

He could picture a crabbed old man to match the voice. "I thought I was calling the front desk. Did I get your room by mistake?"

The voice snorted. "My room! I ain't got a phone in my room, this ain't the Ritz. You got the pay phone in the lobby, fella."

"I'm sorry I bothered you. I'll call the front desk."

"No bother. I don't get many calls."

Andy hung up. A pay phone in the lobby of the Carolina Hotel, in Palo Alto, and the guy had called from there to trigger the failure of the switch in the Palo Alto office.

Andy would bet good money that the phone calls on the night of the storm had been made from a pay phone somewhere near his house—a restaurant, a gas station, maybe another hotel.

He picked up the handset. What if he dialed one of the patterns? What would happen? He punched in the Stanford prefix, stopped, then hung up. Whatever the pattern did, he didn't want it on his call records. Not with Feferman on the prowl.

There was a pay phone at the gas station on the corner. He turned, heading for the door, then stopped. Wayne stood in the doorway, in his pajamas, watching him.

"You're up early," Andy said.

"You earlier," Wayne signed.

Clearly, Andy thought, he looked as ragged as he felt.

"What you working on?"

Andy sank back into the brown chair and regarded his son. Wayne's pajamas were emblazoned with the *Star Trek* logo, a birthday gift from his mother. Sandra's presents were always more appropriate for a younger kid; she seemed to think that because he was deaf he grew up slowly. But Wayne always wore or used whatever she sent.

Tell him you're working on the bills, Sandra would advise, he wouldn't understand all this stuff about switches.

Andy said, "I'm trying to figure out how someone made the switches fail."

Wayne came into the room and took Andy's desk chair. He rolled it back from the computer, spun it, and stopped to face Andy full on. Like the captain of something. "Maybe put something in the TDDs. Bad . . ." He switched to fingerspelling. "Component."

"No, the TDDs were clean. Good idea, though." Andy frowned. Why the TDDs? Did it have something to do with data versus voice transmissions? But no, you said "hello" on the phone and the word was broken down into electronic signals to be transmitted over the line; you typed "hello" on the TDD and the tones were broken down into electronic signals and transmitted over the line. The switch didn't recognize the difference between voice and data traffic; it didn't give a shit if you called with a TDD or a Mickey Mouse phone, it just processed the call.

The pattern of calls he had just discovered seemingly had nothing to do with TDDs. It was only when Andy or Wayne made a TDD call that the switches died.

Andy's skin prickled.

"What? What?" Wayne was mouthing.

Andy realized he was holding up the printout like a trophy. He said, slowly, more for himself than for Wayne, "Someone called two phone numbers in a certain pattern before each failure. When you pick up the receiver to make a call, you have access to the switch. All you have to do is communicate. Punch in your numbers."

Wayne's eyes riveted on the printout. "He could tell the switch what to do?"

"He could if he had set up some kind of communications channel." His own private hot line.

"How?" The stark sign.

"I don't know how he set up the channel." Andy gripped the printout. "But we seem to have a record here of how he used it."

"To stop the switches."

"To instruct the switches to fail when a call came through on one of our telephone numbers."

"Then we've got him!" Wayne's fingers played over the handles of the chair, as if he were triggering laser beams.

"No. We've got something. But we don't have evidence of how he set up the channel."

"Then look!" Fingers flying.

"We did look." If this channel really existed, there had to be instructions, a few rogue lines somewhere in the programming code. He and Lloyd and Candace and Speedy had combed that code looking for the virus that wasn't there, looking for anything bogus. No, they had *started* the job. "I looked, everybody's looking. It's not like one of the programs you use.

The program for the switch runs millions of lines of code. It's . . . well, it's complicated."

Wayne stared at him. Finally, he mouthed, "I'd look again."

"I can't." Andy stared back. "I don't have access to the code."

"What's that?" Wayne pointed at the printout.

Andy suddenly grinned. "A start."

He stood up, told Wayne to grab a jacket.

They went together to the gas station at the corner. As they crowded inside, Andy wondered if this was the phone the guy had used the night of the storm. He dropped in the coins and dialed 725-6652.

A young voice answered, a student. "Telecom." It sounded like "talcum." The voice was slurred with fatigue and Andy knew how it was, spend your Friday night in the lab and still there Saturday morning.

"Sorry," said Andy, "wrong number."

Eyes on his wristwatch, he hung up. He counted fifteen seconds, dropped in the coins, and dialed 767-2676. Just as the guy had on the night of the storm.

Ring backs, then a recording. "Good morning. At the tone, Pacific . . ." The second number was the recording for Time. He hung up, counted forty seconds, then paid and dialed the lab number again.

The kid answered right away, "Talcum."

"Sorry again." Andy hung up.

Wayne was watching him with a kid-intent expression. Worried or impressed, Andy couldn't tell.

Twenty seconds, and he put in his coins and dialed the last number in the sequence, Time again.

He stood there, the receiver locked to his ear, and waited through sixty seconds of Time, but as far as he could tell, no back door into the switch opened to him.

Finally, he hung up.

He undoubtedly needed some kind of number code, a password. That's the way he would have done it, so that no random caller could dial the sequence, unlikely as that was, and find himself on a private hot line to the number five.

He had found the guy's covert channel, but he couldn't use it.

Like a phone phreak whose blue box wouldn't work.

He pulled Wayne out of the booth. "Let's go get some breakfast, Spock."

On the walk back home, he replayed the story about Strowger, just as Amin had told it. For the life of him, he couldn't figure out how Strowger and the channel fit together.

But if Candace had seen a connection, then by God there was a connection.

13

•

REMOTE SECURITY CAMERAS
ARE IN CONSTANT USE
ON THESE PREMISES

Andy must have read the sign before, but it had never seemed to be addressed to him.

In fact, he had never noticed before how secure the grounds around the AT&T building were. Acres of grassy carpet rising into berms, well-trimmed trees, low flower beds; no one approaching the building would be out of range of those cameras. The private road curled through the grasslands and parking areas; speeding would be difficult.

Andy pulled up in front of the main entrance and parked in the visitors' lot. Without an ID badge, he supposed he was a visitor.

He walked past the side-by-side flags, the red, white, and blue American flag and the baby-blue AT&T flag, past the big concrete planters sprouting red and pink geraniums. Lloyd once had told him about the time the flowers had been ripped out of the planters and replaced with weeds. The joke went around that the deed had been done by someone irate over his phone bill. Whether or not Security nabbed the culprit was a topic of speculation; the flowers were replaced before lunchtime.

Inside, Andy glanced around a lobby he had rarely entered. This wasn't the way he came to work. He used a side door, quick access from the parking lot to R-TAC, and just slapped his badge against the scanner.

The lobby was huge, done in the smog sunset colors of brown, orange, tan, and red. Huge paintings on the walls, huge indoor plants in copper planters. He looked around for remote security cameras and then realized there was no way to check without appearing furtive.

The curved reception desk, too, was huge, like the side of a cruise ship. He identified himself to the receptionist, was verified, and was pinned with a visitor badge.

A gofer appeared and led him at a brisk clip up the stairs and into the Security district of the building. He had been here just once before, escorted by Colson into the conference room where they had suspended him.

The gofer bypassed the conference room, and Andy heard voices behind the closed doors. He wondered if the tiger team was meeting in there.

Security had assigned its chief special agent a corner office, no secretary. The gofer knocked, opened the door, delivered Andy, and closed the door behind him.

Feferman was standing in front of his desk, arms folded. "Mr. Faulkner."

Andy had seen a bear like Feferman on one of Wayne's nature shows, a full-grown adult male standing on his back legs in a stance of power and challenge.

Andy stepped forward. "I have some information for you."

Feferman said nothing, did not move.

Andy waited. He was certain that Feferman, whatever game

he was playing, wanted the information. Behind Feferman were a wood-grain desk, padded desk chair, speakerphone and a six-line telephone, gold pen and pencil set. No papers on the desk, one folder in the Incoming box. A secure desk. The desk abutted two oversize corner windows. Feferman had a sweeping view of the entrance to the AT&T building. Feferman could have been the remote security camera constantly in use.

"Sit down," Feferman said.

Andy found a straight-backed visitor chair. By the time he was seated Feferman had silently circled into his own padded desk chair.

"Feferman, I know how the guy got into the system."

Feferman just waited, as if Andy had told him that he knew what time it was.

"Do you understand? I figured out how the guy got into the number fives."

Feferman made a sound, a groan or a heavy sigh. He rubbed a broad white hand across his face. "The 'guy'?"

"The person who garbaged the switches."

"The person who set you up."

The person who killed Candace; neither of them said it.

"That's right."

Feferman swiveled his chair to face out one of the corner windows.

It was a game, Andy reminded himself. The chief special agent was a student of psychology. He said evenly, "I see that I'm wasting your time. Your tiger team's already figured it all out?"

Feferman swung his heavy head around to face Andy, swiveling his chair back to the desk. "Tell me your story, Mr. Faulkner. And don't waste my time."

"You be the judge of whether it's worth your time," Andy said, keeping it neutral; he was catching on. He explained the

pattern match, the calls, clear and brief as they did in R-TAC
when they presented a solution to Colson.

"Uh-huh." Barely a grunt from Feferman.

"It's clearly the same pattern."

"And so?"

"So the same pattern of calls before each failure can't be a
coincidence."

"Oh, I agree, Mr. Faulkner. I don't buy coincidences."

Andy tightened his hand on the chair arm. "So someone
intentionally called that sequence both times."

"And so?"

"And so . . ." Andy relaxed his grip and smiled at Feferman.
"Cause and effect, Mr. Feferman. We have a pattern of telephone calls and a switch failure. Twice. We have one of your
crosspoints. I assume the chief special agent can reach the
conclusion."

"My title is head of Security." Feferman smiled back at
Andy and leaned forward until his body touched the desk. His
face caught light from the window and the light disappeared
in his small dark eyes.

Andy said softly, "I think that the telephone call pattern
gives him a covert channel into the switch."

Feferman was nodding.

"Once he had his channel into the system, he programmed
the switch to fail when someone made a call to or from my
telephone."

Feferman kept nodding.

"Do you see? My number was just the trigger."

"What about the TDDs?"

Andy frowned. "I don't know. The switch can't tell the
difference between a TDD call and a standard call."

Feferman's eyes narrowed, nearly closed. "All right. Then
explain something else. How did he program the switch to
recognize this trigger call?"

140

"I don't know."

"There's a lot you don't know."

"If I had access to the code, maybe I could figure it out for you."

"So the answer is in the code."

"Candace seemed to think so."

"Ms. Fuentes made a cryptic reference to the story about Strowger. Are you going to explain how Strowger fits this whole scenario?"

"No."

"You don't know." Feferman was on his feet, starting to pace. "I deeply regret the loss of Ms. Fuentes. But I still have a tiger team, and my tiger team will find whatever is there to be found."

Andy did not turn. "Your tiger team didn't find the pattern match in the call records."

"Mr. Faulkner, you don't know what my tiger team had for breakfast, and you don't know what they found in the call records."

Andy could smell Feferman, piney, close; the chief special agent had stopped dead behind him. "Breakfast? Probably cold cereal and strong coffee because you don't give them time for more. The call records? They looked for patterns but they couldn't find a match."

"Why not?"

"Because the match is in the intervals of time between the calls. But it would be damned near impossible to look for a match of time intervals between calls when you don't know which calls, out of tens of thousands, you're checking the times of."

"But you managed."

"Only after I recognized the telephone number from Stanford. Anyone on your tiger team from Stanford?" Candace, Andy thought again, had gone to Berkeley. If she *had* found the pattern, she apparently had not shared it with Feferman.

"Stanford," Feferman said. He circled back to his desk, sat down. "Hotshot school. And you're a hotshot Stanford man. You think that's part of the setup? The Stanford number?"

"I thought of that."

"Or maybe this person is connected with Stanford."

"I thought of that."

"But if this person were connected with Stanford, why would he choose a Stanford number as his channel into the switch?"

"To set me up."

"And risk exposing himself?"

"I sure as hell hope so."

"So who is it?"

Andy stared. Feferman seemed genuinely curious. No games. "I wish I knew."

"Brainstorm. What's the first name you come up with when I say Stanford?"

Amin al-Masri. Andy was silent.

"You're thinking of your former professor? Your thesis advisor? Perhaps your mentor? Dr. Masri."

"I had quite a few professors at Stanford. I had lab partners, classmates . . ."

"All of them experts in telecommunications?"

Expert enough to sabotage those switches? Stanford students were bright, cocky as hell, but Andy wondered which of his former classmates was today that expert in telecommunications, which one hated the telephone system, which one hated him enough to set him up. And if there was one who qualified, was he capable of murder?

"No suspects?"

What about Zot? He didn't want to give Zot to Feferman, not yet anyway. "No. I wish I knew."

"Well, Mr. Faulkner, shall we just dismiss the Stanford connection as a coincidence?"

"We don't believe in coincidences."

Feferman smiled. "So what is the significance of Time? Why that number?"

"I don't know."

"Once again."

"Well, Mr. Feferman, maybe he's telling us that he has time on his side, so maybe we'd better work together and figure this *out*."

Feferman was on his feet again, charging around the desk, looming over Andy. "Mr. Faulkner, how did you get a tape of the call records?"

He couldn't answer, not without involving Nell. "I managed."

"You *managed?* I ordered *all* records connected with these failures to be confiscated by my people. Now I'm going to have to browbeat them and find out how and when they disobeyed my orders."

"They didn't."

"Then who gave you the tape?"

"I managed to get it."

"You're cleverer than I am?"

Andy stood. "I'm more desperate. You took my job."

Feferman looked surprised. He backed up to his desk, folded his arms. Stood as he had when Andy came in. "Thank you for the information, Mr. Faulkner. We'll take a good look at your theory and we'll take a good look at the Stanford angle."

"That's not enough."

Feferman waited.

"I want my job back."

Feferman shook his head.

"I've cooperated."

"You brought me an interesting pattern of phone calls, which may or may not be a channel into the switches. You brought me a possible Stanford connection." His tone became soft, friendly. "What you didn't bring me was any evidence that the channel could not have been created by you."

Andy felt sick. He was clutching the rail of a bridge, he was tethered to a telephone pole forty feet up, he was letting go and falling. He said, "Why would I tell you about the channel if I were the one who set it up?"

Feferman's answer followed him down. "The old bait and switch, Mr. Faulkner. Bait, you give me this channel, only you don't give me the entire thing, you just couldn't manage to figure out the final piece that makes it work, the password. So I get my tiger team busy trying to find the password, trying to verify your pattern matches, but—and here's the switch—there's another channel that really works. You keep me distracted with the dummy channel and I won't find the real one."

"Yeah, you got it, Feferman. I set the whole thing up. I bugged my own telephone. And I . . ." Andy just shook his head. "Jesus, Feferman."

"You might be telling the truth. But you're clever, you're an expert, and you brought me a pattern match that no one on my tiger team would have found. You see how it is?"

Andy saw.

Feferman smiled gently. "As the lawman always says, don't leave town."

"FLAME ON *********"

Andy read the message on his computer again, trying to see it as Feferman would see it.

"Hey troll have u seen this????? This is hi level secured stuff Im passing on ****** I didnt get it off the bulletin board u cn be sure. Read this NOW!!"

Andy obeyed, rereading the message that Zot had passed along.

> One switch, two switches . . . Two switches down, but I let them back up. What if the next 5ESS to go down doesn't come back up? And the next? And the next? How many will it take to convince you that your fives belong to me? Think about it. 5ESS is your major local-traffic switch. It's your most elegant switch. It took you years to develop and I can bring one down in seconds. Does that make your blood run cold? It should.
>
> Is 5ESS worth two million dollars to you? Two million in fifty-dollar bills. I'll let you know where to send them.
>
> One switch, two switches, three switches, four. Five switches, six switches, how many more?
>
> Yours truly, Interrupt.

Andy stared at the screen. Interrupt. I have a name for you now, he whispered. He wondered if Feferman would know that an "interrupt" was a facility in ESS processors that stopped a program in progress to run a program more urgently needed.

Interrupt. It was to the point. Andy thought that even Feferman's blood would run cold.

He reread the rest of the message.

"WELL TROLL how do u like that? A flaming sicko huh???? Thot u wld be interested,,,,,,still out of the loop huh? Think the telcos gonna PAY??????? Sincerely, Zot. **********
FLAME OFF"

Andy wondered briefly how Zot had copied a message sent

to top telco officials. No matter; phreaks undoubtedly had their methods. He hit a key and printed a hard copy of the message. He unlocked the desk drawer and put the message in the folder containing the tape of the call records and his program run. As he relocked the drawer, he realized that his security was laughable.

Two thoughts overloaded his mind.

One, if Interrupt planned to shut down another number five, shut it down permanently, whose phone number was going to be the trigger?

Two, if Feferman had ordered all records confiscated, and Robocop had checked Andy's file cabinet at R-TAC, why hadn't he taken the mag tape? And if he had, where had Nell gotten the tape that she brought him?

14

●

She wore a dress and carried a purse. The dress was yellow, soft-looking, modest—cut just below the collarbone and reaching below the knees. The yellow of the dress burnished her eyes, so that they were more gold than ever. Her hair was loose and wavy, catching in the neck of the dress as she turned her head. She wore white sandals, the ones she had worn in the van. He had expected her to show up in jeans and workshirt, carrying tools. The purse was small; it couldn't hold much more than a tiny screwdriver.

"Thanks for coming, Nell." He opened the door to her.

As she moved past him, he saw that her hair was damp. He shut the door, closeting them in the narrow entry hall, and caught the smell of shampoo.

She smiled and leaned toward him, tentative. The dress, the sandals, the washed hair—he thought this was all for him and he should kiss her. He could remember the press of her lips.

But if he kissed her now, it would be impossible to do what he had asked her to come for.

He said, "The phones . . ."

She straightened. "To business, then?"

"I'm sorry. Would you like something to drink?"

"No," she said, "let's get to work." She was the lineman then, striding into his living room. She headed straight for the gray Trimline on the corner table.

His wife had bought this phone, and agonized over the color choice. But she had neglected to take it with her when she left. Nobody remembers a phone when listing community property, he thought.

"I need a screwdriver," Nell said.

He got her one from his workroom.

She followed the phone cord to the wall junction, unscrewed the plate, and inspected the box. "It's clean." She turned to the phone set, disassembled it, studied the insides, and shook her head. He wanted to take the phone from her, tell her he'd already gone over it as thoroughly as she had, and his fingers actually twitched as he watched her work.

"They trained you to do this?"

She answered without looking at him, "They train us to check for devices while doing routine installation and repair. Basically, anything that we could find in a phone set or hooked to a line. They also train security people to look for stuff."

Feferman, he thought.

"Don't worry," she said, glancing at him, "I know my stuff."

He nodded.

She turned back to the phone. "Actually, a wiretap is pretty easy to install because it takes advantage of the basic operation of the phone. You have a microphone," she tapped the mouthpiece, "and a speaker," she tapped the earpiece, "and a wire to transmit your signals. And that's what the eavesdropper wants to do, pick up your conversation and transmit it."

"Yeah, I know how a telephone works." Having her do this was a mistake, but they were into it now and he was feeling a cold nervous dread.

Her eyes narrowed, hooded; he saw Colson in her. She abruptly returned to inspecting the phone. "Nothing there."

"Then this phone isn't tapped."

She replaced it on the table and faced him, all business. "There's no device on this phone. But all the eavesdropper needs is access *somewhere* within the phone system to the wires that carry the signals of your telephone. There could be a tap spliced into the wires between here and the central office. The problem then is, obviously, where."

Andy thought a moment. "But he'd need cable and pair information. He'd need to know which two wires are connected to my phone."

"Congratulations," she said. "You know how the telephone system works."

He flinched. "I deserved that."

"You sure did." Her mouth, taut like Colson's, relaxed into the familiar smile. "Okay, Andy, any more phones?"

He regretted that he hadn't kissed her when she came in the door, hadn't thanked her for the yellow dress and the damp hair.

He led the way into his workroom and stopped just behind her as she examined it. He turned his head in unison with hers, seeing the racks of electronics parts, the desk and computer, the brick and board bookshelves, the worn brown chair.

She traced the cord from the brown desk phone to the wall junction and checked out the box. She paused there, kneeling a moment as if in prayer, then shook her head, and he wondered if she had considered a way to avoid the phone set. But she stood and went to the desk. No, he wanted to say, stop.

But he let her disconnect the jack from the phone, take it apart, and look inside. It didn't take long.

"Andy!" In a quick, expert movement she plucked out the transmitter and whirled around to face him. Her dress flared out like a dancer's. Her eyes sparked, flashes of gold, and she held up the transmitter between thumb and forefinger for him to see.

He remembered Feferman plucking out the same transmitter with a grunt of success.

"Andy, it's a drop-in bug!" She held it out to him, forced him to take it. "It's real common. You replace the microphone capsule in the handset with this bug. It looks just about the same as the real transmitter, and it operates off the line voltage. You wouldn't even have known it was there. It doesn't add any noise on the line." Her cheeks flushed. "People sometimes think that a bug or a wiretap is going to make noise. People call us up and report that they're being tapped because they hear clicking noises on the line."

Andy closed his hand over the transmitter, felt it cold and hard against his skin as he had felt it when Feferman had given it to him.

"Well," she was saying, "you *were* bugged."

He stared at her. Unlike Feferman, he was not a student of psychology. He hadn't known what to expect: she would be cool and detached, or surprised, or furtive, or excited, as she was now. He didn't know what that meant; maybe she could hide surprise, she could act detached when she was excited, she could pretend to be excited when she wasn't. Or she could be excited for reasons he could only guess at.

She had brought up wiretaps, in the van before they made love, and a student of psychology might wonder whether she wanted him to take up the idea, look for a wiretap, look for a bug, and find it. It wasn't hard to find if you thought you might be tapped; it was, as she had said, real common.

Why would she want him to find this bug? He opened his hand, rolled the thing around in his palm. Maybe, the thought coming to him like a nugget uncovered, it was a decoy.

Andy walked over to the dismembered phone and dropped the bug beside it. "Well, whoever put it there, it's dead now, thanks to you." He didn't look at her.

She moved closer to him, he could smell her hair. "I'm glad I could help."

"Nell, could there be another one?"

"What?"

"Maybe this is a decoy." He kept his eyes on the cleverly designed little bug.

"What do you mean?"

"Maybe someone wanted me to find this. If I found it, I would feel that I had cleared my phones and I was secure. Then if there was another device, I wouldn't be likely to look for it." Bait and switch, he thought. He sounded like Feferman.

"Andy, a couple of days ago you didn't even believe that you could be bugged." She lowered her voice, mimicking his. "No one is going to bug a telephone engineer."

"*You* believed my phones might be tapped. A good guess."

She crossed her arms over her chest. "What are you getting at?"

"I'm wondering if you missed something."

"Well, then, maybe you better hire an expert." Her voice was pitched low, but no longer mimicking. "If you have several hundred dollars to spare. Or buy a wiretap detector. Or build one yourself; you're the Ph.D. engineer from Stanford."

"Stanford didn't offer a course in hunting down wiretaps."

"Then what do you want from me?"

He wanted her to say that there were some things she wouldn't do to impress her father. He wanted her to say that she had found the call records tape in his file cabinet and that's all she knew about it. He wanted her to say that as far as she knew, her father had nothing to do with any of this, and if he did have something to do with it, that she would not help him. And he wanted to believe her.

He said, "I'd like you to finish checking for taps. There's a phone in Wayne's room."

She glanced down and plucked at her dress, as if regretting the choice. "Let's go, then."

He led her across the hall into Wayne's bedroom. She looked around curiously, at the computer, the printer, the TDD, the shelf full of disks. He thought, expensive gear for an eleven-year-old.

"Like father like son," she said.

He glanced, like a guilty man, at Wayne's bookshelf and saw the biography of the Roeblings shoved in between a C. S. Lewis fantasy and an Ameslan handbook.

"Where is he?" she asked.

"At a friend's."

She inspected Wayne's phone and wall jack. "It's clean."

"So no more taps? Or bugs?"

"Andy, I don't know. Yeah, sure, there could be something. I mean this stuff gets really weird, sophisticated." She brushed past him to the wall, snatched down a framed photo of the space shuttle, and peered at the picture hook fastened into the Sheetrock. "I heard about a bug that's hidden in a picture hook, in the spike that goes into the wall. I don't know what it looks like, this looks okay to me, you want to check it out? Maybe you'd better check out all your picture hooks."

He stared at the picture hook. It was perfectly normal as far as he could tell.

She said, "Andy, why do you think I'm checking out your phones? Why do you think I got you the tape?"

"You said you wanted to help me."

"And?"

152

"Why did you?"

She crossed her arms. "Are engineers physically unable to describe their feelings?"

"Oh."

"Oh?"

His heartbeat ramped up. How many engineers would constitute a fair sample? On the basis of Ray Colson and himself, she had a good case.

He took her hand, pulling her out of Wayne's room into the hallway, and faced her squarely. "I'll give it a shot," he said. "I really like you."

"That's nice." She sounded amused.

It was a fair description, he thought. Was liking somehow devalued because people could like both their neighbors and their lovers? How did you calibrate the degrees of difference? She was right: engineers were probably innately unable to describe their feelings because they were always striving for accuracy. He suddenly thought that the only feeling that he could describe accurately was love for his son.

He felt the warmth of her hand in his. "I'm very attracted to you," he said.

"Do you trust me?"

His stomach clenched. "Yes," he said, because it was what they both wanted to hear.

"You don't act like it."

"I trust you."

"Then tell me if you found anything on that tape I brought you."

"Yes," he said. "Some interesting calls."

"Tell me."

"Just some interesting patterns of calls."

"Well, what does that *mean?*"

He had just told her that he trusted her. The lying came more and more easily.

She looked at him coolly. "Forget it."

He let go of her hand. "The calls could give someone access to the switch. A way of triggering the failures."

Something flickered in her eyes: interest. Like Colson abruptly homing in on a piece of data he found provocative. "Pattern," she said softly. Then she grinned. "Well, why didn't you say so? Doesn't that clear you?"

"No. It's just part of the puzzle. There's something missing. I need to look . . ."

"Andy."

"What? You know something?"

"Are there any more wall jacks in your house?"

He shook his head. Wiretaps again. "Just the three phones."

"Wall jacks, Andy. Is there a wall jack anywhere that you didn't hook up your phones to?"

"Could be, I don't know."

"How about in the master bedroom? People always want to have a phone in the master bedroom."

He didn't. If the phone rang while he was asleep, he liked to get out of bed and wake up before he answered it.

"This is your bedroom?" She was already moving across the hallway.

His bedroom, more than any other room in the house, looked like a rental, as if the occupant had just arrived or was about to vacate the premises. The only piece of furniture that was his was the bedside table, a slab of birch from the Adirondacks, mounted on wrought-iron tripod legs and stacked with books and journals. The walls were bare but for a print, a birthday present from Wayne: a close-up drawing of a printed circuit board with the capacitors and resistors sticking up like buildings and the soldered joints like roads winding through the miniature city. The focal point was a train chugging along silvery soldered railroad tracks. It was a joke: a reference to the fact that many people thought that what engineers did was drive trains.

He had heard it said that a room reflects the person who lives there. If he could have afforded it, he would have bought a Seurat and hung it on one of the bare walls. Seurat's pointillist style appealed to him. The pictures were made entirely of tiny dots, done with a technician's skill, but when the viewer looked at the picture all the dots merged into a whole that became an image of life.

"Andy, is there a jack behind the bed?" She tugged at one edge of his double bed.

"I don't know. The bed was here when I came. I haven't moved it." He took hold of the other side of the bed and helped her pull it away from the wall.

She crouched onto the bed, her dress pooling like sunlight on the spread, and peered down at the wall. Seurat had painted a girl in a yellow dress, a circus bareback rider in a yellow dress flying up as the horse galloped. Thousands of yellow dots.

"Andy, look."

Her voice was quiet; this time, she was controlling her excitement. He leaned forward on the bed, taking his weight on his knees, and looked where she was looking.

There was a wall jack behind the bed. A telephone cord was plugged into the jack, and it led under the bed.

He reached down, took hold of the cord, and gently pulled. A small rectangular box slid into view. Andy reeled in the box like a fish on a line and let it down on the bed between them.

The box was thin, made of beige plastic. There was a switch, which could be moved to positions marked *A* and *B*. There was a dial, which could be turned to number *1, 2, 3,* or *4,* and below the dial it said *Area Selection*. The dial was set on number *1*. Andy touched a fingertip to the switch, then withdrew it. "Do you know what it is?"

155

Nell didn't touch it. "It would have a microphone inside, and use the phone line as a carrier."

"Nell, what the hell is it?"

"It looks like an infinity transmitter."

It sounded like Wayne's science fiction.

"The idea's simple. The eavesdropper hooks it up, calls your number from another phone, and presses a button on the phone dial that activates the transmitter. Then the microphone picks up whatever is said here and transmits it."

"For how long?"

"For however long someone leaves it on."

Jesus.

"This isn't like the bug," she said. "That just picks up what you say on the phone. This picks up what you say . . . anytime."

He asked, tight, "Why is it called an infinity transmitter?"

"Because the eavesdropper can call from just about any phone anywhere in the world. Infinite."

Andy stared at the box. A microphone and a transmitter: a crude telephone. But this wasn't a telephone lying on his bed, it was a perversion of a telephone.

What was Interrupt trying to pick up, bedroom talk? An icy fury coursed through him. "What's the range?"

She glanced down at the bed, then back at him, her face suddenly flushed. "That depends. On how sensitive the microphone is."

A decent mike, he thought, would pick up sounds from the hallway, from his workroom across the hallway, maybe from the living room. What the hell had he just said in the hallway? The pattern of calls; he'd told Nell what he found in the call records. His heart pounded. All right, all right, what else? The personal talk, between him and Nell. Was Interrupt listening to that? Some kind of goddamned voyeur.

Was he listening now?

"Disconnect it," Nell said, reaching for the box.

Andy grabbed her hand. "I'll do it." He let go of Nell and twisted the phone cord once around his hand.

Wayne had come into his bedroom a couple of nights earlier, awakened by a nightmare. Throwing on the lights, signing furiously, he had told Andy that he dreamed he heard a noise, terrifying, like a funnel of color, blood-red and orange-rust, that swirled over him and filled his nose and mouth and ears and gagged him. He saw the colors and dreamed they were noise. And he woke up screaming, he said, but Andy hadn't heard him scream, and he thought he had really *heard* the noise. Then, as he came fully awake, lying there in darkness and silence, he realized it had been a nightmare. He had finished signing, his hands dropping limp, and a sob broke out of him, in itself a terrible barking noise. Finally, embarrassed, he told Andy he was glad he was deaf, he never wanted to hear a noise like that for real.

Had Interrupt been listening to that? He would have heard that barking sob and Andy's efforts to comfort his son, some of it signed and some of it spoken aloud. Andy didn't remember what he had put into spoken words.

Was he listening now?

"Get out of my life." Out loud; spoken words; spat out; Andy's voice now like Wayne's terrible noise. *"Keep away from us."*

Nell flinched. "Andy, he's . . ."

"He's a coward and a thug." He jerked his hand, ripping the plug out of the wall jack.

"Andy. Was that wise?"

"No."

"I know how mad you are."

"No, you don't." He unwrapped the phone cord from his hand.

"You warned *me* not to take risks."

"Nell." His voice was hoarse, his breathing ragged. "It wasn't wise, but it's done. Drop it."

"If he was listening and he heard you say . . ."

He picked up the box, looped the cord around it, and placed it on the birch table. "He's not listening now."

"I just don't want you to get hurt."

He shifted his gaze from the transmitter to her, crouched on his bed, fetching, as if there had been no business conducted in this room, as if she had settled there solely to entice him, and he felt a sudden weakness, almost giddiness, shoot through him. Precarious.

"Andy, you shouldn't . . ."

He put his hand to her lips and pressed hard. "I'm not wise." He touched her shoulder with his other hand, then slipped it around to her bare neck, beneath the waves of hair.

She leaned back, to look at him fully. Surprised, he thought.

"I really like you, Nell, I'm very attracted to you, and I want to make love with you," he said. "What about you?"

She swallowed, a rippling down her bare throat. "Yes."

As he helped her out of the yellow dress he saw dots, thousands of dots. Then he closed his eyes and she was the image of life again.

15

•

At Stanford, we design elegance.

Looking in through the wall-size window, as if for the first time, Interrupt took stock of the telecommunications lab. State-of-the-art. Sun workstations, IBM 3090 mainframe, experimental switch components, load simulator, peripherals from half a dozen vendors.

And the students. Diligent, industrious, *rigorous* as only Stanford EEs could be rigorous, hunched over keyboards, crouched before switching components as if praying.

Smug.

Interrupt remembered, only too well.

As a teenager, at the kitchen table, heatedly filling in the application to Stanford, not bothering to apply to any other school. Then the letter in the mail, regrets, a stunning letter. With the embossed Stanford letterhead. In shock, sick at heart, Interrupt had gone on to another school, worked like a dog. Excelled. Then, finally, one more application, as much a prayer as a petition, for grad school, for admission to Stanford's Department of Electrical Engineering, to the innovative Center for Telecommunications.

This refusal was like an execution.

In the graduate program at the second-choice school the recurring nightmare had begun. Interrupt was working at Stanford, brilliant work, when the police burst into the telecom lab with a warrant for the imposter's arrest. Humiliated, Interrupt was led away in handcuffs. The other students and faculty in the lab did not even bother to look up from their work; the imposter's removal was of no consequence.

Interrupt could still feel the disgrace.

Now, in the far corner of the lab, a kid was bent over an array of circuit boards. Could be Andy Faulkner as a student. Running a hand through the brown hair, tangling it, worrying it, the neck tendons standing out, tautened, the fingers flicking as though they carried a charge, the kid wiring his soul into the boards.

So like Faulkner.

From the start, Interrupt had known that there would have to be an "Andy," indeed, had defined the parameters and steadfastly waited to find the man who fit them. The target had to be a Stanford man, he had to be both intelligent and technically fluent, and he had to possess what was conventionally considered moral fiber. He had to personify Stanford. He had to be a star. Faulkner fit the parameters. The TDD and the boy had been bonuses.

The kid in the corner, young Faulkner, as Interrupt now thought of him, suddenly straightened and looked directly at the window. Obviously, he was not seeing it, or Interrupt outside; he was facing outward but looking inward. Then his mouth curved into a scowl; he shook his head, pushed away from the bench, and walked over to the soft-drink machine.

No, not like Faulkner. Andy Faulkner would not have abandoned the challenge as easily as that. Interrupt rubbed at the headache, digging in knuckles in a futile effort to erase it.

The man did not give up.

Faulkner had done what he was supposed to do. Find the Stanford lab number, find the channel into the switch, make it look as if Stanford's innovative engineering stars were out of control. Give the telco tiger team a shove in the wrong direction.

But he wouldn't give it up. He would worry it to death, like a dog on a bone, until he had figured out the missing pieces.

Like hell, Interrupt thought.

The kid, lounging against the soft-drink machine, said something to someone, brusque.

Coward and a thug. Faulkner's words.

Coward and a thug.

The headache flared, as familiar, insistent, as hunger pangs. How dare you, Interrupt thought.

Interrupt spun away from the window, from the telecom lab, from the young students in their scowling glory, and cut across campus. At the computer center one could anonymously open a guest account and log onto a terminal to send an E-mail message.

Something bound at Interrupt's left wrist. It was just a wristwatch, strapped too tight, but it bound like a handcuff.

16

•

Once, this place had been a second home to him. Sandra, alone days and many nights in their married student apartment, would have deleted the *second*.

Andy glanced around the telecom lab. Some new equipment, new paint on the walls, old posters. Benches and tabletops littered with twisted wire ends, hardened drops of solder, IC chips, boards. Styrofoam cups, donut boxes, balled-up plastic potato chip bags. Odors mixed: sugar, salt, and the analogous acrid smells of heated solder and cold coffee.

It was as it always had been, except that every student in the room looked too young to belong there.

Every one of them looked too young to be Zot.

The E-mail message on Andy's screen had said simply, "Meet me at the telecom lab in one hour." Andy turned so that he could watch the door.

The lab phone rang, and the student closest, no more than

a chubby kid, picked up the handset without shifting attention from her computer screen. "Telecom."

Zot could be a woman, Andy suddenly thought. He recalled what Candace had said about their phreak—*only men play games like that.* Maybe not.

"A recording," the student said, holding the handset aloft, eyes still on her screen. "Says, please activate your TDD. Who wants it?"

Wayne. Andy reached for the handset. "I'll take it."

By the time he put the receiver to his ear, all he got was dial tone.

He knew this game.

Phase change, he thought. It was a phenomenon of nature, in which a solid, liquid, or a gas changed from one form of matter to another. Andy had heard once about a small isolated body of still water that underwent a sudden, dramatic phase change: ice crystals spontaneously formed, branched, connected, and covered the surface of the lake with a sheet of ice. To the onlooker it was as if the water froze before his eyes.

Andy could see it, could see himself undergoing a phase change, a chill down his spine, an icy knob in his gut, a cold tingling in his arms and legs, and the crystallization icing his whole body until he stood frozen in place in the middle of the telecom lab.

The E-mail message had not been from Zot. The message had been from someone who used a TDD as a weapon. Interrupt. In the frozen depths of his being, Andy was certain of it.

He thought first, I'm on to him. And second, he has killed. Then, with fingers gone cold and stiff, he punched in his home number on the phone. He got Helen; no, she said, Wayne hadn't called the number he had left, the lab number, and neither had she. He hung up.

There were five people in the room, excluding himself. Too young to be Zot, he had thought. Too young to be Interrupt?

The five students worked intently, ignoring the man rooted, stock-still, staring at them. Assuming, perhaps, that he was one of those grad students who never graduated.

The phone rang again, and the chubby student answered. "Telecom." She swiveled her chair to face him. "You Andy Faulkner?"

When he nodded, she handed him the phone.

This time, it was the cheerful voice of the TDD relay operator. Call from Mr. Wayne Faulkner. "Meet me at the admissions office, urgent," the operator relayed. "Reply?" When Andy stumbled, she said, never mind, Mr. Wayne Faulkner has rung off.

Andy stopped himself from calling home again; there was no chance in hell that Wayne had placed that call. If he called home, his call would be switched through Stanford's PBX system, and Stanford, he knew, used a 5ESS for its system. His first call home had gone through, had not crashed Stanford's system. If he called now, would this call be so benign? The telecom lab without telephone service; good joke, Interrupt.

But he wasn't going to bite. He moved away from the telephone.

Why the admissions office?

Go home. Or go to Feferman.

He left the telecom lab and started toward the parking lot, to lay it all in Feferman's lap.

Meet me at the admissions office, urgent, from Mr. Wayne Faulkner. But it couldn't be from Wayne.

Urgent.

Where was a phone?

He turned back toward the center of campus and broke into a jog. It was afternoon, a sunny day in late spring with finals still a month away, and students clogged the walkways. Students on bikes and students on foot, like electrons and protons accelerating toward each other, then repelling at the last microsecond. He pushed through the crowd, through the tangle of shoulders and elbows and handlebars. The students all seemed to belong to Interrupt, recruited by Interrupt to enmesh him.

He found himself outside Encina Hall, the administration building. There were phones in there.

Pounding up the steps, he passed a man who looked familiar, someone from the past. Stark white hair and a square workingman's face. Someone on the engineering staff, Andy thought. What was he doing all the way across campus at the admin building? The man stopped on the steps and turned to watch him, and Andy realized it was because he himself had stopped to stare.

The man nodded and passed on.

Andy sprinted up into the building.

He found the admissions office before he found a pay phone. He asked a clerk if he could use the phone for an urgent call, and she quickly stood up and backed away from her desk, giving him space, access to the phone. He dialed and caught her wary look on him, and while he counted the ring-backs he wondered if this call was going to go through without taking the system down.

Helen answered. No, again; Wayne hadn't called him, she hadn't called him. Everything was fine. Was he all right?

He hung up. His hand was shaking. He backed away from the clerk's desk.

The admissions office was a bullpen of clerks, crowded desks, crosstalk, ringing telephones.

So he had come here, after all.

For minutes he stood rooted, flinching every time the phone rang, waiting for the call that would be for him. Finally, he approached the same clerk and asked if there had been any calls for Andy Faulkner. She was uncertain, new at the job; a more experienced clerk would have grilled him, screened him, but she didn't ask the questions and for that he was grateful. She inquired around the bullpen and finally came back to him with a sheet of slick paper in her hand. She handed it to him with an expression of relief; clearly, someone had expected him to be there and that made it official.

The paper was a fax: A. Faulkner—Stanford Hospital emergency room.

He bolted out the door.

The hospital was back across campus, well beyond the engineering corner. His car was in a parking lot in the opposite direction. He ran.

Running on a warm day, not dressed for a run, sweating, he cut in with runners in shorts pounding the footpath that wound between the main campus and the hospital, through groves of eucalyptus. Sun heat baked the long leathery leaves, drawing out the medicinal oils, scenting the path like a hospital ward.

As he had known he would, Andy thought of a funeral when he drew in the eucalyptus-drenched air.

He thought of someone who could kill to prevent the revelation of a conjecture about switch failures and an undertaker named Strowger.

He reached the hospital light-headed and clammy with sweat. He knew precisely where the emergency room was. He had rushed Sandra there when she went into labor with Wayne, a sudden acute labor that had alarmed them both before settling into a thirty-hour medicated wait.

The emergency room waiting area was occupied by a small cluster of men and women speaking a hushed stream of Spanish, dressed up as if for a wedding.

Interrupt? He didn't know any of them.

From a treatment room came yelling, more in protest than pain, it seemed, and a staccato voice commanded, "Stop it, stop it, stop it, stop it."

The emergency room had been redone in pastels since his visit eleven years ago.

From behind a partition he heard a new voice, gentle, or weary. "Dr. Kolsrud here. Brief me."

His head still pounded with his runner's heartbeat. He knew what to do; he had learned the rules.

"What kind of explosion?" the gentle, weary voice asked.

Andy approached the check-in desk. "My name is Andy Faulkner . . ." he began.

"Faulkner?" The receptionist straightened, recognition flashing across his face.

He knows me, Andy thought. This man with spiked blond hair, a sunburn, and three stud earrings in each ear knows who I am. "Yes, Faulkner."

"Got a message for you." The receptionist glanced down at a notepad. "Wayne Faulkner is being transported to the Stanford Hospital emergency room." He looked up and smiled, in sympathy or reassurance, a mouthful of crooked teeth bright white against the sunburn. "You're supposed to wait here."

He could have done nothing else but wait here.

From behind the partition the doctor's voice droned, an edge to it now. "Vitals, BP one-sixty over one hundred, pulse one-twenty, respirations, thirty-two. That's correct?"

Andy found himself counting his own pulse. His blood pressure must be dropping, he was seeing red spots flicking across his eyes. He focused on the receptionist's earrings and drew in a deep breath. "How did the message come?"

"Some kind of phone operator. T something."

"TDD?"

"Yeah."

"Apply burn packs and start a nasal oxy at six liters per minute," the doctor said slowly, distinctly. "You have the IV established?"

"When?" Andy said.

"When what?"

"When did the call come in?"

The receptionist checked his watch. "Five, ten minutes ago."

About when he'd left the admin building. He, always now like Feferman, didn't buy coincidences. Interrupt had to know where he was and when he was there. Interrupt was on a bike, and with his head down and his shoulders hunched he looked just like any other student racing across campus. Or he was sitting in a car somewhere on the street in front of the admin building, with a cellular phone and a TDD. Or he was the white-haired man from engineering, from the past, forgotten but familiar.

There was no way in hell, he thought, an echo, that the call had been from Wayne.

"What?" All weariness was gone from the doctor's voice.

"You can wait over there." The receptionist motioned toward the cluster of formal men and women.

"Look, I want you to monitor those respirations closely."

Why, Andy thought, does he keep using Wayne's name? This has nothing to do with Wayne.

"Vitals again, please."

My son has nothing to do with this.

The receptionist picked up his empty mug and sauntered over to a counter where a coffeemaker shared space with stacks of hospital forms.

Andy remembered Sandra in the wheelchair, doubled over her inflated belly, her wail of pain, the debate whether they had time to make it from the emergency room to the delivery room. Wayne then was barely real to him, a bulk in Sandra's belly that was propelling them both toward panic. When he was born, when his fuzzed head crowned, Andy was stunned to find himself headlong in love.

Andy grabbed the receptionist's phone and dialed his home

number, his pulse and respirations pumping high. Only one ring-back and then Helen was on the line. He thought her voice sounded funny but he didn't have the chance to pursue it because the line went stone dead.

"Blue hell," from the partition, "I've lost him. What's the matter with the phone?"

Mechanically, Andy tried again to get dial tone, because it was second nature to try again, because no one, not even a telecom engineer who had a damn good idea what was happening to the switch, could accept without trying again that the phone didn't work. He tried again and got what he expected, silence.

Dr. Kolsrud appeared, face taut. He snatched up the handset of the receptionist's phone, listened, then slammed it down. Andy could see the darkened skin around the man's eyes, weariness indeed. "They know what they're doing," the doctor said, to himself, but it sounded more like a wish than a statement of fact.

The emergency room doors banged open and a gurney shot inside, driven by two paramedics, one holding aloft an IV bottle. Andy twisted to see the form strapped under the blankets. A beefy arm was exposed, impaled by a long needle. Not a boy's arm.

Already, Dr. Kolsrud was bent over the form on the gurney, and the IV paramedic stood respectfully by, tending the needle in the inert arm. Dr. Kolsrud had to move on; his phone patient was lost to him.

The phones were down, Andy thought, and his car was all the way across campus.

He ran.

17

•

Andy couldn't get the key into the lock; he cursed, tried it again, and Helen yanked open the door.

"He's gone," she said.

Was this the end of the game? His clothes smelled of eucalyptus.

She followed him as he pushed past her to Wayne's room. "He's not there. He's not anywhere in the house, he's not in the garage. What do you want to do?" She was calm, the kind of practical let's-prioritize calm some people mustered in emergencies.

Wayne's room looked normal, untouched by any intrusion. "What time did you say?" he asked Helen, and his own voice sounded amazingly calm.

"I don't know what time he left," she said. "After you called, the last time, that call that was cut off, I went to check on him and he was gone."

He left. That sounded voluntary. Through the door that led from his room to the back patio, how else?

"I checked out there, Andy."

The backyard was small, enclosed by a fence. There was the patio with the basketball hoop where Wayne shot endless baskets. Browning grass, a stretch of pyracantha clawing up one side of the fence, and the hedge of oleanders.

That's where Interrupt was the night of the storm, obviously. Easy to hide in the oleanders. Andy pawed through the branches, snapping off stems and scratching his arms. Christ, Wayne was too old to be playing hide-and-seek.

Nothing.

He circled to the side yard and ransacked the oleanders that hugged the windows.

He wound up in the front yard. If Wayne left through his door, he came out around the side yard to the front. Then where? Andy scanned the street. Tree shadows, felled by the late-afternoon sun, striped the sidewalks and asphalt. Cars roosted at the curbs, in the driveways. No movement, nothing, not even squirrels on the phone lines overhead. Where were the neighbors? This was supposed to be a neighborhood, that was the point of the suburbs.

Someone was walking out to the mailbox on the other side of the street. Mayerle.

Andy sprinted across the street, shouting, startling the old man. He made himself ask slowly, but his voice shook. Yes, sure, Mayerle knew who Wayne was. No, he hadn't seen him lately.

Helen was in the front yard. He sprinted back. "Did you check the neighbors?"

"No," she said, "he doesn't play with anyone in the neighborhood."

"Maybe someone saw him."

Helen took one side of the street and he took the other. He

172

knew by sight and an occasional exchange of greetings most of the people who lived here.

The first two houses, no one was home. At the third house, his banging on the door brought an angry response and he forced himself again to calm down.

Wayne wasn't with the neighbors, nobody had seen him, one didn't even know who he was.

It made no sense anyway. Wayne didn't go for walks in the neighborhood. Andy crossed the street, looking for Helen. Maybe he did this time. He was under stress, Andy's stress, he bled when his father bled. Maybe he just had to get out of his room, out of the house.

Three houses down, a beige mirror-image of his place, Helen was standing on the porch with a girl and yelling to Andy.

He ran.

"She saw him." Helen's voice had notched up; she was ruffled.

"Walking down the sidewalk toward the intersection," the girl started before Andy could reach the porch. "I passed him on my bike." She still wore black bike shorts, shiny and tight over plump muscled legs.

"Did you stop him?"

The girl gave him a look of teenage disdain.

Helen took hold of his arm and questioned the girl. She had seen a tall boy, brown hair, wearing jeans, she thought, walking head down like he was looking for something on the sidewalk. Maybe an hour ago. He was carrying a small suitcase, something like that, maybe not a suitcase, it was pretty small.

The portable TDD. Andy felt a letdown of relief. If he took the TDD, then there was some logic in where he was going.

They hurried to the intersection. It was a four-lane road, a major road. Gas station and liquor store on the opposite corners. Check there.

"Oh." Helen had a hand up, finger extended as if checking for wind. "Andy, there *was* a phone call."

He snapped around to her. "What call?"

"Well, let me get the time straight. The bus came at two-thirty as usual, and Wayne came in and we talked some . . . you know he's teaching me sign?"

"Helen."

"Then he went to his room. As usual, he closed the door, he wanted his privacy. The first two times you called, I went in there, and he was on the computer."

A bus rumbled by; Helen raised her voice.

"Then, oh, three-thirtyish, a TDD call came in on Wayne's number. You know, I heard the two short rings and I waited for Wayne to take it in his room. As usual."

Three-thirtyish; when Andy was on his way to the emergency room. Wayne got a TDD call around three-thirty and then he disappeared.

Andy started back to the house, running. He felt he'd been running for days.

The front door was still locked, his fingers couldn't even find the keys this time, he dashed around to the backyard and through the open door.

He didn't see the message on the TDD printer until he looked closely.

It was short, words like quick thrusts of a knife. "Be deaf and dumb, like your son. Forget the switches. Remember Candace Fuentes."

He ripped the strip of paper from the printer.

Andy's throat muscles constricted. He saw Helen in the doorway but he couldn't hear what she was saying, indeed he was deaf like Wayne. A nauseating pain bubbled up in his chest and he cried out in rage, only Helen wasn't hearing it, the howl stayed inside him. He gulped a breath of air.

"What does it say?" She was coming toward him, reaching for the paper in his hand.

He crushed it.

She stopped and looked at him with that damned motherly calm.

He forced himself to think. When had the message come? While they were out? Before? She couldn't have seen it or she would have told him, she might have called the police. Call the police. No, not the police. Call Feferman? No, especially not Feferman. Forget the switches.

He faced her. "He sent a message. It's okay, he's with Jacky."

She looked at the TDD, at the crumpled paper in his fist, at his face. "Andy, that boy wouldn't go out without telling me."

"He's with Jacky," Andy repeated. "He was going over to Jacky's today, I'm sorry, I forgot."

"He walked?"

"It's not far, a few blocks." This was unbearable, he had to get her out of here.

"He left without telling me?"

"He's been under a lot of stress, he forgot."

"That's impossible."

"Are you calling me a liar?"

Her head jerked as if he had slapped her.

"I'm sorry, Helen, we've been under a lot of stress." Stiff, he put his arm through hers and guided her out of Wayne's room toward the front door. "You can go, he's okay, he's with Jacky. Thanks." He might as well have told her Wayne was on the moon. She stopped like a mule by the door. Please, Helen, he begged silently, I can't keep this up. "Do you want to call Jacky's?" She didn't know Jacky, she didn't know his last name, she didn't have the number. She didn't believe him, she couldn't possibly have believed him, but she shook her head and said, "Call me if you need me."

His legs weak, his whole body icy cold and weak, he walked back into Wayne's room and sat at his son's desk. The bookshelf, pine boards painted black, hung on black brackets, was slightly crooked; Wayne had helped to paint it and hang it. One book protruded, as if Wayne used it often and never pushed it all the way back in line with the others: a book of slang. Hearing people picked up slang and idioms without conscious effort, part of everyday life. The deaf had to study.

He closed his eyes, a mistake, throwing him back eleven years.

"Will he talk?" Sandra had demanded of the neurologist, loud, angry, almost shouting, and Andy had pressed the baby's head against his chest so he wouldn't be scared by his mother's voice. Still not accepting that the baby couldn't hear his mother's voice. "Unlikely." The neurologist, talking fast to get them out of his office, his job over with the diagnosis. Unlikely with this kind of sensori-neural hearing loss. At best, speech distortion. Flattened inflections, articulation poor. The high-frequency consonant sounds slushy: *s, z, ch, sh, zh,* the neurologist hissing like a snake. Wayne struggling and crying because Andy had been holding him too tight. The neurologist abruptly leaving, giving them time to "compose themselves," and Sandra already talking about a lawsuit, the obstetrician should have given her something to prevent the premature birth, there were drugs. Andy light-headed, as if like the baby he had been deprived of oxygen.

Andy opened his eyes, opened his hand and let the crumpled strip of paper drop on Wayne's desk. *Be deaf and dumb, like your son.* Did the bastard know Ameslan, did he know how to speak so the boy could lip-read?

No, he wouldn't give a shit.

But he knew how to use the TDD.

Think it through, that's what Andy always preached to Wayne.

Andy took a pencil and a pad of graph paper, AT&T paper, from Wayne's desk and roughed out a timeline, beginning at 2:30 P.M. He entered the data points: W comes home, W into room, TDD call, bike girl sees W, H checks room and W gone, A arrives home.

He stared at the paper. Then he entered one more data point: A gets message from Interrupt, thinks it's from Zot. Meet me at the telecom lab in one hour. And A went.

Interrupt got him out of the house before he called Wayne.

Andy gripped the pencil.

But what about Helen? Did Interrupt assume that Wayne was home alone? Or didn't he care?

Data point: TDD call for W. Interrupt assumed that Wayne would do whatever Andy told him to do. And that included leaving without telling the baby-sitter. Good assumption.

With a TDD, Interrupt could be Andy.

Interrupt had been in the house to tap the phones, he knew Wayne's room, he knew about the door to the backyard.

Interrupt could instruct Wayne to leave the house and say nothing to Helen, and Wayne would think he was obeying his father. Did Interrupt make it a game, a secret? How had he manipulated the boy? Meet me . . . where?

And Wayne had typed back, sure, Dad.

This time the rage boiled out of him. *"Sonofabitch."*

He slammed out the back door, he could feel his boy's anxiety, curiosity, around to the front, pounding out to the sidewalk.

Wayne, head down, carrying the TDD, going toward the intersection. Wondering what was wrong with his father.

Andy followed.

Now, at the intersection, where now? Keep on walking, which way? A car stops, a man says get in and I'll take you to your daddy. But he doesn't sign, does he? He forces Wayne in.

Oh, Christ.

He bolted across the intersection. Cars honking.

The gas station attendant doesn't know him because he gets his gas at Rotten Robbie's, cheaper, blocks away. The attendant doesn't remember a boy with a small suitcase and he's got gas to pump, he's busy.

The liquor store, kids in here for candy sometimes, not today.

Outside again. Panting, pain in his chest, the cars chasing past, rush hour.

Andy froze.

There, across the street, the blue sign.

He waited, growing certain, then grabbed his chance and recrossed the intersection.

There it was, you looked at it and didn't even see it because it was common as telephone poles. Metal pole, blue sign, wooden bench.

A bus stop.

Leave the house, don't tell anyone, go to the bus stop at the intersection, take the . . . a number, a time . . . bus to . . .

A metal box was bolted to the pole. Andy seized a slick brochure out of the box, the bus schedule and route map.

He tried three times to read it, then sat on the bench, put his head in his hands, and waited. He looked again, and the fine print of times and numbers became legible, more data points. The timeline was in his pocket; he didn't remember taking it but there it was. He spread it out beside the bus schedule.

Only one bus fit the time Wayne had left. He followed it on the transit map. After this intersection, the route crossed four city boundaries, made eleven stops, and ran along one of the busiest arteries in Silicon Valley. It intersected hundreds of side streets, thousands of buildings.

He would have to go to the police, or the FBI. They knew

what to do, they had the people to do it. Every kidnapper warns the family not to go to the authorities, but they know what to do.

No. Interrupt was spliced right into the telephone system. He would know just what Andy and the authorities were doing.

Go to Feferman. Only, right about now, Feferman would be checking the call records on the Stanford switch failure, and then he would be getting up a posse to nail Andy. Your son is gone? How do we know you haven't stashed him somewhere, made it *look* as if he's been kidnapped, how do we know you haven't concocted this whole scenario?

There was no one he could go to.

If his father had been alive, he might have gone to him. He just might have asked Joe Faulkner for help.

But John Roebling was dead and Washington Roebling ended up crippled.

Talking to the dead. He can't hear you.

18

•

Andy sat at a polyurethaned orange table near the pay phone in Burger King and waited. County transit wouldn't tell him who had driven that bus, they didn't give out personal information about their drivers, but they had agreed to leave a message for the driver.

Call.

The Burger King staff had begun to take notice of Andy. The tense guy in the corner, been here for a couple of hours, fidgets whenever someone uses the phone.

Sorry, can't use my home phone. Could be tapped; may be a device on the line. Maybe Feferman's on my doorstep.

Andy got up and bought a hamburger. When it was cold he dumped it and bought a cup of coffee.

A man headed for the phone and Andy tensed, but he bypassed it and went into the men's room.

The phone rang, and Andy lunged.

181

It was a driver named John Carelli. He was beat, and he hadn't even had his dinner yet, and this better not be a joke.

No joke, Andy told him. Eleven-year-old boy, tall, brown hair, green eyes, wearing jeans, carrying a small case. Deaf.

Yes, Carelli said.

Oh, my God. Andy's hand tightened on the receiver. *Don't lose this call.*

Andy swallowed, his throat dry, and asked if anyone sat with the boy. No, nobody. How did he know? Carelli knew because he kept an eye on things in the rearview mirror, he didn't want any trouble on his bus.

How far did the boy go? Where did he get off the bus?

Carelli didn't know. The bus had a back door.

Maybe some of the other passengers saw him get off. Did Carelli know any of the passengers, any regulars who Andy could get in touch with? No, no regulars on that run, you get regulars on the commute runs. And Carelli had a run tomorrow morning at seven and if that was all, he wanted to get some dinner and sleep. Click, dial tone, and Carelli was gone.

Andy left the Burger King and began to walk. What now? It was dark; Wayne didn't like the dark, because it deprived him of one of his remaining senses. Andy checked his watch. It was nearly nine o'clock.

What now? Follow his boy, as best he could.

Andy waited at the bus stop. Morning traffic: cars, trucks, buses, vans, bikes. He thought, you notice the colors more. And speed is altered, everyone looks like they're going too slow.

Huge, close, out of the blue, it was suddenly on top of him. His neurons fired and he jumped, even as he turned to get a good look. The bus stopped at his feet, tires hard against the curb, and the door swung open in his face.

This is what it was like to be deaf. You were out of synch with the world.

He hadn't remembered it this way. They had run the exercise on the school grounds, just an hour in a controlled environment. Families of the deaf students soundproofed themselves and became "aware" of what it was like for their loved ones. Of course, it was impossible for hearing people to actually reproduce profound deafness; instead, they wore hearing aids set to create white noise, a random background buzz that drowned out most everyday sounds, including speech. The teacher had encouraged them to try it on their own, out in the world, to really get a feel for it. But Andy had felt uneasy at playing deaf, like a voyeur, and had not continued the exercise.

Until now. He had gone to Sears last night and bought a pair of hearing aids.

He gathered his wits enough to check the bus number, then boarded. John Carelli, ID'd by his badge, gripped the handle holding the door open, jiggled his knee, stared right through Andy. He looked like a cop with his thick mustache and slit eyes. Carelli's arm flexed and the air compressed behind Andy. He felt the door snap shut.

Carelli's lips moved, fast, unreadable under the mustache, unintelligible through the white noise.

A flash of anxiety, then Andy knew what was wanted. Exact change only. He dropped the coins in the fare box and Carelli yanked the bus into gear.

Andy grabbed the handrail for balance and moved down the aisle. A man sat in the first seat, in a sports jacket, face turned to the window. Then a young woman, dressed like a hiker, head bent over a book, a neat part in her dark blond hair. He thought of Nell. Three old women, two together and one across the aisle, heads pivoting back and forth like birds, hands flying as if they were trying to sign. Unfathomable. At the back of the bus he dropped into a seat. From here, he saw only the backs of heads, he didn't have to look at the mouths. He figured Wayne would have sat back here.

Carelli's eyes watched in the rearview mirror.

Out the window, storefronts slid by, everything was for sale. Dinette sets, cheap; automotive transmission overhaul; eyeglass frames; frozen yogurt. Like a TV commercial with the mute on.

The bus stopped, released passengers, took on more. Did Wayne get off here? Andy was jarred to one side, the bus was starting. He looked out the window. A savings and loan, a drugstore, a video rental. Here?

He was in a zone of silence, he was in Wayne's reality. *This is how it was.* How had it looked to Wayne, what did he notice, what did he do? What might Carelli have noticed in the rearview mirror that he didn't think to tell Andy, that Andy hadn't thought to ask?

The bus stopped, an exchange of passengers. Out the window was a Radio Shack. He sometimes bought components there. Did Interrupt too? Did Interrupt tell Wayne, get off at Radio Shack, figuring that the son of an engineer would be familiar with the place, would believe that his father asked him to meet there?

Andy stood. A pain, an elbow in his side. He turned and a woman was shaking her head, saying something, apologizing. He wasn't sure, so he said "I'm sorry," wondering if his voice sounded right. The bus started, jolting, and they swayed back down to the seats.

She hadn't noticed that he couldn't hear. Carelli hadn't noticed, because Andy had the exact change and there was no reason for them to communicate. Was that what it was like for Wayne? Nobody noticed? Did he pretend that he was just like everybody else, try to pass for hearing?

How had Carelli known that Wayne was deaf?

Andy had asked if a deaf boy got on the bus, and Carelli had said yes.

Andy pushed to the front of the bus and took the seat by the door, where he could see Carelli's profile. He pulled out the hearing aids and for a moment the real-world sounds were as featureless as the white noise. Then his hearing stabilized, was normal, and he blessed it.

He identified himself to Carelli.

Carelli's head turned, is there trouble on my bus?, then snapped back to traffic. The mustache, in profile, pulled down.

Andy leaned forward. "How did you know the boy was deaf?"

A long dead silence. Carelli ignored it, thinking about it, milking it. Finally, "He got on the bus, put his money in the fare box, and just stood there. He wanted something but he didn't say nothing." Carelli's eyes flicked to the mirror, to Andy, to the next lane, straight ahead. "I ask him what he wants and he still says nothing, just starts in with the hands. Sign language, I've seen it on TV, and that's how I know the kid's deaf."

"What then?"

"Nothing, I dunno what he's saying, the kid gives up and goes back to get a seat."

Andy watched Carelli's hands on the wheel. "Do you remember any of the signs he made?"

Carelli's hands twitched, as if struggling to recall. Then he held up his right hand, his index and middle fingers extended in a V.

Andy frowned. V for victory, or the sign for peace. That made no sense. It was as if an unskilled interpreter were at work, garbling the language of the deaf.

But Carelli was flexing the V. "That ain't all of it. Something with the left hand too . . . both hands . . . but he does it so fast that I can't get it. I tell him I dunno what he's saying, then I remember that he can't hear me so I just shake my head. So he does it again for me, but I got other passengers, I can't sit there all day trying to figure it. So he gets upset, or mad, I guess, and gives up." Carelli glanced at Andy, shrugging, nearly an apology.

Andy extended the fingers of his right hand in a V. All right, he's signing with Wayne, he makes the V and . . . what? There's more to it. Which signs begin that way, maybe use the left hand too? He couldn't think, he was struck dumb, his hand cramped and he couldn't find the sign. Come on.

"A crab," Carelli said. Resting his right forearm on the wheel, he made the V again, bent it, and pinched the fingers together, apart, together, apart. "Then he pinches his left hand with the crab."

Andy stared, as if Carelli's crab were about to nip him, and the word slipped into his mind. Ticket. The sign wasn't a crab pinching a hand; it was a conductor's punch validating a ticket.

But why would he ask for a ticket?

He looked at the fare box, at the small sign listing the prices for regular service, midday service, day pass. *Oh yeah.* "How much did he pay?"

The silence again. Then, "Seventy-five cents, the regular fare. The kid just puts the money in the box, snap-snap-snap, and I'm telling him the youth fare is fifty cents but the money's already in the box and I don't make change." His voice rose, defensive. "So what's a quarter? It won't even buy him a Coke."

"He was asking you for a day pass." Andy pointed at the fare box. "Seventy-five cents youth fare for a day pass."

Carelli flexed his fingers, making the crab again, then gripped the wheel. "No kidding? Well, why didn't he write it down?"

"Maybe he didn't have a pencil and paper."

Wayne had never ridden a public transit bus by himself. He wouldn't have known about a day pass unless Interrupt told him to get a day pass. Faced with impatient Carelli, the jiggling knee, he would have frozen. Andy touched his ears; he thought he knew. The wits left you at the first sign of intolerance. You withdrew.

Carelli pulled the bus over to a stop and swung open the door. The three old women funneled up the aisle and down the steps, chattering, and Carelli jiggled his knee.

A day pass. Wayne wanted to transfer to another bus. Get off at stop X, transfer to bus Y. How many transfers, how many buses? The permutations increased by at least an order of magnitude. "If he was going to use a pass to catch another bus, what's the most likely stop?"

Carelli turned to look full at Andy. His mustache lifted, he was grinning. "You got to be kidding."

"I'm not. Just help me out. What's the most likely transfer point for another bus?"

"Listen," Carelli said. "My route starts up in Menlo Park and I go all the way to San Jose. Then you can take another S.C. transit bus down to Gilroy. You start in Menlo Park"— he held up one hand "and three and a half hours of bus time later you end up in Gilroy." He held up his other hand; his arms were stretched wide. "You get what I mean? My transit system, just Santa Clara County alone, is bigger than the state of Rhode Island."

"Let's go!" from the back of the bus.

Carelli turned in his seat, closed the door, and started the bus in one fluid movement. "Can't tell you more than that," he said into the rearview mirror.

Weary, as if he'd ridden the bus for the full three and a half hours, Andy said, "Just give it your best shot. A hunch, anything. Where's a likely transfer point?"

Carelli's hands raised briefly from the wheel, the universal sign for defeat. "Okay, we got a big one coming up, Monroe and Franklin in Santa Clara. Ten, twelve, maybe fourteen buses gonna branch out from there."

Monroe and Franklin. Fathers of Our Country. Why not? He got off at Monroe and Franklin. One more intersection, they were all looking alike.

All right, he's Wayne, he's instructed to catch bus Y but he didn't get his pass. He checks his pockets; maybe he doesn't have the exact change. Andy crossed the street, asked at the 7-Eleven. Wayne didn't get change there; maybe he already had it. So he goes to the bus stop, sits on the bench. Waits for bus Y, one of ten, twelve, fourteen buses. What's he thinking, is he thinking that this is a great game?

Andy pulled out the transit map and spread it on his knees. Routes from Monroe and Franklin, follow the blue lines, the blue circles, maybe transfer to the orange lines and the orange circles. His eyes blurred.

A bus heaved up to the stop, and the door gaped open. Andy shook his head. The door slammed shut. He felt dizzy, short of breath. He checked his watch: eight thirty-five. Wayne had been gone seventeen hours.

The first rule was, never panic.

What now?

Be deaf and dumb, like your son. Forget the switches. Remember Candace Fuentes.

Forget the switches?

Why? Andy gripped the edge of the bench. It was a little late for that. He had already told Feferman about the Stanford number and the channel into the switches. Interrupt wouldn't know that; or would he? But then he had talked about the pattern of calls to Nell, about figuring the whole thing out, and if the infinity transmitter was on . . . It must have been on. Why else would Interrupt worry about Andy pursuing switch failures?

What else could it be?

Andy sat bolt upright. Bait and switch.

You kidnap my son and I think it's because I got it right, because I couldn't keep my mouth shut about the channel. So now I'll keep it shut, I won't even think about channels or switches because I'm feeling scared and guilty as hell.

But he couldn't help it. He was thinking about switches.

Somewhere in the switch software there had to be instructions that opened the channel and let Interrupt into the switch. That let him set a trigger to shut down the switch.

Interrupt had threatened to take out a lot of number fives. But how . . .

Strowger.

Andy's head buzzed. Remember Candace Fuentes, Interrupt had warned. Candace had told Andy to remember something too. Remember the story about Strowger.

The story about Strowger was the story of manual versus automatic switching. Amin's point in telling the story had been that an operator using a manual switch could be biased, and an automatic system was unbiased.

But there was another point to the story. An operator using a manual switch could place just one call at a time. An automatic switch could place many calls at a time.

So far, Interrupt had been like a manual operator, taking down one switch at a time. But he was threatening to take out a lot of number fives. Taking out a lot of switches one at a time would be cumbersome. He'd have to keep dialing, and waiting for Andy to trip the trigger. Or he'd have to reprogram the trigger. That was clumsy, and Interrupt was anything but clumsy.

What if he had a sexier way to do it? What if he had built an automatic system, one that would take out as many number fives as he wanted, all at the same time?

Candace, Andy wanted to ask, was that what Strowger meant?

Then how did this automatic system work?

Start again. There had to be lines of code somewhere that let Interrupt into the switches. Somewhere in the millions of lines of programming that told the machine what to do. Andy had checked part of it, looking for a bug or a virus that could spread from the code of one infected switch to another.

I'd look again, Wayne would say.

Fine. Where, Spock?

Wayne, eyes trained on his father's hands, locking onto every sign, damned if he was going to miss anything.

All right. Andy held his son's image steady. Let's walk through it one more time. The software that runs the machine is written in a programming language that reads like English. We call that source code.

Problem is, the machine can't read English. So the source code is converted into object code. Object code is written in a language of numerals, just a string of ones and zeroes, something the machine can read.

I never had a chance to get to the object code, Spock, but Candace must have had a crack at it. Maybe she found something. But she never had a chance to tell Feferman. If Interrupt's hidden instructions are in the object code, the tiger team hasn't managed to find them yet, because they haven't managed to stop Interrupt from shutting down switches.

Maybe it's not there, maybe it's . . .

Hang on, Spock, I'm trying to figure it.

Okay, the way I'd do it is to go deep. Don't hide it in the source code or the object code, hide it deeper.

Andy suddenly pictured Carelli, fumbling over the sign for "ticket." The bad interpreter garbling the language.

The interpreter.

Look, Spock, Andy thought, excited, there's a special program in the machine, a software tool, that can manipulate other programs. It's called the compiler. The compiler is an interpreter; remember, the machine can't read English so it needs an interpreter to translate the source code into the object code that it can read. Like you need an interpreter when someone's speaking English to translate it into sign for you.

Think about it. If an interpreter is translating for you, he can slip in some extra comment, something the speaker never said, and you'll believe that's what the speaker said and the speaker will never know his words have been altered.

Shit. His son, to the point.

Yeah, Andy thought, shit. He took in a deep breath.

Long time ago, Spock, there was a war between the Greeks and the Trojans. The Trojans believed in a god that looked like a horse, so the Greeks built a giant wooden horse and hid their soldiers inside. When the Trojans found the horse, they thought it was from their god and brought it inside the walls of their city. And that led to the fall of Troy.

A Trojan horse attack. What if we contaminate the compiler, hide a few lines of enemy code within the useful compiler program, lying in wait to be brought into the system?

It would work.

It would work like gangbusters, because every piece of software that was developed to drive the number five switches had to be run through the compiler.

So, as the compiler is translating source code into object code, the Trojan horse within the compiler is inserting its own instructions into the object code, more Trojan horses. Then the software is shipped to the switching centers and loaded into the processors. And the Trojan horse is within the walls of the city.

And the beauty of it is, Spock, it would be damned near impossible to find.

But isn't the tiger team checking the object code?

You bet. But, remember, object code is just a string of ones and zeroes and it's a real bitch to wade through.

So what you have to do is run a test. You've checked out the source code and certified it as clean. Now you suspect the object code. So you take the clean source code and run it through the compiler again to produce a "test" object code. You assume it's clean because it was translated from clean source code. Then compare the test object code to the suspect object code that's running on the machine. If the two object codes don't match, if there are lines of instructions in the suspect object code that don't exist in the test code, then you've found the Trojan horse.

But, you see, the two object codes will match. And when they match, you will assume that the real object code is clean. And you will be wrong. Because in recompiling, you have unknowingly spawned another Trojan horse. Every time you run clean source code through the compiler, the master Trojan horse goes to work and contaminates the object code.

So when your test code matches your object code, it is not because both are clean, but because both contain Trojan horses. You're fooled, like the citizens of Troy.

So can't you find the horse in the compiler?

Not likely, Spock. You see, the compiler itself is a program, with its own source code and object code. And the master Trojan horse would be buried in the compiler's object code. That code is so arcane that there are tools, debuggers and decompilers, made expressly to examine it. But the tools themselves must first be compiled, and as they run through the compiler the master Trojan horse hammers a few instructions into them. Mask me.

Andy shuddered. It was an elegant piece of work.

Candace had seen it and tried to tell Andy. Candace had liked to say, to the five-E team, to any male engineer she worked with, that women engineers brought a unique perspective to a problem because they saw the big picture while male engineers got hung up on the details.

She had said it, he recalled, to him and Nell and Amin at the cutover. He couldn't argue the point. He had gotten hung up on the details of the Stanford number and totally missed the big picture.

If he was right, there was a Trojan horse in every 5ESS in the country. Good Lord, if he was right, it went far beyond that. Interrupt's automatic system was every bit as powerful as the invention of Mr. Strowger.

Candace had seen it, and talked about it, and gotten herself killed for her trouble.

Now he saw it. He couldn't forget the switches. What he'd just thought up was the equivalent of grabbing hold of a live wire.

Interrupt could have *made* him forget the switches, the way he had made Candace forget the switches. But he hadn't. Because he needed Andy, Andy the flesh-and-blood Trojan horse sent to gull Feferman. If Andy died, Feferman would rear up in surprise and start sniffing around, and Interrupt would be left without a decoy.

So he went after Wayne instead.

Where was Wayne? What in the hell was happening to his son? He had found a Trojan horse he wasn't even looking for but he couldn't find his son. Sitting at a bus stop, without a clue as to where to go next.

I'd look again.

Where?

I'd look again.

"Shit!" Andy slammed his hand down on the bench. Give me a break, just give me a break, I'm looking, I've looked, where do you want me to look? Dammit, boy, where in the hell are you?

A bus approached, brakes screeching like tortured metal,

and Andy viciously waved it on. He watched the bus as it shifted back into traffic, until it was gone.

Spock was gone too. He'd lost the image of his son.

Okay, he told himself wearily, look again. If you can't find Wayne, look for Interrupt.

He had.

He stiffened. No, he hadn't. He had looked for Interrupt's channel, not for Interrupt. *Look for Interrupt.*

The first rule was, never panic. Start again.

Okay. If Interrupt planted a Trojan horse in the compiler, he had to have access to the compiler. Somehow he had to get to the compiler program. Maybe he worked at the software development center and was able to insert his Trojan horse, but that meant he would have shut down the system and reinitialized without anybody . . .

FLAME ON!!! One more shot through his tired brain. On-line with Zot, what was it the phreak had said? He'd been doing this ten years, he'd started when AT&T was implementing D . . .

Yeah. Software for the 5ESS switches was written in the programming language D. D was developed ten years ago. And when they developed D, they had to write a compiler to translate the D source code into machine language.

One way, one very elegant way, to plant a Trojan horse in a compiler would be to do it when the compiler was being written.

The crosspoint. Ten years ago?

Andy spun off the bench.

19

•

His son had been gone eighteen and one-half hours.

Andy gripped the book and thought about crosspoints. A crosspoint was the place in a switching network where two communications channels intersected. The switching element sat right at the intersection and connected the channels.

The Faulkner family had been like two communications channels that could never manage to intersect.

Elaine and Tammy Faulkner, wife and daughter to Joe, mother and sister to Andy, had of necessity formed a unit, one channel. Joe Faulkner, and for a time Andy, had formed the other channel.

Elaine and Tammy had never been invited to a bridge construction site; they were taken to the opening ceremony and allowed to admire the finished product. They appreciated, as Joe told Andy, the "aesthetics" of it. Bridge as art. If Elaine and Tammy had been aware that women were cracking the

195

male fraternity of engineering, they kept that awareness to themselves. If Joe had thought of his women in connection with engineering, then the image was crystallized in the form of Washington Roebling's wife. After the crippling accident confined Washington to a room overlooking the rising girders of the Brooklyn Bridge, he used his wife as a messenger to convey his blueprints and instructions to the workers below.

So Elaine and Tammy created their own channel. Art. They studied, they took lessons, they collected on a very modest scale, they talked about Monet and Motherwell when Joe took Andy to his workroom. Tammy revealed a true flair for drawing, but she never, ever took as her subject one of Joe's bridges.

After Andy fell from Joe's grace, he had more time with his mother and sister. He tagged along on trips to galleries and museums. He made his own discoveries, developed an appreciation for one or two artists, but Elaine and Tammy affectionately dismissed him as a "nuts-and-bolts guy." He had been in Joe's channel too long, had been firmly cast in the Roebling mold. He had an engineer's heart, an engineer's soul. They loved him, they laughed at his jokes, they took him along, but they did not take him seriously.

Andy had seen a crosspoint in the two channels of his family and he tried to explain it to Elaine and Tammy, to Joe. There was art in engineering and there was engineering in art—the two channels met at a crosspoint. But he was the only Faulkner who saw it. A switching element that could not perform its job, could not connect the channels to form a communications path.

Now, holding the book, he knew the same frustration, of seeing a crosspoint as clearly as if it were drawn in fine black lines on cross-section ruled graphing paper, and knowing that the lines would not intersect for other eyes. He thought about trying to explain *his* crosspoint to Feferman. A remark made by a phone phreak. A bus driver's faulty attempts to interpret sign.

And what is the crosspoint? Feferman would ask.

Where the language intersects the compiler, Andy would answer. When they developed a new language, they had to develop a new compiler. And Interrupt had to have been there to plant the Trojan horse in the compiler.

That was ten years ago, Feferman would say. Are you proposing that we look back ten years for the solution? Are you claiming that Interrupt would wait ten years to set off his Trojan horse?

Remember the story about Mr. Strowger, Andy would say. You wanted to know what Candace meant about Strowger. Here it is: the big picture. Interrupt has built something that will shake the telephone system to its foundation, just as that undertaker shook it. I *know* him. He's single-minded, he never gives up. He's like John Roebling. Did you ever read the biography of the Roeblings?

Feferman would look at him blankly.

Put it this way, Andy would sum up, holding himself steady. Interrupt has killed to protect his Trojan horse. He has kidnapped. You think him incapable of a ten-year wait?

That's a long time to wait. Feferman, bland and obstinate. Just as Elaine and Tammy had, as Joe had, Feferman would refuse to see the crosspoint.

So Andy needed data, he needed proof. If Feferman and his team could use the data to thwart Interrupt's Trojan horse, fine. But that wasn't Andy's agenda. He was going to discover the identity of Interrupt and prove it to Feferman, and Feferman was going to have Interrupt arrested and forced to reveal where Wayne was. Torn apart if necessary.

The book in his hands was the first data point. AT&T documented everything, especially a major project like D, the first new switching language since its predecessor C was developed in the early 1970s. The engineers who contributed to D deserved recognition.

He found it in Appendix iii: a list of seventeen names, seventeen engineers who worked on the D project.

One of them had to be Interrupt.

Andy took the book into the library's copier room and photocopied Appendix iii. He replaced the book on the shelf and walked outside.

It was a perfect May day, with a bright sky clean as if scraped by a knife. He sat on Wayne's favorite bench, favorite because sitting at one end was a statue of a man so lifelike that people hurrying into the Sunnyvale library often mistook him for real. Holding a book in one hand, a sandwich in the other hand, head bent over the book. The book was in Spanish. Andy and Wayne had looked once, snooping over the statue's shoulder. As lifelike as he seemed, the metal man had the kind of stillness that Andy noticed in the deaf.

Andy read through the appendix list and read it again. He knew nobody on the list, it was as unilluminating as the Spanish text. Several names were familiar, but he couldn't be sure whether he had seen the names on technical papers or heard them at AT&T. Or at Stanford.

Three of the engineers were women. He had built Interrupt in his mind as a man, but he supposed that Interrupt could be a woman. Nell, her name pierced his mind, but she wasn't an engineer. Was she? *I took some engineering.* Her voice was clear and amused in his mind. No, not Nell.

He realized that one of the names on the list could be Zot.

He folded the paper. There were two things that he was certain of. Number one, that Interrupt had been on the D team, because he must have had access to the compiler as it was being written at the AT&T software development center in Morristown, New Jersey. Number two, that Interrupt had some connection to Stanford. He wouldn't have chosen the phone number of the telecom lab, he wouldn't have known it otherwise.

He needed to find the crosspoint here, where the channels intersected. Which name, or names, on the list had a Stanford connection?

"Hoover Tower is two hundred and fifty feet high," the student guide was saying, her hand resting on the control panel. Andy fixed his gaze on her hand, on her fingers splayed beneath the red emergency stop button, and silently counted, counting off the feet, feet rapidly dropping away below them, lost, and feet gained as they were hauled upward.

". . . really safe?"

Laughter. They were crowded in, close. A student showing his parents the campus, two Japanese in suits and cameras escorted by a third Japanese in jeans and a Hawaiian shirt, and Andy.

"Sure, Hoo Tow survived the '06 and '89 earthquakes," the guide said, and one of the suited Japanese, misunderstanding, nodded and laughed and shielded his head with both arms.

His back pressed against the paneled wall, Andy felt the vibration of the motor that was propelling the elevator two hundred and fifty feet into the sky.

Abruptly, the elevator reached its ceiling and halted, settling a few inches as its cables and counterweights and landing-zone detector found an anchorage in the shaft of air.

The door sucked open and they pressed forward, out. No one lingers in an elevator, Andy thought.

Amin was there waiting for him, leaning against the cage that enclosed the giant bells of a carillon. "You are right on time, my chick."

Andy had thought twice before calling Amin. He had intended to gather his data quietly, quickly, but he hadn't got past the Stanford records office.

Beyond the carillon, he could see viewpoints, fenced in by wrought-iron grilles embedded in concrete columns. He thought it might be possible to squeeze between the grilles; he thought he remembered a story of some long-ago student who jumped from Hoover Tower.

Amin laid a hand on Andy's shoulder and directed him toward one of the viewpoints.

Andy swallowed hard. He would have agreed to meet Amin on the tower of one of Joe Faulkner's bridges if it helped him find out who Interrupt was.

Amin gazed down from the summit, his body inclined like a high-diver about to take flight, his hands clasped loosely behind his back. "I enjoy watching the Terman building from here. I can see the window of my own little office, I can locate myself in the faculty hierarchy. I have not yet achieved a corner office. I once wondered whether Stanford harbored a certain prejudice, whether a Jordanian could reach the top here. What do you think?"

Andy stood well back from the grillwork, focusing hard on Amin's clasped hands, on the thin gold watch circling his wrist. "Sure."

Amin turned and smiled. "I have three names for you."

Three names out of seventeen. "Who?"

"Desjardins, Smith, and Cheney. Their Stanford careers are summarized here." Amin extracted a paper from his pocket, then moved over to Andy to place it in his hand. "Desjardins had graduated before I arrived, but Smith and Cheney, according to their files, did quite well in my classes."

Andy scanned the printout. A cold sweat broke out along his spine; it was the height. "Tell me about them."

"Andy, I have taught a multitude of bright young men and women but I could not make them all my chicks. All that I remember about Ms. Smith and Mr. Cheney is in your hands."

"This doesn't say where they are now."

"I'm afraid I do not know. Engineers, as a rule, are inactive alumni."

Desjardins, Smith, and Cheney. One of them had to be Interrupt. Somewhere, somehow, he had crossed paths with Desjardins, Smith, or Cheney, but it couldn't have been at Stanford because they had left before he came. They had all gone on to AT&T and come together on the D project, and then—where? Maybe still at AT&T, but AT&T guarded its personnel records at least as fiercely as did Stanford.

"You might ask Mr. Colson."

"Colson?"

"Your supervisor at R-TAC." Amin smiled. "I take it that you were unaware that I am acquainted with Ray Colson."

Dizziness, like gentle strokings of a feather, was settling down on him. He shouldn't have been unaware that Amin knew Colson; it would have been surprising that two people like Amin and Colson were both working in this valley, in telecom, and did not know each other.

"Why would Ray know where they are? Even if they stayed at the telco, AT&T has sites all over the map."

Amin steepled his hands, regarding Andy over the tips of his fingers. "Perhaps one of them, or more, were Ray's chicks."

Dizziness, or Amin's gesture, made him feel like a student who had missed a week of class. "Ray's chicks? Where?"

"At Stanford."

"Who, Amin? Who was at Stanford?"

"Desjardins, Smith, Cheney, and Ray Colson, among the several thousands of others who are beside the immediate point."

"Ray Colson was at Stanford?"

Amin looked disappointed, a slight wilting of his youthful face. "Andy, my friend, you take me aback. I had thought that . . . well . . . people work closely together, they both have connections to a nearby school, connections that many would brag about, and they naturally discuss what they have in common."

"What was Ray's connection to Stanford?" He suddenly thought of Nell, ruffled at every mention of the place. He had assumed she considered him one of the braggarts.

"He came as a visiting lecturer, stayed a year, then left. Of course he was brilliant, ninety-ninth percentile, but I don't believe he succeeded in the role of teacher. Still, he was at Stanford when Smith and Cheney were students, and they may have attended his class. Aha!" Amin smiled like a Cheshire. "You see, we have already ruled out Desjardins in connection with Ray, since Desjardins had graduated well before Ray's unfortunate academic career."

People worked closely together and they naturally discussed what they had in common. Certainly, Colson knew that Andy had gone to Stanford. The whole team knew, because that was one of the things you just found out about coworkers. Where did you work last, where did you go to school, do you know so-and-so? He knew that Speedy had gone to Rice, Lloyd had made some joke about white rice and black engineers, and Lloyd had gone to the University of Illinois, and Candace to U.C. Berkeley. More jokes, about the Stanford-Berkeley rivalry. But they didn't know where Colson had gone, what he had done out of grad school, and, surprising now, it hadn't seemed strange because that was the essence of Colson. They knew next to nothing about the man, and what they thought they knew was sometimes proved wrong. They thought Colson had no family, and then Nell showed up.

Colson had been at Stanford.

All right, but he hadn't been a member of the D programming team ten years ago.

Like Amin. Amin was at Stanford, but he hadn't been on the D programming team.

And that was the crosspoint that counted.

Where the hell *had* Colson been ten years ago?

The Japanese were edging around them, knotting together at the grillwork and blocking the view. The dizziness receded, and Andy's head began to clear. He gave the Japanese a silent thanks.

He remembered where Colson had been ten years ago.

Amin took him by the arm, heading for an unobstructed viewpoint. "I consider this place part of the engineering complex, although slightly removed from it geographically. Did you know that Hoover Tower is named for Herbert Hoover, who was a president of the United States, but more importantly was a mining engineer trained at Stanford? And the tower itself, naturally, is a feat of engineering. Never forget, my chick, that towers and bridges are engineering just as much as computers and integrated systems are engineering."

Crosspoints, Andy thought. He pulled his arm away from Amin, before Amin could lead him to the edge.

He pushed out of the elevator as it touched back to earth and went straight to a pay phone. These days, he kept a heavy supply of coins in his pocket.

Nell had told him that Colson was at an AT&T facility in Connecticut about ten years ago. But "about" could have meant nine years ago, or eleven years ago.

He got the number of the Connecticut facility from Information and called. Then he lied. I'm trying to locate Ray Colson and all I have is this number for him and does anybody remember him? Somebody did, and within a few minutes he learned that Colson had worked there nearly three years. He had come from Stanford, eleven years ago, and he had been there while the D language was being developed in Morristown, New Jersey.

Andy hung up.

Nell had told him that Colson was at AT&T Connecticut when he took off on one of his sabbaticals and turned up at the pole farm. Didn't you know? she had asked, wearing the unbuttoned blue workshirt. He remembered everything about that day, everything they did, everything they said.

Andy ran out of the Hoover Institution and ran next door into Stanford's world-class reference library.

It was a piece of data that should be easy to locate. Nontechnical, of no proprietary value, not protected by layers of passwords and access codes.

Where was the AT&T pole farm?

He had read once that you could find information on just about any subject published somewhere in a book. The third book he pulled off the library shelf supported that observation; the index had an entry for "telephone poles." He paged through the book to find the citation, fingers leaving damp marks on the paper.

AT&T documented everything. According to this book, it ran two telephone pole farms, one in Bainbridge, Georgia, and one in Chester, New Jersey.

Andy slammed the book shut. He needed a map.

The reference librarian, busy and tolerant, handed him a how-to-use-your-library pamphlet and found him an atlas.

Chester, New Jersey, was less than fifteen miles from Morristown, New Jersey.

Andy must have made a sound, for the other patrons at the table looked hard at him.

He didn't buy coincidences; it had become an article of faith that he shared with Feferman. If Ray Colson was climbing telephone poles in Chester and the D team was writing a compiler fifteen miles away in Morristown, Andy knew with a mounting rage that there had to be a crosspoint. Colson intersecting with Smith or Cheney. Or maybe Colson alone, climbing in a window like a thief in the night.

Then he reminded himself that Colson might have taken his sabbatical at the pole farm in Bainbridge, Georgia.

Bainbridge or Chester?

Nell would know.

20

•

"How did you find me out here?" Her eyes, two captured suns, flashed merrily.

"I asked around Pac Bell. I told them I was your boyfriend."

"Are you, then?"

"I told them it was urgent that I talk to you."

"Okay." She looked down, to her work, grasping a length of cable in heavily gloved hands.

"Nell. Tell me about Stanford."

Silence from her; noise from a passing car.

"Why do you hate the place?"

"Can this wait?" Her head was still bowed over the cable. A hard hat covered her hair.

"No."

She straightened. "Bill?" she called to the lineman unloading gear from the Pac Bell truck.

"Yes, angel?" He was an older man, muscled like a combat veteran, tattoos on both arms.

"Can you take the line up?"

"Yes, angel." He winked.

"I hate that," she said softly.

"Bill," Andy said.

The lineman paused, a thick coil of rope slung over one shoulder.

"Andy." She mouthed "no."

Andy stared at the man's scarred hands. He didn't care.

"Nothing, Bill," she said.

The lineman gave Andy a hard look and walked over to the pole.

"I have to work with him, Andy."

"I don't care about him," Andy said. "But don't hold back with me. Tell *me* what it is you hate."

The suns darkened. "Stanford."

"Why?"

She pulled a pair of wire cutters from her belt and snapped blades through cable.

"Why?"

"Because of Ray."

"Because he taught there?"

She showed no surprise, at the news that he had taught there or that Andy knew about it. "No."

"Nell, for God's sake, I need to know."

"Why?"

"I'll tell you. But tell me about Stanford first."

Her hands went to her waist, then slid down until her thumbs looped through her tool belt. Behind her, Bill was starting to climb, with a telephone line lashed to his tool belt.

"Ray wanted to go to Stanford, he wanted a Stanford degree, he said Stanford was the best engineering school in the country. And Ray had to be the best."

"He wasn't accepted?" The *admissions* office.

"I assumed it was because we couldn't afford it. My mom wasn't working, she was taking care of me, and Stanford cost a lot."

"Ray couldn't get a scholarship?"

"I don't know. I guess not. I don't know exactly what happened, I just know that he wanted to be at Stanford and not stuck at some second-rate school with a wife and a kid."

"He said that?"

"No. I don't know. Ray never puts things into words like that but you know what he thinks. I knew. I knew he blamed her, blamed me, and I hated him for it and I hated Stanford because that's what he wanted instead of us."

Ray Colson wanted to study at Stanford and he couldn't. But he made it there, after all, to teach. And teaching in telecom, he knew the phone number of the telecom lab. And then he went pole climbing.

Andy stared at Bill, halfway up the pole, the line trailing. The man knew how to climb.

"Is that what you wanted, Andy?"

"Part of it." He swallowed. He was strung tight, as if he had to climb the pole next. "Where did he learn how to climb poles?"

"What?"

"There are two pole farms. One in Bainbridge, Georgia. One in Chester . . . New Jersey."

"I don't know. I didn't know there were two. Ask Lloyd. He told me about it in the first place."

"You have no idea?"

She stepped closer to him, stopped. He could no longer see her eyes; the hard hat shadowed her face.

"What are you saying about my father?"

He could barely make out the words above the acceleration of a passing car. "Just one more question."

209

"Why are you . . ."

"How did you get the call records for me? Did you break into Ray's desk, or did Ray give you the key?"

"What the hell are you saying?"

He could see her mouth, compressed. Colson's daughter. "I'm saying that Interrupt wanted me to have the call records. It was a setup, a decoy. He wanted me to find what was there and distract Feferman with it." And he needed a Stanford man to find the Stanford numbers. That was it? Nothing personal, Ray just needed a certain component: Andy. "I'm saying that if your father wanted me to have the call records, he could have left his desk unlocked, or he could have given you the key."

"Shit, Andy," her voice rising like a triggered alarm, "you're not . . ."

He grabbed hold of her wrist, tight. "Nell, you said once that you wanted to impress your father, and I'm asking if you did it, if you . . ."

She slapped him with her free hand, and the rough glove scraped like a razor across his cheek.

"Did you?" His cheek stung, raw.

She jerked her wrist loose of his grip and whirled away from him.

He thought she was going to climb up the pole, after Bill. His eyes blurred with tears, from the pain of the slap. "Jesus, Nell, *did* you?"

Now she whirled back around, but not to him; she was looking at the road and her body went rigid. "Bill!" she screamed.

Andy stared up at Bill and he saw the lineman twist his upper body to look down at them.

What the . . .

Nell was running and from the poletop Bill gave a shout.

Andy saw him fumbling with the line lashed to his belt and suddenly he understood.

The telephone line was a drop wire running from the pole across the road to connect to a house. From housetop to pole, the line was pulling taut. A trip wire across the road.

Down the road, a car was coming on fast and if the driver saw the trip wire he didn't have the wit to slow down.

Bill was lashed to the line like a puppet on a string.

Andy lunged for the line where it stretched toward the pole. Nell was already at it, her wire cutters in place, but she was rushing, shaking, and the line would not sever.

Andy pressed his body around Nell and grabbed hold of the cutter's handles, his hands overlapping hers. Channeling all his strength into the hands, like arm wrestling, just pour it on. He felt her hands spasm under his; he was hurting her.

Bill yelling from up above, and behind them the Doppler sound of the car approaching, its engine mounting to a roar as the distance between them closed.

And then the car took them, Andy and Nell spun and went down hard to the ground, the line snapped past his face and whipped into the road beneath the wheels of the passing car.

They had cut it; he could see the severed end.

He reached for Nell but she was already on her feet, limping, bruised, but headed for the pole.

The cut-off part of the line, the part between them and Bill, lay on the ground. Andy didn't know if they had cut the line first or if Bill had worked it loose from his belt first, and he didn't care.

Bill was coming down the pole like a shocked cat.

Nell, right below him, yanked off her gloves and clutched one hand with the other. "Damned idiot stunt!"

Andy's own hands were cramping.

"*Damn* you, Bill," she screamed, and then she spun to face Andy. "You don't *do* that, you don't climb with the drop line,

211

you tie a rope to it and haul it up from the ground and *then* you climb up." She spun back to Bill, still gaffed to the pole. "You should know better, you damned idiot, you've been doing this longer than I have. What were you trying to do, save time? What's the matter with you?"

She stopped, panting, then said low and fast, "If you ever call me angel again I'll report you for sexual harassment." She stalked away, toward the van.

Andy caught up with her. "Are you all right?"

"I should have been paying attention." She turned to stare him full in the face. "Instead of listening to you."

"You're right," he said. His hands hurt, his arms ached, his cheek still stung. "I still want to know the truth."

"Go to hell."

"Nell," he said, his chest tightening. It hurt. "Interrupt has Wayne. Interrupt has kidnapped my son. I'll do anything to find out who Interrupt is."

Her eyes widened, then narrowed. The suns were shadowed with disbelief.

He told her about the D language, about the compiler, explaining it the way he would to someone with an engineering background, and he told her how close Chester, New Jersey, was to Morristown, to the place where they had developed D language.

"I'm sorry," she finally said, her voice raw from the screaming, choked. "But I don't believe it."

He was stunned. She must have nerves of steel.

"I mean I don't believe it was Ray."

He stood there, close enough to kiss her, waiting until it was clear she had nothing more to say, then turned and walked stiffly toward his car.

21

•

From beneath the car came the sounds of ratcheting, staccato, demons hammering on the track. Pitched back hard in the seat, Interrupt latched onto the lap bar and stared up the long steely incline. Above, beyond, blue sky stretched to infinity.

In the cars behind, there were whimpers, giggles, a lone strangled yelp.

Interrupt released the lap bar. The feeling grew quickly: anticipation, keen as a child's, edged by the promise of terror.

Ratcheting from below, the chain lift pulling the coaster skyward. *Clack clack clack,* then a shriek of grinding metal and a double *clack,* as if the demons were sawing at the chain.

Interrupt wondered about the designer of this monster, what malicious surprises had been set in store, whether the design engineer dared ride the thing once it had been erected.

Most coasters were adequate. This one looked promising.

Most engineers, Interrupt thought, did work that was adequate. A few, if they were lucky, created something that drew gasps, that made them stand back in astonishment before their own creation.

Wheels sang on the track, and the car jogged gently back and forth.

What Interrupt had created would shock the entire telecommunications world.

"Eeeeeeee!" from the cars behind.

Elegance. Interrupt had waited ten long years to stand back in awe before its implementation.

Every year of that ten-year wait, in every state in the nation, in towns and cities and metropolises, switching offices were cutting over from their old-fashioned crossbar workhorses to sophisticated electronic switches. Some were even cutting over from the earlier analog electronic switches to digital electronic switches. 5ESS, state-of-the-art.

Interrupt laughed out loud. The boy in the next seat, hands off the lap bar, ready to thrust them into the air, looked over and grinned.

Halfway to the summit.

Good heavens, the telco would be saying, this Interrupt is threatening to destroy our number fives. How many? Dozens, maybe more? How many does Interrupt have access to? We have over fifteen thousand number fives in service across the nation. Good heavens, nearly half the nation's telephone traffic—not just ours, that's bad enough, but other companies' as well—feeds into number fives because they are the major local-traffic switches.

And the tiger team would be sweating blood to figure out how to save them. How many number fives can possibly go down?

Interrupt shrugged. How about all of them?

As the coaster climbed higher, the riders got an angle on the loop-the-loop in the distance. A train of cars hung from the apex; heads and arms dangled down, boneless as dolls, then the coaster tore into the downward sweep of the loop whipping the floppy doll parts along with it.

Shrieks from behind. *"Get me out of here."*

Interrupt's pulse quickened; the loop was elegant.

Elegant. Commanding the number fives would be adequate, more than adequate. But Interrupt had designed elegance.

With a few lines of code, dazzling, like the blinding steel rails in the sunlight, Interrupt had toyed with the language that was used to write the software that drove the 3B20D superprocessor. And the superprocessor was the star of the telco system, the primary traffic-routing processor.

Clack clack clack. Shriek. Double *clack.* Demons at work.

The superprocessor not only drove the 5ESS, it lived in the 1A ESS, the other main local-traffic switch.

Ratcheting, vibrating through the car, vibrating the lap bar, sending shivers—little shocks—through the fingertips. Tighten your grip.

And the superprocessor lived in the 4ESS, the very high capacity toll system that switched long-distance calls. And it drove the autoplex cellular switches and the attached processor system and the inter switch communications system.

Sudden silence from behind as the coaster neared the top.

And it drove the network signaling system, which routed telephone calls along thousands of miles of telephone lines nationwide.

They reached the summit. The coaster poised there, and they existed in their own bubble of time and space, hung on a precipice, unable to see ahead or behind.

Interrupt had designed the failure of every major component in the system.

The boy in the next seat shot his arms into the air as the coaster vaulted down the slope.

Interrupt gasped, the boy gasped, and the coaster seemed to

fall free and silent straight toward the earth. Heart and stomach trailed. Just before they reached bottom, Interrupt lifted one foot, then another, dropping with the coaster.

And then the coaster wrenched into a series of turns that threw the riders hard against the lap bars, the only thing between themselves and oblivion.

The loop was coming up, fast.

God in heaven, Interrupt thought.

They hurtled into the loop and the horizon spun and gravity disappeared. For moments at the top they had a respite, hanging like meat on hooks, then they were flung down the back side of the loop and ejected onto a long arrow of track, accelerating toward another loop.

This is what it was going to be like, Interrupt thought, grinning into the wind, the telephone system plunging into silence and the engineers who designed and serviced the network riding it down, with no more control than the coaster riders catapulting into the next twist and turn. The stars would fall and . . .

The coaster jerked them through the loop, and Interrupt clutched the lap bar and screamed along with the boy as they somersaulted through space.

When they finally shuttled back into the station, the coaster now sedate, the boy turned to Interrupt and with a survivor's fervor shouted, "You should try The Edge next!"

He looked to be the same age as Faulkner's boy.

There was a story, Interrupt remembered, of a man who had been mute for years, who rode the hellacious coaster on Coney Island and was shocked into speech.

Faulkner's boy was beyond such help. Interrupt wondered if Faulkner ever resented the boy, resented the burden.

The attendant released the lap bar and Interrupt climbed out of the coaster, refreshed, a little shaky. The coaster designer had done a more than adequate job.

22

●

Feferman ate with fastidious attention. He had ordered the "magic eggplant casserole" after interrogating the waiter about the ingredients and being assured that it contained only eggplant, mushrooms, tomatoes, water chestnuts, topped with cheese and a Spanish sauce. "No meat?" Feferman had pressed, and the waiter had said, "Certainly not." Andy had ordered the Mediterranean sandwich; he didn't care what was in it.

It was five-thirty, early for dinner, and the Good Earth was not crowded. They had a corner booth and a view of the Almaden Expressway; Buck and Howland shared a table across the room, and they, like their chief special agent, ate as if they had not had a meal in days.

Andy had asked Feferman to meet him alone. He supposed this was as alone as it was likely to get.

Feferman listened without comment, working his way

217

through the eggplant casserole, while Andy laid out the cross-points: Colson and Stanford, Colson and the pole farm, Chester and Morristown, New Jersey. Feferman glanced once at the list of names from the D project, once at the printout of Desjardins, Smith, and Cheney at Stanford, but he did not lay down his knife and fork to examine the hard data.

"What happened to your face?" Feferman finally said.

Andy touched his cheek. Rough, scratched, like serrations on a knife. "It doesn't matter. Colson matters."

"Kidnapping's not my field." Feferman shifted his attention to the bread plate. "You were a fool not to call the FBI immediately, and you're wasting my time bringing it to me."

Andy lunged across the table and grabbed Feferman by the right arm. The chief special agent's bread knife dropped to the table. "Damn you to hell, Feferman, Colson's got my *son*. The *hell* with your time."

Buck and Howland froze, flatware in their hands.

Feferman shook his head at the agents, then glared at Andy. "Let go of me, Mr. Faulkner."

Andy tightened his grip. "I wasn't about to call anyone until I knew who Interrupt was. And I came to you because I didn't have time to give the FBI a primer in software development."

"Let go, Mr. Faulkner."

"Cause and effect, you son of a bitch. Now you know what he did and how he did it, you know who he is, so go get him. Get the FBI to get him, I don't care who, just get him!"

The muscles in Feferman's arm tensed, released, and tensed.

"*Feferman*. He killed Candace."

Howland was on his feet, a street thug poised to strike.

"Let go," Feferman said, a soft growl coming from the back of his throat.

Andy leaned closer, breathing in the after-shave, holding onto the thick bones of Feferman's wrist. "Arrest Colson."

Feferman made a face, a snarl, at his agents, and Howland with Buck at his heels pounded over to the booth.

Voices and movements stopped in the restaurant.

Buck clamped his hands onto Andy's shoulders and forced him down into the booth, pinning him there, his fingers digging painfully close to Andy's neck.

Feferman rubbed his right wrist, then picked up the bread knife and pointed it at Andy. "You do that again, I'll have you in jail until you rot."

Andy could not move under Buck's grasp. "That's real bright, chief special agent, throw me in jail while Colson shuts down the whole network." The hell with the network, he thought, but Feferman's eyes finally sparked with interest in something besides his meal.

The waiter was staring at them, rooted in the doorway from the kitchen.

"Let him go," Feferman said to Buck, "and if he touches anything but his sandwich, break his arm." He picked up a chunk of bread and began to butter it, then looked straight at Andy. "We're not encouraged to do that, but you get my drift."

Andy still felt pain where Buck's fingers had been. "Fefer man, please." If he needed to beg, he would beg.

Feferman spread another layer of butter on the bread, the bear building up fats after a long winter. Working the knife through the butter, teasing it out to the crust, the big white hands taking infinite care. "Feferman, please," Feferman said, putting down the knife and inspecting his handiwork.

Buck moved in closer, and Andy realized he was holding up his own knife with the serrated edge toward Feferman. He sank the blade into the sandwich.

"That sounded nice, telephone man." Feferman picked up the two sheets of paper from the table, scanned them, then handed them to Howland. "Mr. Howland, call Special Agent

Dicker at the FBI and suggest that he run these names through his computer." He shrugged at Andy. "Special Agent Dicker is a real hard worker but this could take a while. You see, you've given me seventeen names, ten years old, and we have to assume that they could be anywhere in the fifty states now, especially if they still work for the telephone company. If the names are in the computer somewhere—DMV records, voter registration, credit records—that speeds things up of course, but in some states information may be only manually available. Hard to believe, isn't it? If these people are out of the country, if they've changed their names, if they've gone underground, if they're dead, that slows things down."

"Feferman."

"And then, Mr. Howland," the chief special agent continued, "request on my behalf that Agent Dicker pick up Mr. Raymond Colson for questioning. Then finish your dinner." He waved Buck back to his table. "Go."

Andy's hand shook on the knife. Feferman, bless him, was acting.

Feferman bit off a piece of the buttered bread, chewed, took a long drink of his berry shake. "I figure," he said at last, "that you owe me. Your case against Mr. Colson is based on coincidence." He frowned, as if he had found a piece of meat in his casserole. "The only reason I'm pursuing it is that I have a natural concern for the safety of your son."

The hell you do, thought Andy. But it didn't matter; Feferman was going after Colson. "Where are they going to bring him? I want to be there."

"As I said, you owe me. For the moment, I am going to assume that your compiler scenario is correct. You are going to tell me how to disarm this Trojan horse."

"I don't know." What if they couldn't find Colson? "I want to be there when they question Colson."

"Colson is not a hot issue right now. I'll be notified when

they bring in Colson, but until then we'll file Colson. Right now the hot issue is the Trojan horse. So you just wait patiently along with me, Mr. Faulkner, eat your sandwich, and answer my question."

"I don't want the damned sandwich."

Feferman swiped out a large hand and slid Andy's plate next to his own. "What are you going to propose to neutralize the Trojan horse?"

"Christ, Feferman, I don't know! Ask your tiger team."

"Right now, I'm asking you."

"I don't know."

"That answer wouldn't be acceptable at Stanford. Or at R-TAC. Come on, problem-solve."

"I don't work for you, Feferman, go to your tiger team."

"I'm lifting your suspension. You work for R-TAC and you're accusing your boss of sabotage. Unless you wish to be suspended again, get to work."

Andy's chest tightened, as if pinned under Feferman's huge paws. It was suffocating. "I can't think about anything but finding my son."

"You thought up a Trojan horse in the D compiler."

"I wasn't trying, it just happened."

Feferman wagged his finger. "No, no, no, it didn't just happen. Remember that I've studied you. You're a zealot with a mission, you're a telephone man, and your mind can't stop working on this any more than a switch can stop processing calls."

"Unless it's shut down."

"Unless it's shut down," Feferman agreed. "But you're not dead, Mr. Faulkner, so your mind is still processing."

"I don't care about the switches, Feferman. Not now."

"You care."

No, Andy thought, I'm not Joe Faulkner. I'm a father before I'm an engineer.

"According to the extortion message that someone—Mr. Colson, in your scenario—that someone sent to the company, a goodly number of number five switches are going to fail. That bothers me, and it should bother you."

"Not just number fives," Andy said wearily. "Everything programmed in D language, and that means everything that is controlled by the 3B20D processor."

"He shuts down number fives, Mr. Faulkner. His extortion message threatens number fives. Nothing else."

Andy sighed. "Think it through. What if the number fives are a decoy, the channel opened up by the Stanford number is a decoy, to make you think that he's only going after number fives, that he can only trigger one switch at a time?"

"You're sure about that?"

"I'm problem-solving, Feferman, I'm not giving you a god-damned money-back guarantee. I figure that when he planted his Trojan horse ten years ago he also planted a piece of code that gave him this access . . . this back door . . . into any contaminated machine by dialing the Stanford telecom lab number. That's the Stanford connection. He had this thing about Stanford and he chose the lab number as the key to open the channel. So now, when he decides to use the channel, he dials the combination of the Stanford number and the number for Time—he can count on Time always being in service."

"What if the numbers are busy?"

"He waits and tries again, just like the rest of us."

Feferman scraped the last of the Spanish sauce from his plate. "Theoretically, then, once he's opened the channel he can choose any phone number he wants as the trigger?"

"I'd say so."

"Mine, for instance."

"Sure." I wish he had, Andy thought.

"But what about the TDDs?"

Andy looked at Feferman in disgust. "The TDDs were decoys, a way to set me up, a way to get you to go after me and not him. And you bit."

Feferman sucked gently on the tines of his fork, then placed it across his plate. The fork and the plate were spotless. "I like your Trojan horse in the compiler. I'll buy that for a while. But I'm still not convinced that he intends to use it on anything but number fives. What makes you think he will?"

"Because he can."

"Faulkner."

Andy leaned forward; the table edge pressed into his ribs. "Remember Strowger."

Feferman's eyes narrowed, nearly squeezed shut. "The message Ms. Fuentes left on your machine."

"Strowger invented an automatic switching system, it could process numerous calls at a time. It changed telephony. I think Candace was making the point that what Colson did was like that. He designed a mechanism to destroy numerous switches at a time. If he got into the compiler, then he had the capability to contaminate every piece of equipment driven by the 3B20D processor. If he had the capability, then I'll lay you dollars to donuts that he did it. He's the downside of Strowger."

"The downside of Strowger." Feferman regarded his empty plate for moments, long moments. "Then . . . *precisely* . . . what can he do to the system?"

Andy watched Feferman's heavy face, still inclined over his plate. "With the Stanford channel, he can shut down one switch at a time. With the Trojan horse . . . you don't want it to happen. If he's designed his Trojan horses to all fire at once, then he can hit every contaminated machine in the country at once. You get it? He can shut down, I'd say, ninety percent of our network. And he can shut down the other long-distance carriers wherever they feed into our local switches. That leaves maybe five, ten percent of the whole U.S. telephone network able to function, if it doesn't crash too, because of the overload." Andy sank back against the seat. "That's an estimate, not precision."

Feferman's head snapped up. He was smiling. "You care."

Feferman was right, Andy thought, numb. He still cared.

Feferman lifted a corner of Andy's sandwich, found chicken in the bushy bed of sprouts, walnuts, and olives, and regretfully pushed the plate aside. "What shall we do about Mr. Colson's Trojan horse?"

"I really don't know."

"Write a vaccine program to go after it?"

Andy shook his head.

"Why not?"

"First of all, he's probably buried the code. It's encrypted or scrambled all the hell over the place, it's masked. A vaccine has to be able to find the code, to differentiate between legitimate instructions and bogus instructions, and from the vaccine's point of view all this code's probably going to look legitimate. I'm not saying you can't write an effective detection program, I'm just saying it would be a real bitch to do. *If* you have the time before the whole thing blows up."

Feferman's small eyes bored into him, bright with interest. "So what shall we do?"

"Find the trigger."

"How?"

"I don't know!" Andy looked at the pager tucked into Feferman's shirt pocket, willing it to beep. How long could it take to find Colson?

Feferman fingered the pager. "Perhaps when we locate Mr. Colson we can convince him to give us the trigger."

"When you find Colson, Wayne comes first."

Feferman shrugged.

It was a game, Feferman was still running the game on him. Andy kept his voice steady. "Look, the trigger's got to be a date, a specific time, and when the clocks in the processors reach that time the Trojan horse shuts down the system."

"What's the date?"

"How should I know? Maybe Colson's birthday."

"Possible, but a little obvious."

"Yeah."

"So how do we find the date?"

Maybe Nell's birthday. He didn't want to think about Nell. "Maybe the Stanford connection," he said. "Maybe the date he found out he wasn't going to Stanford. Maybe the telecom lab number transposed to a date."

"Maybe you'd like to thumb through Mr. Colson's engagement calendar and see if he's circled any dates in red." Feferman winked.

"Damn you," Andy said.

"Then stop playing guessing games and give me an engineered solution."

He wanted to walk away. He wanted to sweep the bread bits and butter and picked-over sandwich into Feferman's glutted face. He wanted to have Feferman's thick bones in his hands again. But Feferman was going after Colson, and Andy had to wait for the pager in the chief special agent's pocket to signal him. As he seethed, his mind began to process, as if it now took its instructions from Feferman. The trigger had to be a date, a time, the time was unknown, unknown to everyone but Colson. No. *The time was known.* It was known to the CPU, the central processing unit, the machine's brain. The time existed in a piece of code hidden in the brain's permanent memory, an instruction to destroy itself when the time and date in the code matched the time and date on its clock.

Andy leaned across the table toward Feferman. "Build a virtual machine," he said, his voice raw. Excited.

"Explain it to me." Feferman laced his fingers like a schoolboy.

"A virtual machine, it acts like the real machine but it's just a simulator, a piece of software and some boards. It thinks it's a real switch. Shouldn't take too many hours to build. Then drive it with the 3B20D processor and contaminated software—from the Palo Alto office, there's no question that there's bad code in there. The trick is to make the Trojan horse in the software trigger a failure in our virtual machine. We're assuming that the trigger is a date, a time, but we can't just wait for it to occur in real time. We have to speed it up. So we advance the clock in the virtual machine one second for every real minute until we hit the trigger. Then we'll have the trigger, we'll know when the Trojan horse is set to go off in real time."

Feferman held out his big hand. "You work well under pressure."

"That wasn't pressure, Feferman, that was extortion."

Feferman shrugged, withdrew his hand. "Now we'll assume that your machine has been built and has given us the trigger, let's say"—he looked at his watch—"seven o'clock tonight, just to maintain the pressure. What can we do to stop it?"

"Bypass it."

"Explain that."

"At six fifty-nine and fifty-five seconds, stop the clock in every 3B20D processor. The clocks never hit seven o'clock on this particular date. They bypass seven o'clock, and the Trojan horse doesn't realize that it's missed its big chance. It just keeps on waiting for a time that will never come, has already passed."

Feferman was staring at his watch, shaking his head, again the schoolboy, trying to learn how to tell time. "Stop the clocks," he said.

"Temporarily."

Abruptly, Feferman snapped up his head and scowled at Andy. "But the clock in the processor records the times that calls are made."

"That's right."

"The goddamned clock can't record precise times if it isn't working."

"That's right."

"Then how do we know when people are making their goddamned telephone calls?

"We don't."

Feferman's face slackened, an expression Andy had not seen before. Feferman was surprised, and not happy about it. "We can't bill someone for a phone call unless we have a record that tells us when the call was made and how long it lasted."

"That's right." Andy felt his own stab of surprise, that he could enjoy anything at this point. He wondered if Feferman was going to get this incensed if he had to pick up the dinner check.

Feferman straightened. "Faulkner. If the point is to keep the clocks from hitting the trigger time, why can't we just set the clocks back to this month and day and hour last year? The Trojan horses think it's last year and they're just going to sit and wait, and we can still keep track of our billing."

"Maybe."

"*Maybe?*"

"Look, I'm not current on billing software but I'd assume that the programmers built into it the parameter that time goes forward. You'd be asking the software to change to negative time and you might confuse it so much that it would crash. You'd lose all your billing data."

"Couldn't we adjust the software?"

"Time, Feferman. What if the trigger fires before you've got it rigged up?"

Feferman sagged. "Let's say we do it your way. How long do you want to stop the clocks?"

"I'd stop them until we find the Trojan horse or until we clean out the system."

"And how are we going to clean it out?"

"Go back to development, rewrite the D compiler, take every piece of software in the network that's written in D and recompile it with the cleaned compiler. Then test and debug it."

"How long will that take us?" Feferman asked softly.

"A lot of people, working just on that? A week, more," Andy said evenly. "At a guess."

Feferman blinked, a bear blinded by a sudden light. "You're talking about millions in lost revenues. That may not bother you, Mr. Faulkner, but it sure in hell is going to bother someone in Accounting. You think the company is going to approve a plan that gives the entire country free phone calls while we clean house?"

"How much is it going to cost, Mr. Feferman, if Colson's Trojan horses destroy all our 3B20D processors? What do you want to save, our ability to bill or our ability to process telephone calls?"

"Mr. Faulkner, if I'm going to go to the company and suggest that we shut down our clocks, I want your goddamned money-back guarantee that there *are* Trojan horses in the system and not just in your head."

"I'm giving you my engineered solution. Take it or leave it."

Feferman opened his mouth, then closed it.

"You want to talk about lost revenues, Feferman? If Colson takes down the system, you're going to have a lot of unhappy businesses at your throat. No customers calling, no way to contact branch offices, no way to check inventory, no way to order supplies. And banks, Feferman. Cut off from the Federal Reserve. No way to process checks and order cash and wire money. Automated tellers shut down. And transportation, Feferman. Air traffic controllers can't transmit data to each other, and the airports have to shut down. And probably trains. The commodity and stock markets get shut down, the . . ."

"I get your point."

"You do? *You* can't use your fax machine. You can't call your broker. You can't call a restaurant and make reservations. You can't call an ambulance, Feferman, or the fire department or the cops or 911, you can't call the power company when the power goes out, you can't call home, you can't call your kid's school." Andy drew in a breath. "You know the expression 'high and dry,' Feferman? Yes? Not just here, not just one switch, high and dry all across the country. How much do you think that's going to cost?"

Feferman's hand flew to his chest. For a moment, Andy thought the chief special agent was suffering a heart attack, and then he heard the beeps coming from Feferman's shirt. Feferman pulled the pager out of his pocket. "I have to check in." He heaved out of the booth, scattering crumbs.

Andy was on his feet, blocking Feferman from the phone. "The FBI? I'm coming."

"You have work to do. Go build me a virtual machine. Show me where the trigger is. I'll authorize whatever resources you need."

"I'm *coming*."

Feferman laid a hand on Andy's arm. "Mr. Faulkner, leave it to the FBI. They know what they're doing, and they don't want you there to screw it up."

"I have a right to be there."

"No, you don't."

Andy thought he saw sympathy in Feferman's eyes, but the remainder of the chief special agent was unyielding.

Graceful failure, Andy thought. Processors were designed for graceful failure; when an element failed, the processor promptly shut it down so that the machine's total capacity was reduced only fractionally. He saw Feferman's point. If he were let into the same room with Colson, he might screw it up. He might not be able to control himself, and there would be no graceful failure then.

His skin crawled under Feferman's heavy hand. "Let go of me, Mr. Feferman."

Feferman removed his hand. "Go build the machine. We'll notify you the moment we have something on your son."

"You can notify me at home." Wayne's room, he thought, where it had started, about this time yesterday. Just a day since Wayne disappeared, but those hours belonged to Colson.

Feferman said quietly, "I'd like you to work with us. This is a request, not an order." The gentled bear. "You're good. And it will keep your mind occupied while you wait."

Andy stood aside for Feferman to pass. It doesn't work now, he thought dispassionately, game's over. "Occupy your fucking tiger team. I'm going home."

23

●

She lay in darkness, wrapped in white.

Andy sat bolt upright, heart slamming. The bedroom lights blazed and he was surprised that he had fallen asleep with the lights on, had fallen asleep at all. A sheet covered him, nothing else. The sheet was old, abraded times without number by granules of soap to a thinned chalky textile that clung to his limbs.

He had just dreamed of that sheet, only in his dream it was a shroud wrapped around Candace Fuentes.

He collapsed back flat on the bed. All in white. Like the Lady in the Snow.

It had been before Wayne, when he and Sandra were still kids playing at marriage. Up in the snow at Bear Valley. On a lunch break outside the ski lodge Sandra had started to build a snowman. Somehow, it became a contest. He had scraped up his own pile of snow and started to carve. As her snowman rose in classic great humps, he roughed out a snow body lying on its side. Quickly, it took the shape of a woman. Skiers clumped over in their unbuckled boots to watch, heating up the contest. Only by now it was no contest, because the on-lookers were openly admiring as Andy sculpted the arms and shaved away snow crystals between the curled fingers. Sandra suddenly stopped, leaving her snowman headless. "Where'd you learn to do that?" she'd said. "From my mother and sister," he'd answered. It was a half-truth. Art in the snow in the harsh Adirondack winters, his snow sculptures ornament-ing the whitened lawn to impress Elaine and Tammy. When he finished, the watching skiers applauded. "The Lady in the Snow," somebody said. Andy straightened, stretching, and looked down on his work. It was good; the lady could have been real, fallen asleep and dusted with snow, a true Snow White. "She looks dead," Sandra had said. He got angry, childishly angry, and stalked up the wooden stairs to the lodge and found the counter where condiments and utensils were laid out. When he returned she was smiling tightly, arms crossed, her familiar irritation that stopped short of real anger. He knelt beside the snow woman, ripped open a packet of catsup, squirted it onto her chest, and stabbed a plastic knife between her breasts. Behind him, Sandra gasped. "You're right," he'd said, twisting away from his Lady in the Snow, "she's dead."

He flung off the sheet and shoved out of the bed. He had to move.

He went into Wayne's room and checked the computer screen for messages, not really expecting any, but it was a habit by now, stop in Wayne's room and check the screen every time he passed down the hall. He had left the computer on, connected to the phone lines through a communications board, ever since he had found Interrupt's message on the TDD printer.

He sat on Wayne's bed, then got up to turn up the ringer on Wayne's phone, so that he could hear it when Feferman called again. Feferman had called once and said that Colson was "stonewalling," and Feferman had never seen anyone do it better.

He went back to Wayne's bed and stretched out. He had never been so wide awake. He had never been so tired. He pulled the pillow out from under the bedspread, dragging something along with it. Wayne's pajamas. *Star Trek* pajamas with the U.S.S. *Enterprise* blazing across the chest.

Nothing to do but wait for Feferman to call.

Suddenly, he broke out in a sweat. What if Colson wasn't stonewalling?

Call Feferman.

No. Let the FBI do their job, he'd only screw it up.

What if Colson wasn't Interrupt?

Call. He was dialing, but the phone went dead. No sound but Colson's rare laughter, a dry deep-toned laugh, coming over the wire. Andy yanked the wire out of the wall but he couldn't silence Colson. Colson was broadcasting on an infinity transmitter but Andy couldn't find it.

Someone was flashing a light in his eyes. He froze, listening. Colson's laugh had stopped. Just the light, on and off, on and off. He opened his eyes.

The lamp on Wayne's desk was flashing.

He stumbled out of the bed. He'd been sleeping again, he'd been dreaming, Colson had been laughing in a dream.

The lamp went on and off. It was Wayne's Signalman control unit, flashing the lamp to signal an incoming telephone call.

Feferman.

Andy lunged around to Wayne's desk. It wasn't the telephone, it was the computer alarm that Andy had rigged up to work the Signalman, a visual alarm clock for his son.

Someone had set the alarm.

Andy focused on the screen. The time flashed back at him, in unison with the lamp. 4:10 A.M. He'd been asleep for hours. He felt as if he could sleep for days.

The alarm. He hit the enter key and the lamp stopped flashing, the time disappeared from the screen and was replaced by two words.

Call Mommy.

Call Mommy?

He rubbed his forehead, trying to rub out the fuzziness. Wayne must have set the alarm before he disappeared. But why would he set the alarm that far in advance to call his mother? At four-ten in the morning?

Not Sandra's birthday. Sandra's birthday was in November, he thought sourly, and he had helped Wayne buy her a TDD for her birthday so she could take calls from her son.

Call Mommy? What was the date? He'd been talking dates and times with Feferman and he didn't know the date. May something. He found the calendar in Wayne's drawer and then he understood. Today was Mother's Day.

And 4:10 A.M. in California would be 7:10 A.M. in New York. Wayne was planning to call early, before the telephone lines got tied up with sons and daughters calling mothers in every town and city and state in the nation.

Mother's Day was the busiest calling day of the entire year, busier than Christmas. So busy that nearly a quarter of the calls got blocked at some point during that day.

Andy's head cleared.

Ten years ago, Colson had to choose a trigger, a date ten years in the future that would unleash his Trojan horses in a massive attack on the telephone network. If he had wanted a date that would cause maximum disruption, he couldn't have done better than to choose Mother's Day.

If Feferman's tiger team had the virtual machine up yet, they could confirm the Mother's Day trigger. If the machine wasn't ready, they would have to take his word for it.

Within an hour, he suspected, they would have a real-time confirmation on real switches.

Andy grabbed the telephone handset, thinking, maybe it's already started. But he got dial tone and punched in the number Feferman had given him.

This year, Mother's Day was going to be a real bitch.

24

•

The United States, with a thin slice of Canada above and
Mexico below, floated in a sea of phosphorescent blue.

The rear-projection screen covered the entire back wall. The
blue shimmering down from the wall and the glow from work
station screens cast a haze over the room, giving Andy the
sensation that he was underwater.

Feferman, beside him, stared up at the screen. Bathed in
blue, doused more liberally than usual with after-shave, the
chief special agent complained that he had not slept well.

But they'd let Colson sleep.

"Mr. Colson's got a lawyer, we had to let him sleep." Feferman yawned. "He's awake now. Your wake-up call got everybody up and going. Mr. Colson and his lawyer and the FBI
and my agents are having a very serious talk."

On the wall, the United States pulsed with neon-green dots
and crisscrossing green lines, real-time data on the state of the

AT&T telephone network transmitted from the Network Operations Center in Bedminster, New Jersey.

Andy closed his eyes and the United States went black as night. Systems crashing, switches failing, the network dying. Would that buy Wayne back? He opened his eyes and the United States was still on-line. What if the system didn't crash, what if they bypassed the trigger? How would a guy like Colson react to a ten-year failure? They could break him; he would crash. Would that buy Wayne back?

"Does your blood run cold?" Andy said, glancing at Feferman.

Feferman's expression was unreadable in the blue glare.

"Colson's will," Andy said. He moved away from the chief special agent, but the whole room was Feferman's territory. It was the conference room where Andy had been interrogated and suspended, converted to the tiger team headquarters, and now cobbled into the "situation room." That's what the guy on the security comm lines was calling it, the situation room in Sunnyvale talking to Network Operations in Bedminster and corporate headquarters in New York. Four forty-five in the morning, in a controlled-atmosphere room, and people were already sweating. Agents, tiger team members, third-line managers, all pressed into the situation room and most of them staring up at the wall.

The neon green flickered; every twelve seconds the circuits were sampled and updated; more green now.

"We're still alive," someone said.

The heaviest concentration of green was along the eastern seaboard, where it was 7:46 A.M. and people were up and calling. Happy Mother's Day, Mom, transmitting over thousands of wires. The midwest was darker, it was only 6:46 and traffic was just beginning to pick up. The mountain states were darker still, at 5:46, and the west coast at 4:46 was still sleeping off Saturday night; only the intrepid few were on the lines.

Sunnyvale at 4:46. Wayne had been gone thirty-eight hours. But the hours no longer belonged to Colson.

Andy found a place against the opposite wall and stared at the map along with everybody else. Heads were angled to the right, watching the east coast because if the network was going to go down it would start there. If the trigger was 8:00 A.M., it would fire first on the east coast, then again and again across the nation as each time zone struck 8:00 A.M. Of course, if it did fire on the east coast, they would have the exact trigger time and they would know when to stop the processor clocks in the other time zones. But it would be a costly victory: the entire east coast lost, and the rest of the country saved only by shutting down the clocks.

At the Palo Alto switch office, tiger team leaders were trying to boot the virtual machine. If they could get it running in time, they could find the trigger before it fired, and they could save the east coast. But the word from the Palo Alto switch office was "wait."

Feferman was straddling a chair in the middle of the room: a great hulk with its head turned toward the east coast.

Voices, low and vibrant, transmitted tension around the room like the high-speed telephone signals flashing around the map.

A strained voice. "East is gonna have to TORC."

"Par for Mother's Day."

Already, the Mother's Day traffic was overloading on the east coast. The Network Operations Center would be doing a traffic-overload reroute control, hustling to divert calls from the overloaded area to open circuits. A call from New Jersey to New York, blocked by busy circuits, might be shot from New Jersey all the way out to Sunnyvale, where the circuits were free, then back across the country to reach New York. Detouring through the time zones.

Andy scanned the east coast. Green lights flowered up and

down the seaboard, traffic going toward maximum. In New York, was Sandra expecting a call from Wayne? She would be up, she never slept late, not even on Sunday, because "life's too short." He wasn't sure anymore what she'd be doing on a Sunday morning, but he wouldn't be surprised if it involved the telephone. Sandra was an arranger, she didn't like surprises, she liked to plan for the day to go the way she wanted, and she usually did it on the telephone. "Keeps you in business," she used to tell him. Sunday mornings, they would have bagels and cream cheese with the Sunday paper, and she would not let him go for the bagels until she'd called to be sure the deli hadn't run out of onion bagels, and if they had she'd keep calling until she found a place that had not.

He tasted the old anger; it wouldn't be a tragedy if Sandra's line were cut.

But this wasn't any Sunday morning, this was Mother's Day, a day when love, duty, guilt, or habit drove nearly every mother's son or daughter to the phone. If she didn't get a call from her son, she just might pick up the TDD and try to call him. She might, Andy thought coldly, because she didn't know that Wayne was missing. If Andy had called to tell her, she would have been shocked, she might even have volunteered to catch a flight out to California, but he had thought that she would prefer not to be shocked.

The east coast was bright green, Sandra and several million other callers burning up the lines.

Andy followed the green lights up the coast through Connecticut, Massachusetts, New Hampshire, up to the far edge of Maine. The map turned dark as he followed it across the Maine border into New Brunswick. No neon-green dots or crisscrosses lit up the slices of Canada and Mexico that showed on the map, because Mexico and Canada were not part of the AT&T telephone network.

"Oh, my God," Andy said, louder than he'd thought, for all the heads in the room snapped around in his direction.

Feferman was up, knocking over his chair. "What, Faulkner?"

"Time zones."

"Yeah?"

"Atlantic time hits first . . ."

"That's Canada," a tech said.

People turned to the screen again, to the time zone divisions, to the blacked-out hunk of the map that jutted into the Atlantic Ocean: Nova Scotia, Prince Edward Island, New Brunswick, Labrador, and the far eastern slice of Quebec, where it was 8:47 A.M. Atlantic daylight time. The Island of Newfoundland had its own time zone, half an hour ahead of Atlantic.

Objections flew.

"What's Canada to do with it?"

"Atlantic's off the monitor, Network's not even tracking the Atlantic zone. What the . . .?"

"Canada switches with Northern Telecom."

"Some GTE there too."

"Are we in Canada? What's Canada . . .?"

"Northern Telecom *is* Canada."

Feferman's voice cut through the crosstalk. "Faulkner, what are you saying? Are you saying that he got to the Canadian network too?"

"No!" one of the managers broke in. "It's marketing. We've had a joint venture with GTE for years comarketing equipment, their small switches and our big ones." She swept a hand up high from right to left, from the Atlantic to the Pacific zones. "Ask any product manager. Been trying to crack the Canadian market for years."

Andy nodded. "That's what I'm saying."

Feferman was on point, heavy head swinging between the manager and Andy. *"Do we have switches in Canada?"*

241

The manager shook her head; she didn't know.

Canada was touchy about the United States, about domination by its southern neighbor. Northern Telecom built good switches, and if the Canadians could buy good homegrown equipment, they would. But AT&T built good switches too, and if it could sell to the Canadians, it would.

"Faulkner!" Feferman said.

"I don't know, but I think you better find out."

Feferman was already across the room, commandeering the line to New York.

Andy was counting on the chief special agent. Right now, Feferman owned AT&T, he *was* the telco, and he would charge through bureaucracies, across touchy international borders like a maddened bear.

"Number five ESS, number four ESS, anything that uses the 3B20D processor," Feferman was growling into the phone. "No, just the Atlantic time zone—and that Newfoundland zone—I don't give a rat's ass about the rest."

Andy watched the map, framing Feferman's huge silhouette. 4:57 A.M., 5:57, 6:57, 7:57 across the time zones. Coming up on the hour. Green lights multiplying like bacteria in a petri dish. 8:57 A.M. Atlantic time, 9:27 Newfoundland time; if they'd been sampling Canadian circuits, the darkened eastern provinces would be pulsing green.

Did they have Mother's Day in Canada?

8:58 A.M. Atlantic time. 8:59, coming up hard on the hour.

Feferman was sputtering into the phone.

Nine o'clock, Atlantic time.

"Ha!" Feferman shouted, stiffening every body in the room. He muffled the mouthpiece with one big hand and grinned fiercely at Andy, showing teeth stained blue by the light from the wall. "Couple of cities in Nova Scotia, been running our number fives over a year. They're down, Faulkner. The poor

Canucks were still running diagnostics when we got through on our emergency lines."

This was it, Andy thought coolly, this was the trigger. The minute, the second, the time that Ray Colson had been waiting ten years for. "What time did they fail?" he said, his throat tight, not cool at all.

"Eight-thirteen, on the nose."

Eight-thirteen. The day, the hour, the precise minute had arrived, the Trojan horses had finally received their orders of attack. *Go.* Seize control of the operating system and take the switches down.

The room fell quiet as techs, tiger team members, managers, security agents, and the chief special agent himself looked silently up at the darkened patches of land jutting out beyond Maine.

"Which one is Nova Scotia?" someone asked.

"Forget Nova Scotia," Feferman boomed out. "In ten minutes our whole east coast is going high and dry. Nobody'll be able to call their shrink, and we're going to catch hell for it." He glared around the room. "And rightly so." His glare caught on Andy. "Unless Mr. Faulkner's bypass surgery works." Feferman snatched up the comm line again

Andy wanted to get his hands on the machines, get to the closest switching control center and do it himself. Here in the situation room they could do nothing but wait. Now it was up to the maintenance engineers, good solid people who handled the switches with the fond discipline of seasoned parents. In control centers for every 3B20D processor on the map, they were ready to stop the clocks just shy of 8:13 A.M. Piece of cake, just tap in a couple of instructions and take a bite out of time.

Suddenly, the upper right corner of the map lit up with neon-green traffic: Network Operations had gotten a display of the circuits in Canada's Atlantic provinces. In the bottom-

243

most patch of land, Nova Scotia, a black hole was punched into the busy network of green. Two number five electronic switching systems, dead in the water.

Damn you, Colson, Andy thought. Didn't even know you were taking down Nova Scotia, did you? What did people do in Nova Scotia, shipping, fishing? What did a fisherman do before going out to sea? Call some weather service and find out how the tides and currents were running, find out if he was going to get caught in a squall. He wouldn't be calling today.

"Eight-nine, eastern," a tech near Andy said.

The Trojan horses were set to take down the east coast in four minutes.

A roar barreled through the room, Feferman on the comm line, circling the table like a maddened bear, bellowing into the handset: "Why didn't you inform *me?*"

Andy shot over to his side. *"Colson?"*

"Hold on!" Feferman bellowed into the phone, and every person in the room froze.

Feferman yanked the receiver from his ear and buried it in his chest. "New York informs me, *now,* that we're going to do a two-minute bypass. Two minutes only, then the clocks start."

"Jesus!" Andy said. "That'll suit Colson just fine. Feferman, tell them . . ."

Feferman clamped a hold on Andy's arm. *"Them?* You know who *them* is? Not just our honchos, our honchos have to consult with the honchos from all the operating companies because they own a helluva lot of the switches you want to diddle with. Seems everybody's been arguing about it since yesterday, since they first heard the words 'stop the clocks and the billing' and they couldn't decide whether to shit or get off the pot. When they heard that today was the magic day they apparently decided to get off the pot, they couldn't swallow more than two minutes without billing on Mother's Day."

"Eight-ten, eastern time," the comm tech said.

Feferman released Andy's arm and bellowed, "Did any-body in this room know about it?"

The product manager finally spoke up. "It's a tough call. What do we do, bankrupt ourselves? We *know* the trigger now, and I think the two-minute bypass is a clean solution."

"You want to bet the store on it?" Andy said. He pushed up close to Feferman and bored in on the small angry eyes. *"Listen.* All we know is that eight-thirteen is one trigger, maybe just the first trigger time Colson programmed. Colson's not an amateur, for God's sake. He would have gone for a greater-than trigger. It costs him nothing and he gains everything."

Feferman's eyes locked on Andy. He jammed the receiver back to his ear and hissed to New York, "My tiger team says it's a greater-than trigger."

"Eight-eleven, eastern," the tech whispered.

Feferman smothered the mouthpiece with his hand. "What the hell is a greater-than trigger, Faulkner?"

"Greater than eight-thirteen. The trigger fires at eight-thirteen or at any time *after* eight-thirteen. Greater than."

Feferman seemed to have frozen. Then he targeted one of his tiger team and bellowed, "You buy that? Greater than?"

"Yup."

The big head swiveled back to Andy. "Okay, I'm going to bat." Feferman turned his back, hunched over the phone, and lowered his voice to a mutter.

A chair creaked, then another and another. Someone coughed, muffled it. Someone started to tap a pencil. Heads turned back toward the screen on the wall.

Andy couldn't tell what Feferman was saying to New York.

"Eight-twelve, eastern," the comm tech said.

"Eight-twelve and twenty seconds," someone amended.

"No, I've got fifteen seconds."

"Somebody call Time."

Laughter erupted and the guy who'd said "call Time" and not meant it as a joke joined in, laughter triggering laughter, all of them stretching it, chuckling after the hard laughs ran out. But they kept their eyes pinned to the giant eastern seaboard.

Andy pressed close to Feferman. Still on the line, Feferman looked at him and mouthed, "They're discussing it."

"Hurry them up," Andy said.

"That's it, we've got eight-thirteen eastern, to the tick," the comm tech said, and rapped his knuckles against the table.

The room fell silent, the tapping and creaking and coughs stopped. Up on the wall, across the United States floating in its sea of blue, neon-green signals glowed. It was 5:13 A.M. Pacific time and traffic was still sluggish on the west coast. Mountain time at 6:13 showed more activity; traffic at 7:13 Central time was hopping. On the east coast it was 8:13, 8:13 and ten seconds, 8:13 and eleven seconds. Then the neon green flickered; every twelve seconds the circuits were sampled and updated. The flickering stilled, and every man and woman in the room took a breath and held it. The east coast showed a forest of green. Mother's Day, the busiest calling day of the year, and the east coast was still on the line.

They had bypassed the first trigger.

A roar surged through the room, people shouting, whooping, pounding each other on the back and yelling their throats raw.

The comm tech and Feferman were both on the lines, hands pressed against their free ears. Feferman, trying to talk to New York, caught Andy's eye and shrugged.

Andy watched the roomful of people yelling themselves silly. They had saved the network. In two minutes, when the clocks restarted, they might lose the network, but right now, for two minutes, the network belonged to the good guys. Andy couldn't help it: he grinned and thrust a fist into the air.

Suddenly, the comm tech was yelling at them, like someone trying to shout through a thunderstorm. "They got the virtual machine running! It's a greater-than trigger. Stop the clocks," he shrieked. "They said to stop the clocks!"

Feferman blinked, then bellowed into his receiver, a sound that rose above the uproar in the room, a sound that must have blasted them to the walls in New York.

Andy turned to stare at the screen. They had about a minute to get every control center on the east coast to shut down their clocks. If they stopped the clocks in time, if they saved the network, if they broke Colson and found Wayne, Andy vowed, he would call Sandra and wish her happy Mother's Day.

"What's the time?" someone yelled.

"Eight-fourteen and ten."

Feferman handed his receiver back to the comm tech and let his arm swing loose. The big hand flexed, then slackened.

"Feferman?" Andy shifted, bringing Feferman into his sight along with the screen on the wall.

"They bought it." His voice was cracked from the abuse he had given it.

Lights held steady on the big map, the cast a green jewel.

The room was silent again, a hollow silence after all the shouting, silent as a morgue.

"Give me a time, dammit!" The product manager.

"Eight-fourteen and fifty-seven seconds, eastern," the comm tech said.

Andy caught a glimpse of Feferman's hands; the chief special agent's fingers were crossed.

"Eight-fifteen, on the tick."

The green flickered; the circuits were updated. *Green, still green.* On the east coast, callers continued to chatter and laugh and yell and whine, and at the Network Operations Center techs kept on hustling to reroute the Mother's Day overload.

"We did it, then?" someone asked.

One more bellow from Feferman, a full-throated roar. The chief special agent was stamping around the room, his hands locked over his head swiping at the air, the bear who had wrestled down all comers.

People began to grin and shake hands, but they let Feferman roar on alone.

Nice work, Andy thought, a damned nice morning's work. He was glad to have Feferman on his side instead of on his tail.

Feferman circled in on the comm tech and commandeered the line again. "Get some people up to Nova Scotia and fix their phones," he growled into the handset. "I don't care how, I don't care if you have to do it with an operator and a plug-in switchboard, get their telephones working!"

It wasn't Feferman's job to get Nova Scotia's telephones up, it was PECC's job, but nobody at the telco, not the Product Engineering Control Center or corporate headquarters, was going to tell the chief special agent to butt out.

Feferman, still charged, came to Andy and stuck out his hand. "Congratulations, telephone man."

Andy took his hand and they shook, firmly, quickly. "Nice work, Mr. Feferman. Now, *Colson.*"

"Let's go."

Outside, it was not yet dawn, the streetlamps still burned holes in the dark. 5:20 A.M. Pacific time, and Mother's Day had barely begun.

Andy shivered: damp shirt and cold air.

Feferman stopped in the visitors' lot beside a powder-blue Jaguar, same color as the AT&T flag. "Here's how it's going to be. You're going to get in your car and follow me. We're going to pick up some oranges and donuts at the 7-Eleven and then we're driving down to San Jose, 280 South First, you'll see the big FBI sign. You're going to wait in the waiting room, the chairs are okay, I don't know about the magazines. Get some sleep if you can. I'm going to join the conference with Mr. Colson and I'm going to add a little psychological pressure. I will come out and tell you the moment he utters your son's name."

Good enough, Andy thought. He stuck out his hand and Feferman took it.

25

•

The horsewhip was mounted on the wall like a trophy. Fine-grained white leather, braided into tight spirals, sheathed the handle of the whip. Two gold silk tassels, also braided, hung from the knobbed grip end. The actual whip was a slender thong, of the same white leather, knotted at the bottom and curled back around the handle in gentle loops.

Seated at his desk beneath the whip, Amin studied Feferman as if he were an unwelcome quals candidate.

Feferman's huge body had taken on a weary slump. He eyed the whip and Amin with the same leaden expression.

Amin addressed himself to Andy. "I congratulate you on your very clever fix."

Andy started; Amin knew already? Fix. He hadn't fixed the system, he'd massaged it, and he watched Feferman rear up in his chair, also surprised that Amin knew.

Feferman shoved a hand into his coat pocket. "Who told you about that, Dr. Masri?"

"I have a network."

"A what?"

Amin steepled his hands. "An interconnected system of people with common interests, in this case telecommunications."

"Is Ray Colson in your network?"

"I am sorry, no."

"How about . . ." Feferman pulled a notebook from his pocket and consulted it. "Judith Smith, Marc Desjardins, Mark Cheney?"

"No, I am sorry."

"They were your students."

"Judith Smith and Mark Cheney attended my classes, Mr. Feferman. They are not part of my network, and I have no conception where they are today."

"Today, Mark Cheney is parked in a field office of the FBI in Houston, Texas." Feferman tossed his notebook onto Amin's desk. "Ten other names on this list are also in conference with the FBI. But right now, we have no *conception* of where the remaining six are. Your students Marc Desjardins and Judith Smith are among the missing. Please read the list, Dr. Masri, and tell me how you are going to be of help with these names."

Amin bowed his head over the list, then stood and reached across his desk to deliver the notebook back to Feferman. "I am sorry."

Their hands nearly met over the notebook, their shirt cuffs shot back on extended arms, revealing Amin's thin gold watch and one nearly like it on Feferman's blockish wrist.

"Did Zot tell you?" Andy asked, and they both turned to him.

He had waited two and a half hours for answers in a hard-backed FBI chair, beyond sleep, buzzed on strong FBI coffee and functioning on 7-Eleven oranges and donuts. By the time

Feferman came out and grimly reported that they had nothing from Colson, he felt stripped raw. Stripped of dread, worry, suspicions, stripped clean as though someone had taken a pair of wire strippers to him and peeled off every layer of insulation. A raw wire ready to make a connection. When Feferman, frustrated, grumpy from lack of sleep, lack of answers, had said let's go see your teacher, he had experienced a resonance, Feferman's stimulus causing a vibration that matched the natural vibration in his own stripped-to-the-wire system.

"Who is Zot?" Feferman demanded.

"Zot is irrelevant to this discussion," Amin said.

"Who is Zot?"

Both of them were looking at Andy, Feferman impatient, Amin tapping a finger to his lips. A light tap of the horsewhip.

Resonance.

The horsewhip.

When Andy had been a student, Amin's office in the old electronic research labs building had chipped linoleum on the floor, oxidized paint on the walls, and an unguinly steel desk that took up too much space; but the fine leather horsewhip had hung on the wall, and everyone who set foot in the room identified Amin with the elegant whip rather than with the shabby junior faculty office.

The joke was, of course, that Amin kept his students' noses to the grindstone with a flick of the whip. In reality, of course, Amin's "chicks" were self-governing and kept their own noses to the grindstone; Amin did not attract the kind of student who needed goading.

However, the whip was a working horsewhip. In Jordan, Amin had ridden dressage and won the white leather whip in a horse show. At Stanford, he went along with the joke and claimed to use it on candidates in quals and orals "to command attention and demand obedience."

Now Amin had a tenured third-floor-view office in the Terman building with weekly cleaning of the carpet and yearly painting of the walls. But the whip still hung on the wall, defining the office and the man.

The creamy white leather, the gold silk tassels, the soft braiding were all for show, to mask the whip's purpose.

The whip was for control.

"Who the hell is Zot?" Feferman repeated.

Andy felt neither surprise nor excitement, just the resonance of a connection made.

In a switching network, the processor was for control.

Amin was the processor in his own communications network. The network, always the network, and in place of going home to Jordan to build a real telecommunications network Amin had assembled a virtual network in Stanford and Silicon Valley, with trunk lines to London and Rangoon and Los Angeles and New York, and he could not possibly have resisted adding a tantalizing peripheral to his network, the community of phone phreaks. But phreaks were at heart self-governing and to bring them into the network required control that did not look like control. The showy disguise that masked the working horsewhip. And so Amin had created Zot.

Zot was Amin; Amin was Zot.

"Zot is a communications hobbyist who runs an electronic bulletin board," Amin told Feferman. "No, it was not Zot, and I assume that I am not required to reveal the source of my information unless you initiate some sort of legal action against me." Amin's eyes narrowed, a slivering of polished brown almonds.

"If your source of information has breached AT&T security, then you can bet your professorship that I'll require an answer."

"I have nothing to do with a security breach, Mr. Feferman."

"Head of Security Feferman, Dr. Masri."

They watched each other's face, taking measure.

Andy shivered. Completing the circuit. Zot the ghost on Andy's screen. The only reason Amin could masquerade as Zot was that he did not have to show his face. A phreak was just electronic signals, faceless. Like Interrupt. The only reason Colson could masquerade as Interrupt was that he did not have to show his face. Substitute X for Colson. The only reason X could masquerade as Interrupt . . . Give X the value of Desjardins, Smith, or Cheney. He had thought Amin had given him all the available data on them, but he was wrong.

"Amin," Andy said, his voice, too, stripped raw, "what do Desjardins, Smith, and Cheney look like?"

"Look like?" said Feferman, a growling echo.

"Andy, my chick, it has been years I never saw Mr. Desjardins, and I can't recall Cheney to mind . . ."

Feferman lunged to the desk and clamped a hand on Amin's telephone. "Give me your fax number."

Amin rolled his chair back from the desk, away from Feferman's hulk.

"Faulkner wants to know what Cheney looks like, and I'm going to have Houston fax him to us if that suits you, Doctor."

Amin reached to the table behind him to switch on his fax machine. "Help yourself."

The fax hummed.

"There may be a photo of them in some yearbook . . ." Amin began.

Feferman hissed into the mouthpiece, trying to keep his voice down.

"Perhaps in their files, but it's Sunday and the records office is closed."

"I can get the records office opened," Feferman said, listening to Houston and staring down at Amin.

"What about Smith?" Andy said.

"Judith Smith." Amin laced his fingers and brought them to his forehead. "Brown hair, I think, medium-length brown hair, a thin figure, perhaps tall."

"Her face."

"Thin. Not remarkable, Andy, I simply do not see it."

"We'll get her from records." Feferman had hung up and had his back to them, hunched over the fax machine.

"They may not keep photographs."

"Then *think,* Doctor." The fax was coming in; Feferman hunched closer to look.

Amin stood. Beside Feferman, he looked like a delicate boy, but then he stepped around Feferman in one fluid movement, as he might have moved around a big horse, easy with the whip in his hand. "I know where to find her, Andy. WISE."

"Yeah." Andy beat Amin to the door.

A ripping of paper and Feferman pushed out the door behind them. He shoved the fax of Mark Cheney into Andy's hands.

"What's wise?" Feferman said.

They moved fast down the hallway, shoulders, arms bumping.

"Women in Science and Engineering." Amin guided them down the stairs.

"Christ," said Feferman.

"They are a network, as ATT is a network."

Andy passed the fax back to Feferman.

"You recognize Cheney, Faulkner?"

"No."

That left Desjardins and Smith.

Up another hallway and Amin strode out in front to take hold of a doorknob. He turned it once, then twice again, his gold watch flashing.

"You don't keep a key, Doctor, to Women in Science and Engineering?"

Andy shoved Amin aside and heaved his weight against the door. He thought it gave, a fraction, and slammed against it a second time. A pain shot through his shoulder, a wire vibrating, so he turned his other shoulder against the door. Now Feferman was beside him, adding his crushing weight. They slammed together and that was enough. The lock gave with a screech of metal abusing wood.

"Now I know how to pick a lock," Feferman said.

They passed through the lounge to a room lined with file cabinets and bookcases. They rushed, amateur burglars, yanking open file drawers, tossing brochures and catalogs aside like unplayed cards. Then they slowed, Amin settling into a chair to sort through a stack of files, Feferman on his knees at the bookshelf, his head cocked to read the spines. Copies of theses, yearbooks, reference works.

Andy found it, an old recruiting brochure, "Meet WISE at Stanford," with captioned pictures of successful graduates, "went to work for Du Pont," "took a post-doc at MIT," "internship at the EPA," "flying high with NASA." And there she was, Judith Smith, "connected with AT&T."

Andy gazed at her, medium-length brown hair, thin face, but Amin was wrong, her face was remarkable, truly remarkable.

Resonance.

What was it Feferman had said? If they've changed their names, that slows things down, takes the FBI a little longer to find them. Judith Smith had changed her name. She had gotten married.

She was Lloyd Narver's wife.

There was pain. God, he had thought he was stripped raw, but here was one more layer of insulation and this time it burned away, the heat came from his core, and like a wire carrying too much amperage, it burned.

He had gone after the wrong man. He had badgered Feferman into locking up Colson, and then he had felt that Wayne had a certain margin of safety, that if he did not know where Wayne was at least Colson could not get at him, and then he had gone ahead and told Feferman to build the virtual machine and stop the clocks and bypass the triggers. He had thought that, confronted with his failure, Colson would crack and give up Wayne, but it wasn't Colson's failure, it was Judith Narver's failure, and she was not in custody and Wayne had absolutely no margin of safety. Ten long years and then failure, how angry would she be, how would she treat the son of the man who had told the telco how to stop her Trojan horse? The way she had treated the woman who came too close to figuring out the Trojan horse and boasted about it into Andy's answering machine. The way she had treated Candace Fuentes.

A clever fix, an engineered solution. He was a damn good engineer, he might have impressed even Joe Faulkner, but he had gone after the wrong man and left Wayne high and dry.

He rode in Feferman's Jaguar, smelling of good leather and pine-scented after-shave. Feferman drove fast. Andy gripped the armrest, sending spasms through his sore shoulder. He watched the clock on Feferman's dashboard and calculated. Wayne had been gone just over forty-four hours. He wished Feferman would push the Jag faster.

He'd seen Judith Narver just once. She'd come to R-TAC to pick up Lloyd when his car was in the shop. He couldn't remember what her voice sounded like. He thought she worked for 3Com.

The Narvers' street was already roadblocked. Police cars and unmarked dark official cars were stopped at odd angles, converging on a large house. No cars in the driveway, no faces at the windows. The windows were gridded like French doors, decorative, but it made him think of a cage. A Spanish-style stucco house, deep rose with gray slate tiles on the roof, a magnolia tree set in the lawn like a flower in a jacket lapel, everything precise, the way Lloyd wore his tie.

The fat Sunday paper still lay on the lawn.

Andy followed Feferman through the knots of cops and agents, uniforms and suits, shifting weight from foot to foot in professional patience. Feferman closed in on a red-haired man in a suit—FBI, Andy figured— his square black sunglasses jutting up as he conferred with the telco's chief special agent. Nobody apparently at home, the FBI man told Feferman, they were waiting for a warrant to search inside.

The talk of procedures was cut-and-dried like a diagnostics run-through—we'll do this, then we'll do that—and Andy registered the words but there was no more resonance.

Wayne wasn't in the rose stucco house; Interrupt would not have brought him there.

Andy glanced around at the other houses, the Narvers' neighbors. There were faces at some of those windows, staying inside on this sunny Mother's Day afternoon.

Now Feferman pressed close to him, growling into his ear, "Agent Dicker says they've released Colson."

He'd gone after the wrong man. The wrong *person*. He'd got it all wrong, even the sex. He'd assumed Interrupt was a man, and that was a stupid assumption. Oh, he'd certainly suspected Nell, but only in connection with her father. He remembered telling Nell that "guys" included women engineers, he'd thought himself superior to Joe Faulkner, who never even connected women with engineering, he'd considered Candace as good an engineer as he was. Then he'd gone ahead and made the stupid assumption that Interrupt was not a woman, that a woman would not try to sabotage the telephone system.

That a woman would not kidnap his son. That a woman would not kill a woman.

Still, he made one more assumption. That a woman would not harm his boy. He clung to it fiercely.

26

•

An immense slab of mirrored glass slanted over the entry,
shooting upward from the doors to the open spaces above,
and from the angled ceiling far above dangled dozens of light
fixtures, spinning off beams to reflect in the overhead mirror,
in the highly polished walls and the vast floor, in the glass
tabletops of the lobby bar, in the octagonal pool of water
where the floor abruptly turned liquid, beneath crossed angles
of the escalator and the mezzanine balcony.

Feferman glared up at the glass slab. "Californians don't
take their earthquakes seriously."

Andy had to blink, his tired eyes straining against the lights,
and he thought that this was a far cry from the shabby Carolina Hotel, or from the gas station phone booth. But the toll
records did not lie, the call had originated here. Interrupt liked
to call from anonymous places, and the Doubletree Hotel was
anonymous as hell.

The Doubletree Hotel promoted itself as sited in the heart of Silicon Valley; at one end it branched into the Santa Clara Convention Center and at the other it butted up against Techmart, where the valley's premier companies rented showplace suites and staged meetings, seminars, conferences, and multivendor expos.

Even today, even on a sunny Mother's Day afternoon, executives, vendors, and convention-goers prowled the lobby, many of them wearing name tags and dressed for business.

Suddenly, heads turned and voices lowered as agents of the FBI and AT&T Security and officers of the Santa Clara County Sheriff Department fanned out through the lobby. The galaxy of lights caught on badges, sunglasses, polished black shoes, gun metal.

"Where'd they put the front desk?" Feferman complained, charging ahead into the lobby. Feferman was taking the lead now, telco security had been breached again. Andy and FBI Agent Dicker followed in his wake.

They passed a man in a Doubletree jumpsuit reassuring a clump of guests, "It's because of the phones."

Andy stared at the faces, the men as well as the women, but he recognized no one in the jumble of anonymous faces. How long did Interrupt hang around after making a call? Long enough to enjoy the disruption firsthand?

The call had originated here, had been switched through the Santa Clara office to Andy's home phone, had been picked up by his answering machine, and had triggered the failure of the 5ESS that was in the act of processing the call. Just one failure, just one machine down, just many thousands of lines dead, just like the first time.

They had stopped the clocks in the processors, had neutralized the Trojan horses, but they hadn't plugged Interrupt's old channel; indeed, in the face of a total network failure, Interrupt's one-at-a-time shutdown channel had seemed insignificant, noise in the system.

When they had gotten word of the failure, all of them still milling outside the Narvers' house, Andy had had the thought that Interrupt communicated with switch failures the way normal people communicated with telephone calls.

They'd taken Feferman's Jag to the Santa Clara office, gotten the mag tape on which the processor's temporary memory had recorded the calling data, and found a working machine to dump and filter the tape. Familiar now, there was the three-call cluster to the Stanford telecom lab and Time opening up the channel into the switch and then the call to Andy's number triggering the failure. Just like a recurring nightmare, he thought, that comes back when you'd almost forgotten it.

No more assumptions, Andy decided. Don't assume that any switch is safe. Don't assume anything about Interrupt; Interrupt is sexless, faceless, a collection of electronic signals.

Assume only that Wayne is safe.

The front desk was tucked away under the mezzanine balcony. Feferman got the clerk to get the manager, and she led them into her office. It was small, comfortable, with muted lighting, and Andy gratefully took a seat and rubbed his eyes.

Feferman lined up photographs on the manager's desk: pictures of Judith and Lloyd Narver taken from frames on their bedside table, the fax of Cheney, another fax, just come in, of Desjardins, an FBI mug shot of Colson.

Andy looked at Feferman in surprise. Cheney and Desjardins were in FBI custody, neither one could have made the call, and Colson had just been cleared and released. Feferman wasn't making any assumptions, either.

"We believe that one, possibly more, of these people made a telephone call from a pay phone in the lobby of this hotel shortly before your phone service was interrupted," Feferman said. "What we're going to ask you to do is this. You're going to have one of your people make copies of these photographs, if you will, and circulate them among your staff. We haven't had the time to make copies, so I hope that you have duplicating facilities here."

"Of course," she said. Her manner, her clothes, her voice, her neat graying hair were all tailored to Doubletree business, but Andy couldn't help noticing the silver-framed photo beside her telephone and wondering if she'd gotten her Mother's Day call before the phones went dead. "Might any of them have been registered guests?"

"Let's find out," Feferman said.

The manager picked up the phone, started to punch a button, then smiled ruefully. "I'll have to send someone up to our data center. I'm cut off." She went to the door and spoke to the desk clerk.

"How many rooms do you have here?" asked Dicker.

"Five hundred."

Anonymous as hell, Andy thought. If Interrupt had a room here—but why?—it wouldn't be registered under Narver.

A *room.*

Surely, there was bus service to a major hotel and convention center in the heart of Silicon Valley; surely, you could transfer to one of those buses from Carelli's bus. In a dead-calm voice he said, "Can you find out if there's a deaf boy staying in this hotel?" He pulled out his wallet, found Wayne's picture, and placed it on top of the photos and faxes on the manager's desk.

Feferman's eyebrows shot up.

"That's a thought," Dicker said.

The manager glanced down at the picture and frowned. "I don't understand the connection. I thought you were interested in these people who made the phone call."

"Is he here?"

Feferman held up a hand, ready to clamp onto Andy's arm. "We're interested in the boy, too. Is he here?"

"This is an official request?"

"Official as you need."

"Yes," she said. "Room 810."

Simple as that. Ten miles, maybe less, from home, in a hotel in the heart of Silicon Valley. He could probably *see* his home or see the treetops on his street from the upper floors of the Doubletree Hotel, and he could undoubtedly see the AT&T building. He was practically next door to Great America; he could see the Ferris wheel and the roller coaster and what was that god-awful ride he had tried to drag Andy onto? The Edge. He would be able to see the San Jose Airport, would have a fine view of the planes taking off and landing.

Feferman was pulling him up, saying gently, "Come on."

The elevators were directly across from the front desk. They rode up without talking, crowded in with a group in swimsuits and soggy towels. A pool, Andy thought, and probably a gym, and laundry, and restaurants, and room service. A hotel was self-contained, everything you need.

They stepped off the elevator into an atrium area, big plants and a wide window, then the manager led them down a hallway, dark in contrast, dilating the eyes. They passed a lot of rooms and finally came to the end of the hall. Room 810 was an end unit. She knocked, calling out, "Manager."

"He won't hear you," Andy said.

She nodded, then unlocked the door and stood aside.

He couldn't go in. He was like Sandra: he didn't want to know or see anything that would shock him.

Assume that Wayne is safe, *assume it*. But he let Feferman and Dicker go in first.

"Faulkner!" Feferman's voice boomed out.

Andy took a breath and went inside.

It was a damn nice room, spacious, south-facing, light

poured in from the balcony. Feferman stood at the far side of the room, gazing at the bedside table. "This look familiar?"

Andy started toward Feferman, but there was a resistance in his leg muscles, as in a dream when you walk and walk and don't get anywhere, and he could have sworn it took minutes to travel around the two double beds to where Feferman stood.

On the table were a lamp, a Trimline telephone, and a portable TDD. The telephone had been disconnected and the TDD plugged directly into the wall jack.

"Is it his?"

"It's the same model as his."

Dicker came in from the balcony and stopped by the sliding glass door to inspect a writing desk on which books had been stacked and magazines fanned out. "Maid's been here."

Feferman brushed past Andy to the line of dressers and opened a drawer. He pulled out a tee-shirt, held it up. On the chest was a dog wearing sunglasses and lime-green trunks, riding a yellow surfboard through shocking orange waves that spelled out the words "Rude Dog."

"This belong to your kid?"

Andy took the tee-shirt and held it against his own chest. Too big for Wayne, but a boy's size nevertheless. He looked into the open drawer: two more tee-shirts, the same print, a pair of black jeans, three pairs of socks, and three pairs of jockey shorts, everything folded. Wayne didn't fold his socks; he balled them. But Dicker said the maid had been here. "It's all new."

"Is it his size?"

"Close enough."

Interrupt had bought him clothes. If Interrupt intended to harm Wayne, Interrupt would not have bought him clothes.

Andy slammed the drawer shut and moved to the television.

Beside it was a telecaption decoder, with a "Property of Doubletree" metal plate screwed onto the panel.

Dicker called out from the bathroom, "Pair of swim trunks on the towel rack. They're dry, but stiff. You know, chlorine."

Wayne had gone swimming. Andy thought, you didn't go swimming if you thought you were in danger, you tried to get away.

"Two toothbrushes, toothpaste, Crest, a shaving kit, no medications . . ." Dicker reported.

"Faulkner."

Feferman had another dresser drawer open. Andy leaned over to look. More underwear, socks, plain white tee-shirts. Feferman pulled out one of the shirts and unfurled it like a flag. Andy froze.

"Yours?"

"No."

"It's a man's size."

Toothbrushes, *plural,* and a shaving kit.

Feferman had the closet door open. Two small suitcases on the floor, a man's white shirt and slacks on hangers.

"Ma'am!" Feferman called out.

The manager came in "Can I be of help?" As though she had come in response to a guest's complaint.

"You neglected to mention that the boy was sharing this room." Feferman smiled.

"I promised discretion."

"You're going to break that promise. Your hotel has been misused."

She glanced around the room, at Feferman and Dicker, then looked hard at Andy.

He'd pulled on his clothes at four-fifteen in the morning, the first things that came to hand, jeans and a wrinkled white dress shirt and loafers. He'd shivered and sweated in these clothes and torn a hole in his sleeve on a splintered doorjamb. His eyes were red and he hadn't shaved and his cheek was scabbed and his voice was worn to gravel. He knew he didn't look as if he belonged to Dicker or Feferman, to the Federal Bureau of Investigation or to AT&T Security. He swallowed, trying to moisten his throat, and said, "I'm the boy's father."

"Mr. Bell? You?"

"Bell? Mr. Bell, oh, that is cute." Feferman began his slow pacing, keeping eye contact with the manager. "Now you're going to explain to us the precise chain of events that brought the deaf boy and Mr. Bell to this hotel."

She nodded briskly and addressed herself solely to Feferman. "It was an out-of-the-ordinary reservation, so I handled it personally. This was a couple of days ago. Mr. Bell said he was coming to town on business, some kind of government business, well, the implication was, very secret business, I assumed with one of the defense contractors in the valley."

"This was on the phone?"

"On the phone. He had to bring his son along, he didn't say why, but he was going to be very busy, in and out at odd hours, and he wanted to make certain that his son was taken care of. He explained that the boy was deaf, what he would need, the decoder for the television, room service meals, I think that's about it. He was very specific about it. He said his son wouldn't be leaving the hotel, that he was very shy and would want to be left alone, that he could find his own way to the pool and things." She gestured out toward the balcony. "We normally don't guarantee specific rooms, but I thought if the boy was going to be stuck in the hotel that he might enjoy one of our balcony units."

"That was considerate," Feferman said.

"How long did he make the reservation for?" Dicker asked.

"It was open-ended. He sent us an adequate deposit by EFT. Electronic fund transfer."

"Did you see him when he checked in?"

"No. The boy checked in for both of them. Wrote a note and took both the room keys. Said . . . wrote that his father was at a meeting and would come later."

"What name did he use?"

"Bell, like the father. Wayne Bell."

Wayne faithfully carrying out his instructions, secrecy, the made-up name, whatever came over the TDD. From this room his son could see Great America, although Andy was guessing because he had no desire to walk out onto an eighth-floor balcony. Wayne probably thought that his father had picked a pretty neat place for him to hide out. Andy felt a killing fury. "Didn't you think it was strange?"

The manager glanced at him, looked back to Feferman. "Strange? Strange is when a guest wants the desk clerk to call and sing 'Rock-a-Bye Baby' every night."

"Who brought this luggage?" Feferman swept a hand toward the closet.

"It was left near the front desk, later in the day after the boy arrived. I didn't see who brought it. The cases were tagged with their names, Mr. Joseph Bell and Mr. Wayne Bell."

"The boy's name is Wayne Faulkner." Andy started for the door, but Feferman blocked him.

"Hold it a minute, Faulkner." Feferman turned to the manager. "Did you, or any of your staff, ever *see* Mr. Bell?"

She flushed. "No. Not that I know of."

"By God," said Dicker, "that's the first kidnapping I've ever heard of done entirely by telephone."

"Kidnapping?" The manager took a step backward.

Andy tried to shove around Feferman. "He's somewhere in the hotel." *Assume that he's safe.*

Feferman held his ground. "Mr. Dicker, let's get our people asking about a kid named Bell."

Dicker started for the telephone.

"Mr. Dicker, the phones don't work."

269

"Yeah. You just keep on expecting them to." The FBI agent changed direction and headed briskly out into the hallway.

Feferman turned to the manager. "All right, the boy's been told not to leave the hotel, so where does he go?"

She shrugged. "The pool."

"His trunks are in the bathroom," Andy said.

"Maybe the health club, on the third floor."

"Health club, okay." Feferman held up one finger. "Where else? Where does he go to get a milkshake?"

"If he doesn't get it from room service, he could go to the Caffe Milano. Off the lobby."

Feferman snapped up another finger. "Where else?"

"I don't know, he could have wandered all the way over to the convention center, we're all under one roof. We're really not geared to children, we're geared to the needs of executives and . . . oh! I suppose he might have discovered Chips. Opposite the Caffe Milano. That's our high-tech club, it has audio and video entertainment and . . ."

Andy came alert. "Computer games?"

"No, a big screen, music and dancing, like MTV."

"Okay, Faulkner, you're going to take Chips and the milkshake, I'm going to take the health club, and you"—he wagged a finger at the manager—"are going to wait here in case the boy shows up. If you would."

Andy started down the hallway, breaking into a run with Feferman lumbering behind, bellowing, "Rendezvous at the front desk." The elevator was too slow, he found a door leading to a stairway and pounded down, taking it in his knees, every bone in his body hurting by now, spiraling down, getting a friction burn from the handrail, how many floors down was he? He'd lost count.

He hit lobby level, yanked the door open, was stopped cold

again by the lights and glass and mirrors. Men and women strolled by, he didn't see any cops or agents, where the hell was everybody? Then he spotted a Doubletree jumpsuit and grabbed the man's arm. *"Chips?"*

To the right. He didn't wait for the rest of the directions, just sprinted across the lobby. Up ahead was a sign "Caffe Milano," why two *f*s? Inside, bright checked red and white tiles, but it was midafternoon and the place was nearly empty. He came back out and saw the "Chips" sign opposite and spun in there.

The place was a nightclub. Small round tables, chairs, a dance floor, a long bar with a "Happy Hour 5–7" sign, and not a soul in sight because it was midafternoon. No windows in Chips, the lights were off, and the place was dim. The big projection screen was blank, but he could imagine Wayne looking in here, he would have explored the whole place, drawn in by giant flashing MTV images. No sound, just giant flashing images in the crowded high-tech club and the press of anonymous bodies. Andy sagged into one of the chairs and prayed that his son had indeed thought this was a neat place to hide out.

A phone started ringing. Andy stood, looked around. The ringing was coming from behind the bar. But the phones were dead. Then he remembered the first time, the five-E down and not processing calls, and none of them could bring it up, and then it simply fixed itself and Lloyd had said "fairy godmother." Not a fairy godmother, of course. The processor lived and died by the commands of the code hidden in its brain, and the code was under the command of Interrupt. The phones were no longer dead; Interrupt had brought them back to life.

Andy answered the phone. It was the manager, calling from the room next to 810. "You'd better get up here, Mr. Faulkner. The light's flashing on that deaf phone machine in

Mr. Bell's room, and I don't know how to work it. I think someone's trying to call."

"Two hundred thousand," Agent Dicker said.

Andy touched one of the bricks of fifty-dollar bills on the Doubletree's conference table. It had taken Buck and Howland under an hour to produce the bricks. "Are they marked?"

Feferman turned to Dicker. Dicker was silent.

"He asked for more," Andy said.

"All we can do is advise the extorted party how much to pay," Dicker said, glancing at Feferman.

"They know what they're doing," Feferman said to Andy.

"This way," Dicker picked up, "we're showing good faith and we're tempting his greed, but we don't lose our bargaining position. You hand this clown two mil and you may not get your boy back."

Assume he's safe. Andy picked up the closest brick. It smelled like real money. What the hell did counterfeit money smell like?

Dicker opened a small case. "Please take off your shirt, Mr. Faulkner."

"No," Andy said. "No mike."

Dicker stopped with the transmitter in his hand. "We advise you to wear this."

"What if *he* asks me to take off my shirt?" Andy said.

Dicker was silent. Red-faced, but Andy couldn't tell whether he was burned at the question or whether it was his normal redhead coloring.

"He told me to come alone," Andy said. Andy, rooted in apprehension in Wayne's empty hotel room, had obediently typed his reply on the TDD: yes. "Alone," Andy repeated. "You think someone who's bugged my house and spoofed the telephone network isn't going to think of the possibility that I'm wired for sound?"

Dicker placed the transmitter on the table and turned to Feferman. "It's your company's money."

Feferman snatched up the transmitter and tossed it back into the case. "My company owes him. Let him do it his way."

27

•

Interrupt sighted through the ocular lens of the telescopic mount, his left eye squeezed shut and his right cheek pressed hard against the stock. He played with the focusing ring, working it back and forth in smaller and smaller oscillations until he had a sharp image. This was going to be a difficult shot.

He had learned to shoot from Judy, and she was still the better of the two.

The image in the lens blurred. His eyes were watering from the wind and the grasses, and a tremendous headache had built just above the bridge of his nose. He set the .22 down in fury to massage his forehead.

Judy, he thought, rubbing hard against the bone, he really was going to miss her.

Marksmanship was just one of the properties he had valued in Judy. The first, of course, was her Stanford career and the second was her membership on the D team. Interrupt was not superstitious, but he had to believe in serendipity, that state of grace when a great gift comes unsought, unexpected, and is valued all the more. It was serendipity that he had intersected with Judy at the telecom conference in Chicago, and if they had had to live much of their first year of marriage apart because he was in line for promotion at AT&T Lisle, Illinois, and she was working on the D language project in Morristown, New Jersey, then that was the price paid for serendipity. He had existed in a state of grace throughout that year of exchanged visits, his mind soaring on the flights to New Jersey, first the conception like one of the great cumulus clouds forming on the horizon, then the refinement as the hum of his laptop kept tune with the rumble of the jet engines, his code taking wing. Finally, the execution in her Morristown apartment while she slept, exhausted from the grueling final push. The compiler was complete, debugged, it had passed its periodic code audits and its programmer peer reviews and was stored like a ripe plum in the D project mainframe; but she still had access, and with her user name and password and home terminal he logged in and planted his Trojan horse deep within the compiler. Then, with a final flick of the keyboard, he erased the listing of his entry from the access log.

He had loved her then, for she had given him much: access to the project, an insider's knowledge of Stanford, the details and the layout of the Center for Telecommunications. She had told him about the telecom lab and she had recited its phone number for him when he asked if Stanford grads would remember the number. She had assisted him unwittingly, true; she was little more than a flesh-and-blood Trojan horse, but he could not have achieved his state of grace without her.

He remembered that time with a sweet nostalgia. It seemed to have eased his headache.

Interrupt wiped his eyes clear, picked up the .22, and swung it around so that the barrel pointed directly down toward Stanford. He could not see the campus from here. The ridge-line interrupted his line of sight. But he knew where it was and he knew that Faulkner would be appearing from that direction.

Everything was light. His legs, which had dragged like concrete in room 810 at the Doubletree, now felt light, almost weightless. He had heard runners talk about breaking through the wall, running close to exhaustion then breaking through to an untapped energy source and sprinting off light and easy.

That was how he climbed, light and easy. He felt nothing.

And the pack was light. His shirt was damp and warm where the pack rested on his back, but he felt no tugging on the padded shoulder straps.

A man could carry six pounds on his back and barely notice it.

That's what Agent Dicker had said, that the money weighed about six pounds, not counting the negligible weight of the nylon pack. The $200,000 six-pound pile of bricks was their bargaining chip. The bricks for release of his son and Interrupt's promise not to shut down any more switches, with the hint that more might be paid later if he kept the bargain. All of that in six pounds.

He felt nothing but the sweat on his back.

The breeze was light, rippling the calf-high grasses and drying the sweat from his face before he could wipe it away.

There were still clumps of poppies in the grasses. A Bay Area spring, warm sunny days and cool nights. Some nights the coastal fog slipped this far inland and coated the hills.

He stopped and looked back. No one in sight, but then he had not expected to see anyone. Access was limited; the land was part of a state game refuge. This particular slice of the foothills bulged up between Foothill Boulevard on one side and the 280 freeway on the other, at either end it was bounded by major roads, and the entire area was fenced to keep the grazing cows in. But the hills were in Stanford's backyard, and the cows and protected game had to share land use. On the Foothill side a couple of gates led to footpaths for runners and hikers, and a road wound up to the scattered radioscience outposts and satellite dishes of Stanford's Engineering Department. The road and the gates were blocked now by Feferman's and Dicker's people, and every car parked along the perimeter was being checked. Feferman and Dicker had to let him come alone, because there was no way to approach the ridge without being seen.

He resumed the climb. It seemed a lifetime ago that he had climbed this path with Nell and Wayne.

While he climbed he twisted a hand behind his back to heft the nylon bag, taking the six pounds in his palm. It wasn't much.

Not when he thought about the fact that Interrupt had asked for two million. He calculated. Two million dollars in fifty-dollar denominations worked out to forty thousand fifty-dollar bills. If the four thousand fifty-dollar bills he was carrying weighed six pounds, then the forty thousand that Interrupt was expecting would weigh about sixty pounds. He wondered if Interrupt had figured that out when he asked for fifty-dollar bills. He would want small enough denominations to spend without trouble, but he would also want to be able to carry the payoff. Sixty pounds was a heavy load, but a man could carry that. A woman too, but Interrupt wasn't Judith Narver. Dicker's people had located Judith Narver at her mother's in Delaware.

Still, coming up a hill with sixty pounds on his back, a man would not be climbing light and easy. His shoulders would hunch, he would trudge.

He scanned the hill above him. If Interrupt was concealed

in the oaks up there, watching Andy now, watching through binoculars, would he be able to tell that the pack on Andy's back was fifty-four pounds too light?

Shit.

The headache had eased to a dull pressure. He yawned; he had been up since 4:00 A.M. He had set the alarm, but he hadn't needed it. Ten years of anticipation had wakened him with a pounding heartbeat.

He had wakened alone, having surprised Judy two days before with a plane ticket back east to surprise her mother for Mother's Day.

At 5:12 A.M. he had been in his car, cruising slowly through the darkened eucalyptus groves leading into the Stanford campus. Helpnet was on the radio, with some distraught caller telling the psychologist host that she was afraid of people in hats, and the psychologist was asking was she afraid that there was something under the hats, and Interrupt was listening hard. He cared nothing about the hat problem, he cared only that the discussion was being broadcast live from New York, that the host was in a studio talking on the telephone to a telephone caller. He was listening so hard that he no longer heard what was being said, just the rising and falling of voices coming over his radio. He watched the digital numbers glowing on the clockface, and when the 2 was replaced by a 3, when 5:12 turned to 5:13, he knew it was 8:13 eastern time, and he whispered very softly, almost reverently, "Bingo."

But the voices continued uninterrupted.

He had slammed on the brakes, fishtailing the car and nearly throttling himself on the shoulder harness.

It was 8:13 A.M. eastern time on Mother's Day and every Trojan horse in that time zone should have triggered. The telephone lines on Helpnet were switched through a number five, he had checked, and the Helpnet phones should have died, several million phones should have died.

But they had not.

Faulkner. Faulkner had interfered.

The voices kept on chattering over his radio, and in the background phones rang in the New York studio. He had pulled over and shoved the gearshift into park. He had snapped off the radio, his chest beginning to constrict. He had snapped the radio back on, and the voices were still there. He had made himself wait, minutes, thinking *the trigger could still fire,* anytime after eight-thirteen it could fire, *it should have fired.* Calls kept drilling into the radio studio and the psychologist kept on jabbering. His head felt like it was going to explode. He had grabbed the screwdriver out of the glove box tool set and pried off the panel under the dash. He had felt for the radio wires, found them, and ripped them out. The radio died, the voices died for good, the phones ringing in the background died, and he was left in darkness and silence with a handful of twisted wires still warm to the touch and a pressure amplifying inside his skull until he thought it would kill him.

By the time the wires were quite cold his mind burned with a new conception.

He refined it as he drove, and when he located the van with the E.T. bumper sticker in the Pac Bell lot, he knew it would work. He had been prepared to break a window or force a door but it wasn't necessary. The van was unlocked. The ease of it made him cautious, and he incorporated into his plans the variable that his identity was known. There was no pleasure this time, no state of grace, but he was sustained over the following hours of preparation by a steady state of rage.

Finally, in the Doubletree, after calling the boy on the TDD, giving him the instructions, watching him leave the hotel and head for the bus stop, he had experienced a moment of doubt. What if they'd done more than find the trigger?

What if they'd found his code and cleaned it out? No, they wouldn't have had time. He had waited in an unobtrusive place, the darkened nightclub, looking at his watch and giving the boy enough time before he could dial the numbers and find out that he still had a channel into the switch.

Now, with the .22 trigger beneath his finger, he waited again. Candace had said to him once that he waited well. The joke about his tie: he was calm and steady and he knew how to wait. She had no idea how right she was. Or perhaps she did have an idea, at the end.

But the wait had been for nothing.

Andy followed the trail into the grove of oaks, their branches knotted and hanging low like an old man's arms. He paused, knowing he was concealed by the screen of oak leaves. Go to the picnic spot, Interrupt had instructed over the TDD. Above Stanford? Andy had typed back. You understand? Interrupt asked. Yes, Andy had typed.

He understood.

When he moved out of the shielding oaks, emerging onto the ridgetop, he stopped and looked first to locate the large oak standing alone where they had picnicked. Beneath the oak, the grasses tramped down by Nell still lay flat, matted brown husks.

Nobody there.

Up here on the ridge, the breeze was stronger. It ruffled his shirt and combed through his hair, lifting the wet strands off his neck.

Interrupt had to be watching. Andy put his hands to the shoulder straps and reset the pack, as if it were heavy and his shoulders were sore.

Where was he? Andy remembered the concrete building, one of the engineering labs. Yes. It was the obvious place. Interrupt was there. Wayne was there. Wayne and Mr. Bell.

He still felt light, buoyed, the runner's high. He took a couple of deep breaths, easy breaths, and stepped forward to a position that gave him a clear view along the ridge.

He saw the lab and his breath caught, he was right. Although the door to the squat gray building was shut, one of the windows was broken. It was impossible to tell if anyone was at the window, for it was dark inside, and the shards of glass that still clung to the frame glinted in the sun like gold teeth.

No one could approach that building, for a good long way in any direction, without being seen.

As he gaped, halted in his tracks like one of the grazing cows, witless at an obstacle, his peripheral vision picked something up.

The line of telephone poles.

No, he thought, raising his eyes, no.

He ran, the pack slapping his back and his chest tightening, shouting his son's name again and again as if a deaf boy strapped high on a telephone pole could somehow pick up the sound waves, the vibrations, the way he had once picked up a thunderclap.

He ran, thinking that Interrupt was watching from the darkness behind the window.

He ran, praying to God that his son was alive.

Almost there, and he could see how Wayne was lashed tight with a safety belt, arms and knees hugging the pole like some arboreal animal, his feet at angles, the metallic flash of gaffs. His head in the orange safety helmet lay against the pole, his eyes were closed or he was looking up, away, somewhere, but he didn't move.

Andy stared at the feet, the gaffs, and he saw slashes of pink on the boots. Nell's boots. His mind was reeling.

Wayne was high, higher than Andy had climbed, nearly up to the cables.

This was not the pole he had climbed with Nell. This was a different one, and it looked even higher.

He reached the base of the pole, kicked it, but up above, Wayne didn't feel the kicks, didn't move.

A set of climbing gear was heaped by the base, safety belt, gaffed boots, gloves, helmet.

He turned to face the concrete building, maybe a hundred yards away, shouted something, *bastard,* he was shouting *bastard* over and over.

Shaking, hurrying, he dropped to the ground and yanked off his loafers and pulled on the boots. They were too big, and the part of his mind that was working estimated that with heavy socks on they would be about a half size too big. He pulled the laces tight, tighter.

He had climbed in these boots before.

Belt on, gloves on, helmet on, and he started to loop the belt around the pole.

Wait, no telephone pole is straight, find the side that's leaning away.

He had one gaff into the pole, starting to lift off the ground, when he thought of the pack on his back.

Nobody, not even a man sick with fear and anger, would choose to climb a telephone pole with a sixty-pound pack on his back. Interrupt watching out the window would be expecting him to drop it.

"Fuck it," he said, and started to climb.

Heels together, toes and knees out, strike the gaff cleanly, get a good foothold before moving the belt up. The pack did not bother him.

He was climbing okay, he knew what he was doing and he stopped concentrating on the process, heels-toes-knees-gaff, he just did it. Not light and easy, but he did it.

He looked up. Straight up, the pole seeming to shoot up directly from his forehead, up and up, far enough up that the diameter of the pole shrank, and he saw gaffs, pink-striped boots, black jeans, legs jackknifed in a crouch and a boy's skinny butt hung out in the air.

A shudder ran through him, the height.

Quickly, he looked back down, not meaning to look all the way to the ground but it was okay, he was not that far up and he was holding steady. The breeze was strong, it was a wind up here but it didn't move the pole and it felt good on his face. He saw the roof of the building, ashpalt shingles, he did a fast scan of the ridge and there was only grass and trees, no people, not Interrupt or Feferman or agents or cops. He saw the stand of oaks where he had been sick and he glimpsed something brown in there, an animal, must be a cow.

He felt a pain in his shoulder, just a pinprick, where he had jammed it against the door, and a heaviness in his quadriceps, his muscles surprised by the climb.

Move. He raised his right leg, locking his knee into position, and kicked the gaff hard into the pine.

There was a sound, it might have been carried on the wind, a voice, low and throaty, a drawn-out monotone, and it came again. Daaaeee.

His head jerked back and he stared up the pole.

"Daaaeee!"

Wayne's face peered down at him, shadowed by the orange helmet, but Andy could make out the big grin on his face. Wayne straightened his legs, coming out of his crouch, standing up on the gaffs, and Andy could almost feel the boy's muscles stretching in relief. He must have felt the vibrations from Andy's gaff kicking in. Wayne let go with one hand and waved, grinning like a big happy puppy, like a kid who has come through for his father and had a whale of a good time, showing off now, Spock, Rambo, He-man, GI Joe.

"Wayne!" Andy yelled, and he held up his hand in the sign for "wait." Wayne must have climbed up there by himself.

After all, with his boy's fierce attention he had watched Nell teach Andy to climb. But Andy swore that he wasn't going to climb down by himself.

A shudder again. He closed his eyes and willed it away.

When he opened his eyes, Wayne was still waving his hand and he realized that the boy was pointing at the ground.

Andy looked down.

He saw the door to the concrete building standing open, and directly below, near the base of the pole, he saw Interrupt.

He wore a pink shirt and a white tie, the wind had whipped the tie over his shoulder, he had on dark glasses shielding his upturned eyes from the sun, and he held a rifle in his right hand, its stock tucked up under his arm and its barrel pointed at the earth.

A full shot of nausea hit Andy—the height, the rifle—and he held on tight to the pole.

"Drop the pack," Lloyd said.

Andy was able to glance up, to see Wayne frozen in place above him, the grin gone from his face.

He fought the nausea and looked back down. "Goddamn you."

Lloyd held his right hand away from his body, and the rifle pivoted, the heavy stock dropping and the barrel swinging skyward. With his left hand, he pulled the tie off his shoulder and tucked it into his shirtfront. "Drop it, Andy-man."

Six pounds, Andy thought, eyes on the rifle. He had six pounds to negotiate with.

There were tremors in his leg muscles, and he had to shift position. He pulled out the left gaff, straightened his leg, reset the gaff.

Below him, Lloyd dropped to one knee, bringing the rifle into firing position, his movements as practiced and precise as if he were kneeling at a panel to get at the wiring with a soldering gun.

From above there came a low moan, a sound Wayne sometimes made in a bad sleep.

Lloyd wouldn't shoot, Andy thought. Good Lord, Lloyd wouldn't shoot them, not for six lousy pounds. But maybe for ten lost years. *Candace.* His chest convulsed. "Let us down," he shouted, "and we'll talk," but his words were bitten off by the sharp crack of a rifle firing.

He screamed, pushing out from the pole, letting go, arching his body back to somehow catch Wayne, but Wayne was still tethered in place, he hadn't been shot, but he, too, was arching away from the pole, trying to get out of the way of the thick black thing snaking down out of the sky at them.

The telephone cable.

Andy grabbed back onto the pole, shouting uselessly at Wayne. All he could do was hold on and wait as the cable swung back and forth in smaller and smaller arcs, slapping at the pole like a live thing seeking a place to latch on.

Below, Lloyd stood, cradling the rifle, watching raptly.

He'd shot the cable. Why?

Above him, Wayne was out of position, fumbling with his safety belt.

Andy yelled, then brought out his right boot and viciously kicked the gaff back into the pole.

Wayne's head jerked and he looked down.

"Stay," Andy signed, "not danger."

The cable carried low voltage, only enough to make a telephone ring. It was still writhing near the pole, driven by the wind, but the exposed wires were no threat.

"Faulkner, one more time."

The tone was mild, calm, the tone Lloyd used at R-TAC when there was a major alarm and everyone else was strung tight as a wire, but when Andy looked down he saw Lloyd crouched again in firing position. Only this time Lloyd was not precise and smooth. He took his hand away from the trigger, flexed it, moved it back to the rifle, and Andy thought he saw the hand shaking.

Nerves? No, not nerves. The tension in the man's body was clear from up here, and Andy knew what it was because he felt it too. Lloyd's hands were shaking from raw hatred.

Andy let go of the pole with one hand, slipped his arm out of the shoulder strap, then reversed the process, as slowly and obviously as he could. He held the pack out and let it drop.

Lloyd didn't move, didn't lower the rifle, just kept looking up.

There was silence from above, the adventure shocked out of the boy, he was not Rambo or Spock but a kid scared senseless and he had no senses to spare. The only sound was the *whup-whup* of the severed cable snapping in the wind and the steady muttering of the wind itself.

Andy swallowed, then said loud and clear, "I'm sorry."

He was not lying. He was sorry he'd followed the language, the interpreter, the compiler, Strowger, sorry he'd thought of a Trojan horse, sorry he'd offered Feferman the trigger bypass, sorry he'd screwed up about Colson. Painfully sorry that Candace had called to confide in him. Sorry that his son was deaf and had steadfast faith in anything that came over his TDD.

Lloyd tucked the rifle under his arm and walked over to pick up the pack. He crouched again, laying the rifle across his knees, and unzipped the pack. He thrust a hand inside, then yanked the zipper all the way open and pulled out several green bricks. For minutes, it seemed, he flipped through the bills, counting them, holding them. How the hell long did it take to figure out that six pounds of fifty-dollar bills did not add up to two million dollars?

Finally, he put the bricks back inside, zipped the pack, and put it on his back.

All of a sudden, Andy's ears buzzed and the ground started

to spin. He squeezed his eyes shut, feeling the cold sweat coat his body. No, not now.

"Faulkner!"

He opened his eyes, he couldn't lift his head away from the pole, couldn't stop looking down. The ground, Lloyd, the rifle, the pack, all of it reversed direction and spun again.

"Faulkner!" Lloyd put his left hand to his mouth, funneling it like a megaphone. "You . . . cheated . . . me."

He wanted to be sure Andy heard, he wanted a response. Andy wanted to respond, wanted to say, "Let us go and leave the switches alone and they'll negotiate with you about the rest," but people bargained across a table or on the phone or standing face-to-face, they couldn't expect a man to bargain strapped to a pole with the world spinning around his head.

"Was it you?"

The spinning stopped, and he didn't dare to close his eyes or shift his glance for fear that it would start again. He kept his eyes locked in a tight focus on Lloyd's upturned face. Yeah, you son of a bitch, it was me.

"Was . . . it . . . you?" Shouts.

Can't talk, Lloyd, don't like it up here. But you know that. Nell told you. She was waiting for Ray that day at R-TAC and you two started talking about climbing fucking telephone poles and . . .

Lloyd snapped the rifle up.

Andy flinched. There were no shots.

. . . so you got my kid up here and you got me up here, so what are you waiting for, are you waiting for me to totally lose it, scream, beg, black out . . .

"Daaaeeee."

Andy tore the right gaff out of the pole, forced his leg up, dug in the gaff, gouging the pole, wood chips flying. He moved up the belt, hauled himself higher, his inner ear going crazy, sweats and chills together, but he shinnied higher.

If he could do nothing else, he could get right up under Wayne and shield the boy with his body.

Shouts from below, but his ears were ringing.

What the hell more did the man want?

It suddenly dawned on him. Lloyd, the steady member of the team, good worker, reliable, but Lloyd was known more for his sarcasm than his engineering, Lloyd calling Andy "genius" with the calm voice and the bitter edge. But the man himself had a streak of genius. Look at his Trojan horse, an elegant piece of engineering.

Recognition, that's what the man wanted. Andy shouted back, "An elegant . . . piece . . . of engineering!"

He didn't try to look, just kept climbing, hugging the pole, his body heavy like rocks. The pole filled his vision, rough wood; then it cleaved the horizon, the two lines crossed, and the axis tilted.

Rifle fire.

More fire, crackling, explosions.

In pure terror he watched the cable coming down, twisting and snarling like the first time, only this wasn't the telephone cable. It was the power cable, shorting, spitting fire, tongues of electricity shooting out, whip-cracking the air, 12,500 volts looking for a ground.

The cable danced closer, then with a crack like bones snapping, a pure blue stream of electricity arced from the raw wires to the telephone pole, and at each point of contact where his body touched the pole Andy felt a vibration.

The wood was conducting, he thought wildly, wood wasn't a conductor but it was conducting, it was hot. Then as the cable bucked away, sending down blue bolts to the earth below, he thought moisture, the fog brought moisture and there was moisture in the wood and water was a conductor, and he and Wayne were pinned to the pole like mounted butterflies.

The cable was snapping back toward them. Why didn't the circuit breakers kick in, the cable was live, arcing, the cracking was deafening, deafening, he looked up and saw Wayne's right foot dangling, the metal gaff flashing as the boy tried to scramble down.

Metal.

Andy tore off his helmet and heaved it upward but it didn't go high enough, Wayne didn't see it.

The wind howled into his unprotected ears.

Wayne got his gaff in as the cable writhed past. Blue fire arced into the pole and the wood vibrated and sent its convulsive shivers through Andy's hands and feet.

He climbed; his body was a machine programmed only to climb and he would climb until it failed.

A shout came among the cracking sounds, carried on the wind, and he looked down to see Lloyd with the pack on his back and the rifle slung over his shoulder, and Lloyd was mounting a brown horse.

Then the cable was coming again, jerking and snarling, grounding its fire in the pole as it passed.

If the cable swung much closer, Andy thought, it would find two perfect conductors, two solutions of electrolytes wrapped in skin and clothing, and the ground-seeking current would flow along a path that took it through the organs of the chest, and the heart would be shocked into a frenzy of fibrillation, or the chest muscles would freeze in an uncontrollable contraction, and in either case the two conductors would cease to exist.

He climbed, heels together, toes and knees out, strike the gaff cleanly.

Suddenly, the wind was louder and the sky was brighter and he looked to find the cable swinging more gently, driven only by the wind, limp and relaxed after its exhaustive hunt for ground.

Somewhere, a circuit breaker had finally tripped.

He wanted to hang relaxed and free like that cable, just hang from his safety belt and let the wind rock him, but he climbed, inching up the pole, and he was surprised when he finally felt his hand closing over his son's leg.

Interrupt sighted through the lens, sweeping the .22 across a wide arc until he was satisfied that there was no one within range, then kicked the horse into a hard gallop across the grasslands toward the next shelter of oaks. There were several thousand acres of oak woods and grasslands in this section of foothills, not an easy area to search if indeed the authorities were rash enough to come clambering up here. No, they would concentrate their resources around the perimeter and wait until Faulkner reappeared with the boy, if Faulkner and the boy managed to reappear, or until Pac Bell and Pacific Gas and Electric arrived to locate their downed lines, and then if they did come they would come cautiously. That was precisely how he intended to proceed, cautiously, working his way down as if they were already hunting him.

His eyes streamed and itched; he could taste the grass; his nose and throat burned as he inhaled. He wanted out of this place so badly that he took double care.

When he came within sight of the fence he stopped, watching until he knew what belonged there and what didn't. Trees on either side of the fence, oak and buckeye and others he couldn't identify; blue jays flapping the leaves; dense scrub brush, weeds; telephone poles. He listened. Jays squawking, sound of the wind, traffic noise in the distance. Everything belonged.

The fence was six rows of barbed wire strung between metal posts.

When he was fully satisfied, he dismounted and unstrapped the saddlebag and stuffed Faulkner's pack inside. There was plenty of room, because he had brought a bag large enough to accommodate the gear he had had to transport up to the pole, and large enough to accommodate the bulk and weight of the money he had asked for, but he hadn't got payment in full. He roughly closed the bag.

He set the bag and the rifle on the ground beside the fence and turned back to the horse. He balled his hand into a fist and struck the horse in the neck.

The horse reared, snorting, then settled down and waited, fixing its marbled brown eyes on him.

"Stable horse." He struck again, harder, and this time the horse took the lesson and broke away into a run. He watched to make sure that it was running up the ridge, that it had sufficient motivation to head back toward the stable. He had asked when he rented the horse, playing the beginner afraid of getting lost, does it know its way back? Yes, sir, the handler had said, just give him his head.

They might find the horse in the hills, they might even find it nosing the fence along Alpine Road, although Interrupt doubted that the animal would find its way back to the place where he had cut the fence and entered the refuge. No matter; if they found the horse they would find its stable brand, and they would check out the stable on Alpine Road, which was a five-minute walk from the Stanford campus.

They might also find his car, parked on Los Arboles near the Stanford golf driving range.

It was a gamble. If they found the horse or the car, or better, found both, they might draw the conclusion that he was in that area. He thought that they would suspect that he had been drawn back to Stanford. Given that assumption, they would concentrate their resources in that region, when in fact he was at the opposite corner of the refuge.

That, then, would make life a whole lot easier.

He squinted up the ridge. The horse had disappeared.

He pulled the heavy bolt cutters from the bag and cut through the bottom three rows of barbed wire, sufficient to pass underneath with the bag and rifle on his back.

On this side of the fence, the ground dropped to a creek bed. Trees and brush tangled along both banks of the creek. Doubly cautious now, he could hear the traffic of Page Mill Road just beyond this wood, but he could not see the road. The corollary was, he could not be seen from the road. He scrambled down into the V of the creek bed and followed it downstream. The creek was low, little more than water traps where the rocks piled up and patches of seeping mud that stank of decomposition.

He moved slowly, concentrating on any sounds that were not his own.

After about fifty yards, the creek bed angled to the right, just about where he had expected it to, and was channeled into a concrete culvert. From above, road level, the culvert would be hard to find, if indeed someone knew it was there and took the trouble to push in through the scratchy brush and trees to find it.

He had found the culvert only by chance. When he had scouted the perimeter along Page Mill Road early this morning, while he waited for the stable to open, he had seen a dog trotting along the wide dirt shoulder. The dog, a collie with a blue bandana around its neck, had suddenly veered off into the wood and hadn't reappeared, and that had roused his curiosity. He had parked, followed the dog's route, scratching himself on the bushes, and found the collie sniffing around the culvert.

His original plan had been to simply hide in the wood along the road until he felt it was safe, maybe until nightfall, and then get across the road. But this was better.

He would tunnel under Page Mill while up above the big

cars cruised the road, binoculars scrutinized the hills, and voices radioed back and forth over the police band.

He waited for two minutes, by his watch, listening to the dull automobile rumble from above. There were no sounds of deceleration.

Slipping the rifle sling off his shoulder, he brought the .22 into position and flicked off the safety. The culvert was foul, the ground slick with algae, and his muddied sneakers picked up a coating of scum.

Halfway through the culvert, he stopped. A possibility existed that the authorities had found the culvert and were waiting up ahead for him to emerge. He didn't really believe that they were there, or he would have retreated, but he saw no reason to proceed rashly.

Crouching, he aimed the .22 at the far entrance to the culvert and yelled "Help!" twice.

No response, verbal or physical. He waited, again an arbitrary two minutes, then continued through the culvert to the creek bed on the far side of Page Mill Road. The traffic sounds were behind him now, but the trees and brush and the ubiquitous noisy jays were the same on this side.

The creek, like the collie in the blue bandana, led him to safety. Here, the rolling hills were home to the Stanford Industrial Park: beige and ocher and gray buildings that harmonized with the hills, oak-studded lawns and parking lots patched into the grass and woodlands so as not to violate the spirit of open space. It was a place where a business suit and running shorts were equally appropriate seven days a week.

He settled in the brushy fringe at the edge of the Syntex parking lot and studied the parked cars. Not too many, but then it was Mother's Day. The breeze dried his shirt but he still felt gritty, sticky, headachy, and he smelled of horse and undergrowth. He removed the sneakers and shoved them beneath the thicket of dead oak leaves, then took his pair of clean hard shoes from the bag and put them on.

When he felt rested, when he felt he knew what belonged in the parking lot and what didn't, he broke down the .22 and stowed it in the bag and pulled out his mobile phone and called the number he'd jotted down for the airport limo service.

While he waited, he brought back what Faulkner had said. *Elegant piece of engineering.*

The headache had returned. He pressed his thumbs to his temples, trying to kill the pain.

Faulkner's voice. Mr. Narver, that's an elegant piece of engineering. Faulkner's grin, the whiz kid from Stanford smirk. It's a piece of shit.

He pressed, containing the headache.

His code was still in the system. All the telco heroes, sweating bullets, and his code was still in the system.

28

•

Joe Faulkner leaned far out over the rail of his bridge, like a man who would jump and is testing his will. It was dawn, and fog filled the valleys between the hills and the river gorge below the bridge.

Everything was fog-wet: the leaf-slicked earth beneath Andy's sneakers, the forest behind him, the black asphalt leading onto the bridge. He shivered. The dawn sun was too feeble to burn through the cold.

Joe turned his head, his body still stretched over the rail, and called to him. "Come! Andrew! You have to see this!"

Andy didn't move. He was a man now, not a boy, and he did not have to follow his father onto the bridge.

From where he stood, the bridge seemed to float on fog. Fog licked all the way up to the stiffening trusses of the span, and the suspender cables that soared skyward looked as though they were coated in diamonds, but it was just a layer of ice crystallizing in the sunlight.

"Andrew! Look!" Joe's voice was a tenor, pitched higher in his excitement.

Trembling from the cold and a building wrath, Andy shouted back, "You're not real!"

And indeed, fog had already been drawn up from the river gorge to veil his father.

"Faulkner. *Faulkner*. They're nearly ready to load the tape."

Andy lost it.

"Andy?"

"Yeah. Just trying to remember a dream I had last night."

Feferman hunched his bulky shoulders in disgust, Amin smiled, Colson simply glanced away, and Nell gave him a look that he could not read.

He wanted to smile at her, but he didn't know how she would take it.

He shook off the dream and started across the huge switch room, excitement budding in his gut. He shoved his hands in his pockets and crossed his fingers. Like Feferman. Like Joe Faulkner courting luck with his bag of steel shavings to toss in the river.

The rows of baby-blue and white cabinets looked just as they had the night of the cutover, only then he had left them brain dead and now he found them alive, swiftly and silently processing calls, and he was satisfied.

He wasn't the only one to feel excitement. He saw it in the men and women pressed around monitors in the control center, in the taut faces of passing techs, and heard it in footsteps rapping across the floor.

The supervisor, more anxious than excited, met them at the administrative module processor. They shook hands all around.

Technically, none of them but the supervisor had to be here.

Feferman had come because he was seeing his job through to the end, because he was a bear that didn't let go of his catch until he had flogged it into total submission and consumed it. Amin had come because he was the advisor who had overseen the development of Andy's program, because it would have been impossible to keep him away when something was about to shake the network. Colson was here because he had worked with Andy on the program. And Nell? He supposed Nell was here because she was Colson's daughter and they had both been used poorly. They were owed a certain measure of satisfaction.

And I am here, he thought, because it's my program and because I want to feel and taste the execution of revenge.

Two tape cartridges lay on the workstation table. One tape contained the rewritten switching software; the software development people in Lisle had labored over it for nearly two weeks while everyone waited and stewed.

If this test run went smoothly, the new software would be installed in contaminated 3B20D processors across the nation, and in two towns in Nova Scotia, and there would no longer be a Trojan horse in the entire telephone system.

The second tape cartridge on the workstation table contained Andy's program, and if its test run went smoothly, it would be installed in every ESS across the nation, from small-capacity switches in rural towns to the very high capacity switches that processed long-distance traffic.

Nell linked her arm through Colson's and regarded Andy. "Ray says you program like a bat out of hell."

"That's about what I felt like." He glanced at Amin, then at Colson, and saw a flicker in Colson's shadowed eyes, an acknowledgment.

The program had been Andy's idea, approved by Feferman and all the way up the bureaucratic chain, but it was Amin with his reputation and connections who had successfully lobbied the telco to develop the program out of line in Sunnyvale rather than in Lisle. The engineers at Lisle had their plates full rewriting the switch software, with New York breathing down their necks hot to restart the clocks. So it was Amin who acted as consultant, as mother hen to his chick, it was Amin who checked his code and made suggestions, who caught more than one error.

But it was Colson who had done the dog work with him. Colson knew less than Andy or Amin about the subject, but he knew that he wanted in on it, and Andy welcomed his sharp mind and single-minded attention. They had damn near worked as equals for the first time in his R-TAC career. At first it had been awkward, for his prolonged apology had annoyed Colson, but then it became pure work and the tensions eased.

He had wanted to ask Colson about Nell, but that would have been a breach of their tacit working contract. She had finally called, to inquire about Wayne, and he had told her that Wayne was fine, that the only danger Wayne was in now was the danger of becoming a huge pain in the butt wanting to learn rock climbing. Andy had done his best to apologize, but he still hadn't figured out how to express his feelings to her satisfaction, so they talked for a few more painfully polite minutes, then broke the connection. She had not dropped by R-TAC to see her father, at least while Andy was there, and tonight was the first time he'd seen her since he'd accused her father, accused her, and she'd slapped his face.

She looked changed. Maybe it was just her clothes. She wore a dark dress, plain, tailored like a suit. They had all dressed soberly tonight, businesslike. It was not a casual occasion.

But her hair still made him think of the sun.

*　*　*

The fog was retreating, and he finally stopped shivering. He could see his father again clearly, hands gripping the rail, elbows jabbed out at right angles, his body a cocked arrow ready to let fly.

"Look! Come look, boy!"

I'm not a boy, Andy said, but he wasn't saying it out loud, he didn't dare yell it to Joe Faulkner.

Still, something about the way his father leaned out over the rail, the tight-strung arrow tension of it, aroused him. What did Joe Faulkner see down there, what was so compelling?

"Andrew!"

Without deciding, he was already walking, stepping from the rough earth onto the road that led out to the bridge. The recently poured asphalt had been rolled beautifully flat and level, and a fine layer of grit rasped under his sneakers. It was warmer out here on the asphalt, the black reflecting the sun's mounting heat up his body, while all around him the water slick steamed off the roadbed.

His father watched. Then, satisfied that Andy was coming, he turned back to the rail. Andy could not see his face, only his hair, and it was thick, brown well-streaked with silver; it would turn fully silver as he aged but stay thick as an animal pelt until the day he died. Andy saw his father's head move softly from side to side. He was following something down below, or he was shaking his head in wonder.

Andy began to hurry. Everything was moving rapidly, the fog sizzling away, the river crashing headlong under the bridge. He was not close enough to see the river yet, but he heard it and saw bits of foam sent spinning through the air.

"Hurry, son!"

He ran, tracking the white line that blazed so bright and clean along the center of the road that he could almost see the paint flowing down off the brush.

301

And then he was on the bridge roadway itself, passing beneath the first tower, solid, strong, well engineered.

He reached his father and Joe Faulkner turned, beaming his delight. "Good boy! Come look!"

Andy tried to step forward. He could smell the river below, water running so fast it was cleansed of all impurities, oxygenated as it whipped over the boulders in its path. The river smell cleared his head with a shocking chill and he dared not move to the rail and look down. "I can't," he whispered.

Joe Faulkner turned his back on Andy and thrust his chest hard up against the rail. "Now! Don't miss this!"

His father's command resounded in the gorge, as if he had engineered the river as well as the bridge.

A heavy hand squeezed his shoulder. "Faulkner will."

The bridge and the river and Joe evaporated like the fog. Was that all, had he waked up then? Andy blinked. It was Feferman's hand, and he squeezed again. "What?"

"Good grief, Faulkner, either pay attention or go take a nap."

Amin frowned. "He has earned a nap, Mr. Feferman."

"I'll what?" Andy said.

"Draw us a map. With your program." Feferman finally released him and turned a scowl on Amin. "Then he can go sleep until the cows come home."

"Sounds just fine," Andy said.

Feferman was thinner, he noticed. His suit jacket puckered as if the shoulder pads had been removed, and the padding under his cheekbones was gone. He had fumed during the past days, "waiting for the other shoe to drop," keeping the entire security force ready to pounce the moment a switch went down. But no switches failed. Feferman complained that the channel was like a bomb that had not been defused; it could still take down enough switches to give him nightmares and if it didn't this minute then you had to sweat through the next minute.

Maybe that was the idea, Andy thought. Lloyd knows we'll be more worried about a trigger that doesn't fire than about one that does. Maybe Lloyd was just playing it safe, because if he triggered a failure the toll records would show where he had been, and that was the kind of data the FBI liked to exercise. The FBI already had a few data points; Feferman said that several marked bills had surfaced, but that told them only where Lloyd had been, not where he was now.

As long as he did not leave the country.

"Time," Colson said.

The supervisor had the panel open on the processor, fussing, then picked up one of the tapes, carefully checked the label, and loaded it into the tape drive. He typed a command into the terminal. "Reading the tape."

Lights blinked on the tape drive and the motor whirred in short bursts: confirmation from the machine half of the human-machine interface.

The supervisor smiled back.

The five-E was cleansing itself, feeding in healthy code, dumping contaminated software.

Andy wanted Lloyd to feel the excision of his Trojan horse, the way that an amputee was said to feel the ache of a missing limb.

He listened to the tape drive.

This was like a cutover. Sometimes, you cut over to a new switch bit by bit, always having a backup ready to take the cut lines in case of a screwup. Engineers called that a chicken cut. But it wasn't always workable to cut over that way. So, with most cutovers, you simply cut the life out of the old machine and hoped to hell that the new machine would work. They called that a flash cut.

Cut, and trust.

TONI DWIGGINS

They pressed in closer, attention riveted on the blinking light, and Andy wanted them to feel what he was feeling. Trust, the restoration of trust in the five-E.

The tape drive stopped. It was done.

"Now," the supervisor said, "I understand you've got a new task for our diagnostics processor." He picked up the remaining tape cartridge.

Now, Andy thought fiercely.

"Yup," said Colson, "we're gonna do a little digital signal processing."

The supervisor chuckled and loaded the tape into the second drive.

Amin bent slightly toward Nell and spoke, voice low, his words like an underground current, blurring. Colson and Feferman stood side by side, immobile, the oscilloscope and the bear.

Andy jammed his hand deep into his pocket, feeling for the quarter. It was the coin that had given him the idea for the program, and he trapped it between his knuckles and compressed his hand into a fist.

The tape reader lit up and started to hum.

How did it feel, Lloyd? When you crept into the Carolina Hotel and stuck the coins in the phone and dialed into the switch? Did your heartbeat ramp up, did you feel it in your eardrums? Did your mouth go dry?

The tape advanced and the 5ESS drank in the code.

Andy withdrew the quarter from his pocket. He rotated the coin, so that the ridged edge ground his fingertip.

Lloyd had had to wait ten years for his Trojan horse to spread through the system. Andy wouldn't have to wait much more than ten hours for his code to be running on every ESS in the country.

Then Lloyd was going to pick up a phone. Make a bus reservation, order a pizza. Call Time. Sooner or later, Lloyd

304

was going to use the phone, and Andy pictured it as a pay phone in an anonymous hotel lobby in a city where he knew no one and no one knew him. He would drop a quarter in the coin slot, wait for dial tone, and punch in a number.

Lloyd would be what Colson and Andy had defined, in their software documentation, as an unaware user.

They were going to nail him with his own voice-mail recorded message. "You have reached Lloyd Narver's office at AT&T Regional Technical Assistance Center. I'm not at my desk right now but if you'll leave your name, number, and the date and time of your call I'll get back to you as soon as possible. You may leave a message after the signal tone."

They broke down Lloyd's speech signals to produce a visual pattern of the sounds, a spectogram. A voiceprint. That part was a piece of cake.

". . . pattern matching . . ." Andy caught the words in the current of speech Amin was pouring into Nell's ear.

Pattern matching was the real bitch.

"So you're matching the words?" Nell was saying. "Lloyd's voiceprint to what he says on the phone?" She turned to face Amin; she was exactly his height.

"Not exactly," Andy cut in, and she gave him a polite look of interest.

"Miss Colson," Amin continued, classroom voice now, "we cannot match word for word in this case. There *is* such a system in use, most commonly to identify speakers who wish to transact their banking over the telephone. The user makes a statement onto tape, it is filed, and when the user wishes to gain access he makes the same statement over the phone. If the statements match, his identity is verified. Because he is aware of the identification task, we call him an aware user."

"But that wouldn't work with Lloyd. He wouldn't want to be identified," Nell said.

Amin beamed. Feferman grunted assent.

"So what good is his voice-mail message? He's not going to call up and rattle off that message so you can match it."

Colson leveled a look on his daughter. "Think, Nell."

Andy snapped the quarter over in his palm. "Lighten up, Ray."

Colson stared at the tape drive, mouth compressed. Nell glanced at Andy, her mouth twitching at the corners. Angry or amused? He still could not tell.

"You're right," Andy said quickly, while she was still looking at him. "We don't know what Lloyd's going to say in any given call. But the only record we have of his speech patterns is the voice-mail message. The trick is matching the voiceprint we built from that to whatever he says when he calls. The words won't be the same, so we have to match the syllables."

"To be precise," Amin broke in smoothly, "we used a technique that will break down the words and separately analyze each syllable's frequency response, and then match those of the voiceprint with those of the telephone call. A very difficult task," he said gravely, "a nontrivial task."

"Bully for you," Feferman said.

"Oh, no, bully for Andy and Ray. They did most of the work."

It had taken all three of them, Andy thought, and Amin was dead right. It was nontrivial. He suddenly grinned. It had been a real bitch, and it was more fun than he'd had in a long time.

"It's a damn fine piece of programming," Colson said quietly.

Nell shifted her gaze to her father. "Let's just hope it works."

Andy flattened the quarter between his thumb and forefinger and felt the eagle poised for flight.

It was damned well going to work.

They were going to nail Lloyd with his own voiceprint.

Lloyd would drop in the coin and make his call. Meanwhile,

the switch would be randomly scanning the lines, testing for channel noise, testing to be sure all was well, all part of the normal call processing. And, as the switch scanned and tested, it would perform one added task.

It would carry out the instructions of the program that they had crafted. It would try to match the voice signals on the line to the digitized voiceprint of Lloyd Narver that was stored in its memory.

Andy saw Lloyd calling. He made Lloyd call the drugstore to fill a prescription of Seldane; the man suffered from hay fever. If Lloyd made it a quick call, he might escape detection. A switch took several minutes to scan all the lines, especially in a high-capacity office.

And, even if the random scan caught his call to the drugstore, he had to remain on the line long enough for the program to match the speech signals and verify his identity.

And, given that the technique had a ten to fifteen percent error rate, on any given call the program might fail to identify him.

Statistically, Lloyd could make quite a few telephone calls before being scanned and verified.

Let him get his Seldane and go free, Andy thought, let him order his pizza and find out when the next bus is leaving town. Let him be blissfully ignorant that the telephone system he had abused was going to exact its toll.

Because sooner or later, sooner in all probability, he would make the telephone call that Chief Special Agent Feferman and FBI Special Agent Dicker were waiting for. His speech signals, his cool mild voice droning into the phone, would be matched with his voiceprint on file, with his digitized fucking voiceprint as he would put it, and then the switch would freeze the call on the line, even if he hung up, and that would trigger an alarm in the switch room's master control center. And then a message would appear on-screen, identifying the telephone from which he was calling and instructing the switch office personnel to notify the FBI.

They might not catch him the first time; he might manage to disappear before they arrived. They might not catch him the second or third or fourth time. But each time that the voice-print identified Lloyd as the caller, they would add one more data point to the map. Until they had a crosspoint.

The way Andy pictured it, they would catch him on the phone. He would be in the grubby hotel lobby, still on the telephone, when the FBI and telco Security and the local police burst in and nailed him.

Andy wanted the handcuffs to hurt, and he wanted Lloyd to learn that Andy and Colson from the old R-TAC team had done a spectral analysis on his voice and nailed him to the fucking wall.

Andy and Colson and Amin had given their speech recognition program a name. Engineers usually named things with painful precision. They could have called it "A Speech Recognition Algorithm using the Hidden Markov Modeling Technique." They didn't. Sometimes, engineers named things with a painfully humorous pun, or a painful dose of sentiment. Andy and Colson and Amin had called their program "Candace."

Candace, Andy thought, was going to nail him dead on.

"Done," the supervisor said, snapping shut the panel on the processor.

Andy slipped the quarter back into his pocket.

They stood silent a moment, the way the team at R-TAC fell into silence after wrestling with a major alarm and retiring it, just taking a breath before congratulating themselves or going out for a beer or going home or scrambling to respond to the next alarm.

Then the faintest of smiles broke on Colson's face. "Phone home, Lloyd," he said, and Nell laughed like a kid.

Feferman made a sound like air escaping from a balloon.

They headed out of the switch room, all of them but Amin, who spied an engineer he had met at the previous year's Globecom conference. Amin slipped an arm around his new chick and they walked down one of the aisles into the number five, disappearing into the blue and white army of switching modules. A network had to keep growing, Andy thought, or it lost its competitive edge.

Outside in the parking lot, Andy fell into step beside Feferman. The big man threw off waves of heat that blasted Andy before dissipating in the night chill.

"How long have you worked in Security, Feferman?"

"Eight years."

"Why?"

Feferman grunted in surprise.

Andy could hear a murmur behind them, Nell speaking to Colson. "Why Security, Feferman?"

"What is this, Faulkner, an interrogation?"

"Humor me, please. Why Security?"

"Because I'm big."

"Feferman."

"What is this, you figure I owe you this?"

"I figure we're just about even. But I want to know."

Feferman hunched his shoulders inside the roomy jacket; he'd finished throwing off heat. Andy pressed his arms in close to his sides against the chill.

"What do you feel when you nail someone?"

"Contentment," Feferman said, promptly.

"Is that all?"

"That's everything."

"What about . . . evening things up?"

"An eye for an eye?"

Feferman's Jag was directly in front of them. They stopped,

both of them staring down at the Jag, at the baby-blue paint job turned to a noncolor by the halogen parking lot lights.

"You're talking about a tooth for a tooth?"

"Yeah," Andy said, "I guess."

Feferman pivoted and leaned against the Jag. "Ask her."

Andy spun around as Colson and Nell joined them.

"Mr. Faulkner wants to know why someone goes into the security business." Feferman held his hand out to Nell; she accepted it and they shook.

Andy stared at her hand, buried in Feferman's paw. Colson was looking too, but Colson might as well have been observing the kinetics of the human handshake as wondering why his daughter was shaking the chief special agent's hand.

She let Feferman's hand go and gazed at Andy. "I signed up with Security."

Security. The tailored dress.

He flinched. He was struck dumb, he didn't know what to say and he couldn't form the words, the *syllables,* even if he had known what to say. Why was he always three steps behind her?

Finally, he found a word and the means to produce it. "Congratulations."

"I still have to get through training."

Training. What could be hairier than pole climbing? "You'll be great."

She stood at ease, settling her hands on her hips as if ready to loop her thumbs into a lineman's belt. "Tell the truth."

Truth was, the first time he'd seen her, dressed as a lineman, he'd thought it was a joke and been dead wrong. He said good night to Feferman and Colson and walked over to Nell. "May I drive you home?"

No anger or amusement to her mouth now, just neutrality as far as he could make out. It was too dark to tell what went on in her eyes, what shade of gold watched him.

310

"Nell," he said, "the truth is, I really like you. I'm very attracted to you. And I want a chance to make it more than that."

Still, she didn't smile, or speak. But then, neither did she walk away.

"May I drive you home?"

Night silence, then the roar of Feferman's Jag starting and the slam of Colson's car door.

She must have heard it too. She nodded. "Sure."

As they crossed the parking lot to his car, he angled closer to her and took hold of her hand. The warmth of her hand, their sudden closeness, brought the smell of piney after-shave to him. Feferman's handshake. Security. The truth was, he wished she had signed up to become an engineer.

The fog had withdrawn to higher altitudes, shrunken into thin cirrus clouds. Now the mountains and the river gorge and the bridge, and his father in front of him at the rail, were lit in fierce clarity by the unobstructed sun.

The sun broke the great spans of cable into hundreds of silver flare-ups that made his eyes ache, made him squint.

His father was bent so far over the rail that his head had disappeared from view; Andy could see the hump of his shiny blue poplin jacket, then nothing. Joe Faulkner was stone-still, silent. He might have died right there on the rail. But that was not the way Joe Faulkner died.

"Dad?"

Nothing.

Andy's heart raced, he was left behind. His father at the rail wasn't dead, but he was so absorbed in what lay below that he had forgotten his son was there.

"Dad!"

Andy heard the water crashing below and he tried a third time, roaring to compete with the river. "Dad!"

Was the man deaf?

Andy extended his arm, stretching all the way from his rib cage, but the form at the rail was out of reach.

Without deciding, the way that he had stepped out of the woods onto the roadbed leading to the bridge, Andy stepped forward. He moved stiff-legged, his muscles in contraction, in rebellion. This time it would be terrible. More than dizziness or tremors, he feared he would spin completely out of control to fall and fall and never black out, just fall without end.

Even as his breaths shuddered out, he moved forward toward the rail. His father's blue jacket grew in his field of view until his vision was completely filled with blue and he was standing directly behind his father, staring down at the bent form. "Dad," he whispered, terrified.

Nothing.

He closed his eyes and put a hand out, feeling for the rail. He clamped on with one hand, pulled himself forward, clamped on with the other hand. Bless the solidity of steel.

If he opened his eyes he would spin away and fall.

"Look, son!"

His eyes peeled open and Joe Faulkner was full face to him, not old, not even fifty, flesh still sculpted to the bones, lines just beginning to form around the mouth, a strong straight line between parentheses, and the eyes hard turtle-shell green. Then his father smiled, the parentheses deepened, and Andy saw what Joe Faulkner must have looked like as a kid, full of wonder at the way things were before he had ever thought to try his own hand tinkering with them.

"Andrew, see this!"

His father turned back to the river gorge. They were shoulder-to-shoulder, four hands lined up on the rail, hands nearly the same, broad across the palm, long fingers with prominent joints like hex nuts firmly threaded onto bolts.

Andy raised his eyes beyond the rail and he saw the far end

of the river gorge. The river was a twisting green ribbon that widened as he looked downward, finally fraying into white lace on the rocks directly below.

Andy laughed out loud. He was leaning out over the rail like his father, looking down, far down, and not falling, not spinning away into chaos.

He wasn't afraid.

But that was not why Joe Faulkner had drawn him out on the bridge.

"Son, *look.*"

Andy craned his neck and looked down, under the bridge, and he gasped.

The tower piers were gone. The bridge was anchored to earth only by the roadbeds at either end; the load-bearing piers that should be supporting the hundreds of thousands of tons of steel and concrete were simply not there. The bridge should have buckled in on itself, the spans should have broken and tilted and tumbled down into the river; without support, the weight was too great and the working stresses were too high and yet the bridge stood. With its feet knocked out from under it, the bridge still stood.

They were floating above the river gorge on a bridge no engineer could have designed and no builder could have erected.

"It's a miracle," Joe Faulkner said softly.

Andy fought through the fog, out of the dream, sitting upright in the dark, and he still felt the unanchored bridge under his feet.

So that's how the dream ended.

He got carefully out of bed, so as not to disturb Nell, pulled on a robe, and stumbled into his workroom. By the dim light from the streetlamps outside, he found Joe Faulkner's old brown leather chair and sank into it.

He was dreaming of miracles.

A bridge with no means of support. That was like a telephone network with no means of transmission that nevertheless connected human voices.

An impossible piece of engineering.

Andy laughed softly in the dark. He had dreamed a child's dream and he tried to recall if he and his father had ever in reality shared a moment of wonder like that.

But in reality, Andy did not believe in miracles and neither had his father.

What would Joe Faulkner have thought if Andy came to him in a dream, opened his hand, and said that he held there the basic switching matrix upon which the telephone switching systems of the future would be built? His father would look into his hand and see nothing. Building a switch from nothing—a miracle, like building a bridge without support.

"It's not a miracle, Dad," Andy would say. "It's a photonic switch, the next step into the future from the electronic switch. Photons are the fastest things in creation, and beams of photons—light, Dad—can pass through each other without interference. So thousands of information channels carrying photons can be packed together in a switching matrix so small you need a microscope to build it."

And they would both look into his hand, and neither one of them would be able to see the miraculous switch.

Maybe Joe Faulkner's dream bridge was not impossible. Who knew what the limits would be with high-tensile low-weight structural materials of the future? Maybe his father had dreamed of something like that.

Andy suddenly grinned.

His dream wasn't about miracles, it was a kick in the butt. Get back to work. It's over, Lloyd's good as nailed, he's purged from the system, he's a critical alarm that's been retired, now let him go and get back to work. Go build something that you can eat, sleep, and dream about, and get sentimental about in moments of exhaustion and utmost privacy.

He wondered if anyone was working on a speech recognition system that could be hooked up with a TDD, so that a deaf person could talk rather than type and the system would recognize the speech and print it out on the other end user's screen. Applications like TDDs always lagged the technology . . .

A ringing drilled into his thoughts, and he lunged out of the chair and grabbed for the phone. Feferman? No, he'd just left Feferman a few hours ago at the switch office, and they couldn't have any news yet, and he wasn't on call at R-TAC and no one phoned at this time of night unless it was bad news. "Hello?" His throat was dry.

"Gloria?"

Gloria. He let out a breath. Christ. "No, there's no Gloria here."

"Um, this isn't Gloria Meacham's number?"

"What number did you call?"

"I don't remember, I already closed the phone book. What number is this?"

"There's no Gloria Meacham here."

"Is this Fred?"

Andy sighed. "You got the wrong number. Look it up again."

"You're not shittin me? You sound like Fred."

"It's five o'clock in the morning," Andy said, "and— "

A slam, and dial tone filled his ear.

He replaced the handset gently in its cradle and cursed.

The telephone system was beautiful, it was a wonder of engineering design, it was an irreplaceable convenience, it was a lifeline, and it faithfully transmitted the utterances of genius and fool alike.

Andy returned to the brown leather chair, stretched out his legs, and folded his hands behind his head.

Fundamentally, a TDD speech recognition system was going to have to be able to analyze both discrete speech and continuous speech, and that would take a robust design, but . . .

Andy fumbled for the light switch and grabbed a pencil and paper.

29

•

"FLAME ON ********** HEY troll u did good. May that hacker get HUNG and may u forever write clean code!!!!!! Nice to switch in a good clean network again—& thanks fı all the free calls. Be seeing u in the system. Zot. ********* FLAME OFF"

Andy pushed away from the terminal and spun his chair to face Amin.

Amin leaned one shoulder against the wall, slouching gracefully beneath the horsewhip.

"Then who *is* he?"

"He is Zot. What more can I tell you?" Amin steepled his hands.

Andy braced for the lesson.

"Andy, my chick, just be glad he's on our side."

317